THE LORDS OF GREYSTONE

JOSEPH J. CHRISTIANO

The Lords of Greystone

The Lords of Greystone ©2023, Joseph J. Christiano

Tell-Tale Publishing Group, LLC
Swartz Creek, MI 48473

Printed in the United States of America

History has its truth,
and so has legend.
--Victor Hugo

For my original Oshkosh crew.
The origin of the name remains a mystery…

TABLE OF CONTENTS

CHAPTER ONE

First Impressions

Katie's GPS decided to start working again at the last moment. It had been cutting out and then returning for brief periods since she left the Landing behind. The female voice interrupted the morning deejay on WERD to inform her to turn right. In the split-second before she hit the brakes she thought maybe the thing was lagging and she had somehow missed the turn altogether. There seemed to be nothing on either side of her but trees. She squinted through the windshield and then the passenger window. No side street presented itself. Katie released the brake and allowed her Cruze to inch forward. After a few moments a house came into view ahead on the right. Just before the house a narrow road revealed itself.

There was no street sign, nothing to indicate this was Aldebaran Road. She glanced at her GPS but its screen was back to displaying the *No Signal* message. "This has to be it," she told herself. Her Cruz continued its slow advance. "I mean, there haven't been any other turnoffs. There's no way I could have missed it."

Her Cruze came to a stop at the top of the side street. She paused, looked right and left. Aldebaran—if that's what this was--cut across 26 going in both directions. She saw nothing but trees everywhere she looked. "This has to be it," she repeated.

Katie wondered how she could still be within the boundaries of Deacon's Landing. When she was still on Route 6 she had crossed the town line into Woodbury. That was back when she could still see signs of civilization. The turn onto Route 26 changed that. She could not remember the last time she saw a structure of any kind. At some point she must have reentered

Deacon's Landing but damned if she had noticed. She supposed she was lucky her GPS worked as well as it did. There was no way she could have found this place otherwise, even by accident.

Katie turned the wheel to the right. The lone house on the corner was large with a well-manicured lawn and a Beamer in the driveway. A power line ran from a telephone pole on the opposite side of Aldebaran Road to the house. Katie's eyes followed the powerline away from the house and down the street. It vanished into the thick canopy of leaves and branches that stood sentinel on either side of Aldebaran. Katie put the large house in her rearview and advanced slowly forward.

The woods remained thick on both sides of Aldebaran Road. Their branches met high above and gave the impression she was beneath a dome of some kind. The dome blotted out most of the late-morning sunlight although patches appeared on the blacktop every so often. The leaves had just started to transition to red and orange.

A couple hundred feet in she saw her first driveway and mailbox. The trees were too thick and the driveway too long for her to see more than the roof of the house in the distance. The shingles were black and she counted no fewer than six pitched points. Katie whistled through her teeth; the house had to be massive. "Must be nice," she whispered.

After that she saw driveways and mailboxes every few hundred feet on both sides of the road. A few sported short, stone pillars with engraved metal plates upon them. Katie slowed down to read a few. NIGHT SONG, read one, TAJ MAHAL, another. "It's probably as big as the Taj Mahal," she told herself. She had yet to see any of the actual houses.

Her GPS returned to life and stated her destination was one mile ahead. Katie advanced, her speedometer hovering between fifteen and twenty miles per hour. Eventually—and suddenly--the blacktop ended and the road became dirt. It also widened, forming a circular area. It was the first spot on Aldebaran she had seen where a car could turn around safely. Even her Cruze was too big to make such a turn without scraping the woods on either side of the road.

Katie drove as fast as she felt comfortable on the narrow, dirt surface. "What am I gonna do if another car comes this way? Backing up to that round spot is gonna be a bitch." No other cars presented themselves, nor did she see any other signs of life. There were no runners, no walkers. It occurred to her she hadn't even heard birds since she left 26.

The dirt road inclined and made several sharp twists and turns. Katie spotted an open field on her left. The field sloped up, its top hidden by more trees. The soil had been tilled and the field was covered by what looked to be corn stalks. Katie did not know what she expected when she applied for the job, but a farm was not on the list of possibilities.

She saw another open field, this time on her right. Unlike its cousin on the other side this one was not used for farming. The grass was green and tall. The remains of a rather large bonfire stood in the center of the field. Katie imagined her hopefully future employer hosting late night parties for the neighbors.

The house, or, rather, its main gate, came up on her fast. She rounded a corner and it was directly in front of her. Katie hit the brakes and her car skidded a bit on the dirt. She stopped well short of the gate which preserved her hopes for a positive first impression. The gate was made of wrought iron, and it was ten feet tall if it was an inch. On either side of the gate stood a stone column even taller than the gate. A bronze plaque adorned the column on the right. GREYSTONE, it proclaimed.

Katie craned her neck for a view of the house. Unlike the other residences of Aldebaran Road, Greystone was visible from the road, if barely. It looked like a Victorian mansion from where Katie sat. "Okay, well, you knew they were rich, didn't you? So don't sit here and gawk like an idiot."

A few feet in front of the left column stood the call box. Katie pulled up to it and pressed the button. The reply came back within seconds. "Can I help you?"

Katie leaned a little closer and looked directly into the small camera lens above the speaker. "Hi. I'm Katie Spencer. I have an eleven o'clock appointment with Mr. Exton."

There was a mechanical buzz and the wrought iron gates parted in front of her. "Thank you," Katie told the call box. There was no further reply. She drove through the open gate.

Katie followed the driveway through a few more twists and turns. It was unpaved and her tires crunched gravel quite loudly. She gasped and reflexively hit the brakes when she got her first good look at the house.

It was in the Victorian style; she had been right about that much. Calling it a mansion, however, had undersold its size. It was simply the largest house Katie had ever seen. The façade was made of stone; great, grey blocks that would have looked right at home on an old English castle. The main bulk of it was four stories but there were multiple spires that were a great deal taller than the rest of the house. Large windows, some taller than her, dotted the front and the side. The roof sported the same black shingles she had seen on the first house. Even standing in direct sunlight Greystone looked dark and cold. Katie whistled through her teeth.

She snapped herself out of it and eased her foot off the brake pedal. Her car advanced closer to the house and in front she saw a few other cars lined up one next to the other. She parked next to a pale green Land Rover and killed the engine.

Katie crossed the driveway to the deck in front of the house. It was long and wide and could accommodate a couple hundred people with room to spare. She imagined large, elegant parties where men in tuxedos and women in gowns stood out here drinking expensive wine and smoking even more expensive cigars while comparing their stock portfolios.

The front doors were as tall as the pillars at the end of the driveway. They were made of wood that sounded very thick when she knocked. Katie stood back and folded her hands in front of her and smiled. *First impressions*, her mother told her once. *Nothing is more important.* For what this position paid Katie was very determined to make a great first impression.

The right door swung open and a girl younger than her stood on the other side of the threshold. She wore what Katie could describe only as a classic maid's outfit. "Ms. Spencer? Come in, please."

Katie smiled and walked inside. The girl closed the door behind her.

The foyer was large enough to fit Katie's entire apartment within its boundaries. The floor was hardwood, the real thing, not the cheap garbage available in most hardware stores. The walls were papered in a pattern that reminded Katie of her grandmother's old house in Indianapolis. Aside from the area rug the foyer was bereft of knickknacks or wall hangings. It was the barest room Katie had ever seen.

"This way, Ms. Spencer," the young girl told her, and started off.

"Katie, please," Katie replied as she kept pace with her.

"Mr. Exton prefers a level of formality within the residence." It was all she said on the matter, and indeed, all she said at all.

She led Katie through another room that may have been a living room or a drawing room. Katie really had no idea what the difference was but calling it a living room felt too pedestrian. The furniture was richly upholstered but did not look comfortable. The end tables were free of magazines, books, and dust. It was another room lacking in the small details that seemed to make a home. It was as if the room served no purpose other than to exist.

Katie wanted to make conversation. Walking a step behind the young girl and in total silence made the hairs on Katie's arm stand at attention. Whatever she had in mind to say died a quick death when they entered the library.

The room was large to a ridiculous degree. Three stories tall, all four walls lined with bookcases filled to overflowing. There had to be thousands, tens of thousands, of volumes, Barnes and Noble on steroids. Katie stopped, tried to take it all in. "What is this, the Library of Congress?" She regretted it right away. *First impressions*, her mother had said. *So much for that.*

The girl turned her head a bit and smiled. *Look, hayseed, try not to drool on anything valuable*, that smile seemed to say. She had no other reaction.

Katie cleared her throat and blushed and continued to follow her guide.

They exited the library through another open doorway and proceeded down a long corridor. They passed several closed doors; paintings and portraits adorned the walls. The girl in the maid's uniform stopped at a large door and knocked. The sound was so gentle and soft that Katie barely heard it herself. There was no way anyone on the other side could possibly—

"Come," said the man's voice.

The younger girl swung the door open and stepped aside for Katie.

The room beyond was richly furnished. Unlike the foyer and the first room this one seemed to serve a function. The desk was large and clearly old. The wood had been worked by a master craftsman judging by the ornate designs carved into its surfaces. The single lamp that sat on the desktop would have looked at home on the desk of some old timey politician or head of state. The HP desktop, on the other hand, looked state-of-the-art and completely out of place in this setting. The walls were dark wood and hand-carved with intricate designs. In front of the desk stood a single plush chair. Behind the desk sat Mr. Exton. His age was indeterminate. He might have been thirty or sixty. His features seemed to age in both directions depending upon the expression he wore.

"Thank you, Ms. Palmer. That will be all."

Ms. Palmer nodded and closed the door.

Exton indicated the empty chair. "Please, Ms. Spencer, sit."

Katie smiled and took the chair. She started to fold her hands but changed her mind and held out her right. "Pleased to meet you, Mr. Exton."

Exton shook her hand briefly. It was weak, perfunctory. He turned his attention to the paper in front of him. "I reviewed your resumé. Your credentials seem to be in order. Tell me, why do you seek employment at Greystone Manor?"

I need the money. I'm sick to death of living in this one stoplight town and I want to get the hell out of here. It was true but not something she could possibly say aloud. Her smile in place she said, simply, "Your ad sounded very interesting to me. And now that I've seen the house, I'm very excited for this opportunity."

God, that sounded lame. She nearly cringed but she got hold of herself at the last second and maintained her smile.

"I see," Exton replied, his eyes still on the paper in his hands. He placed it on the desk and typed something on the keyboard. He used the hunt-and-peck method and Katie tried not to smile.

All this money and they can't hire a secretary to do this? Right on the heels of that she thought, *maybe that's why they can afford a house like this. They don't spend money where they don't have to.* But no. Anyone who could afford to own this house could afford a staff of hundreds if they so desired. Maybe she could offer her services as a typist. She couldn't swing 100 words-per-minute but she'd still be much faster than Mr. Exton.

The man turned the monitor to face her. "Who is this?"

Katie's smile faltered. One of Tom's mugshots stared back at her. She froze for only a moment. *Forget first impressions and forget this job.* She swallowed and answered, "My brother, Tom."

Exton left the monitor in place. "But you indicated you had no living family. Can you explain this discrepancy?"

"We're not particularly close," she stammered. That, at least, was the truth. *And I'm sick of this guilt-by-association bullshit. Every interviewer who sees my last name makes the connection and I get the "We'll be in contact" kiss-off.* Katie swallowed again. "I shouldn't have lied. I apologize for wasting your time, Mr. Exton." She started to rise.

"Please remain seated until the interview is concluded, Miss Spencer." When Katie froze halfway to standing up Exton indicated the chair and turned the monitor back to face him. "We do not hold one's family against anyone. If you and Mr. Spencer are not on speaking terms that is your business. I trust the lesson has been learned."

Katie couldn't believe it. Was this man still considering hiring her? She lied on her resumé and got caught. The instant she saw the mugshot she assumed the interview was over. *Maybe he's just toying with you now. You wasted his time so he's going to waste yours.* No, Katie did not believe that for a moment. Exton struck her as far too serious a man to bother with something as trivial. "It has." Katie returned to the chair. "I'm sorry again."

"The position for which you are applying is to last no fewer than six weeks. Depending on several factors it has the potential to last far longer than that. Your duties will be described to you by Ms. Palmer. They should hold no terrors for you. The salary will be as we discussed. Are these terms acceptable to you?"

Katie struggled to return her smile to its former place and sincerity. Exton seemed to have gotten over her lie in very short order. Maybe this was the job for her after all. Her heart picked up the pace and her new smile was honest. It was all she could do not to leap from the chair and throw her arms around her new boss. "Yes, Mr. Exton, they are indeed acceptable."

Exton nodded. "Welcome to Greystone Manor." He reached across the desk and shook her hand again. It was the same brief, weak handshake he gave her when she entered the room but this time Katie took no notice. "Come, I'll give you a brief tour before I see to my other duties." He stood. Katie stood with him.

He exited the room, Katie on his heels. He pointed to various closed doors as they passed. "This is a bathroom. There are fifteen in all. They are not part of your responsibilities, but Ms. Palmer may call on you from time to time to spruce them up for their Lordships. All must be in readiness when they arrive." They passed more doors, with Exton identifying them all in turn. A playroom not used in many years, a closet bigger than Katie's bedroom that stored dishes and cutlery. The armory was impressive; sporting rifles were mounted on the walls alongside swords, daggers, and other medieval-looking weapons she could not begin to identify. The kitchen looked as if it belonged in a hotel or on a cruise ship. The tables and appliances were stainless steel but the floor was covered in tiles of red and black which seemed to absorb much of the light coming through the large windows. Lights dangled from the ceiling on long, slender cables. Katie nodded each time Exton described a room or what she would be expected to do within but kept her comments to a minimum. He seemed to prefer silence.

They encountered Ms. Palmer walking down one of the corridors with a young woman in tow. Katie knew immediately this was another interviewee, one who had apparently already been hired. The new girl smiled at Katie and Exton but said nothing as she kept pace with Ms. Palmer. A very long, black rose tattoo adorned the woman's forearm. The ink seemed out of place in this setting, as if it and the person sporting it had been transported here from the far future.

Exton led Katie into the largest room she had seen so far. There were four fireplaces, one on each wall, and each one of hand-chiseled stone. Various items, all of which looked not just old but ancient, adorned the mantles. Katie could not even begin to guess their origins. The furniture appeared just as old as some of the mantle pieces, but everything was in pristine condition. She doubted she could find so much as a dust mote within the room.

Large portraits were hung, one above each fireplace. "That is Elizabeth Morley," Exton said and indicated the only female subject. The painted woman's hair and clothing made her appear as if she lived in Elizabethan times. "She is their Lordship's sister, the eldest of the Morley children. She has been gone many years now." Exton's expression hardened, just a little, at the woman's image.

Katie frowned. Something about the painted woman's expression, or perhaps it was her eyes, rose gooseflesh on her arms.

"This one is Edgar, their Lordships' younger brother," Exton said as if he were introducing the man in person. "He has passed away as well, I'm afraid."

Edgar Morley's expression, captured for all time, was that of a stern headmaster or perhaps a judge who was used to sending prisoners to the gallows. His clothing, at least, appeared more modern than his elder sister's, if only by a century or two.

Exton strode to another portrait and nodded. "This is William, one of their Lordships." He nodded again at the portrait that adorned the opposite wall. "And that one is Arthur. You look confused. Were you unaware their Lordships are twins?"

"Um, yeah. I mean, *yes*, I guess I was." Katie hated stammering. She especially hated it in this setting. She was unlikely to impress her new boss like this. She regarded Arthur, mostly to put some distance between herself and Exton. She needed a moment to recover from her embarrassment and looking over the portrait was a golden opportunity.

Arthur's expression mirrored his twin's. If anything, both paintings could have been of the same man. Katie could see no difference at all between them. They were both old, dressed in suits that must have cost a fortune one hundred years ago, their eyes pale blue, almost white. Their expressions were identical to their younger brother's.

"Which one is older?" The question was out before she knew she was going to ask. Katie cringed. *First impressions, you idiot. Don't appear too inquisitive. Exton doesn't look like the type to put up with curious employees.* "I'm sorry. I thought only the eldest son was called *Lord.*" *Yeah, in* Game of Thrones. *This is real life. Christ, you sound ridiculous.*

"A family may have multiple sons and daughters with titles," Exton replied. He seemed unbothered by her question. Perhaps he was used to it. "As for who is older, I am afraid no one knows. Their birth records were lost many years ago."

Katie nodded and looked again at the portrait. The hairs on her arm were still standing at attention. She hoped not to spend much time in this room during the next six weeks.

Exton led her from the portrait room into another, smaller room. It was still larger than Katie's apartment and the furniture therein was just as old—and just as well-maintained—as in the last room. Katie decided right away this would be known as the room of masks.

One wall was made entirely of windows. Each pane reached from floor to ceiling and was wide enough for two people to stand in front of without touching shoulders. They looked out onto the grounds, the well-manicured lawn that stretched to the border of more woods. A large, ancient tree stood guard perhaps twenty feet from the glass. Beyond the tree stood a barn. This structure, at least, seemed comfortable showing its age. It had been red once, but the paint was chipped and faded and even from here she could see some of the rot that was slowly overtaking the façade.

The wall opposite the windows was adorned with dozens of masks. Each was pale yellow in color with hand-painted designs of red or black. Some seemed innocuous enough but more than a few gave Katie the creeps.

"That's quite a collection," she remarked.

Exton appeared to anticipate both her comment and her need to make it. "Their Lordships collect them. It is their one indulgence. They were acquired from all over the world. This one, for example, comes from Peru. And this one is German, if I am not mistaken."

"How interesting." It wasn't, really, but Katie had neither the ability nor the desire to guess which mask came from which corner of the globe.

Exton led her to the second floor of the mansion. He described the function of each room as they passed its closed door. Bedrooms, too many for Katie to count, more bathrooms, more drawing rooms. The third floor was more of the same. By the time they got to the fourth floor Katie was becoming winded. Her head was spinning with the information Exton had given her. She knew if he asked her what was behind the last door they passed she would have no answer. She thought her brain might be starting to liquefy.

She concentrated on the details to stay sane. Some hallways had hardwood floors to match the first floor, others sported carpet that was so soft she thought she might sink right through it. Each hallway was lit with wall sconces and little light bulbs in the shape of a flame. The wood paneling of each hallway was hand-carved and with different patterns from the last. Katie wondered, not for the first time, just how much Greystone Manor would fetch on the housing market. *More than you can afford*, she thought. *Yeah, no shit*.

She thought the tour might be over when Exton led her outside. Instead of escorting her to her car he took her around to the other side of the house. They followed the gravel driveway to the barn she had spotted earlier. Up close the rot was in even more evidence. The whole thing looked like it might collapse in a strong wind.

Exton took her inside. There were stalls for horses, but no animals were in evidence. The walls were hung with all manner of groundskeeping equipment and tools. Exton inclined his head toward a man at a workbench on the far side of the barn. "Mr. Johnson, if you please." He motioned for the man to come forward.

Mr. Johnson was not quite the size of the Incredible Hulk, but he was not that far off, either. (*The creature who ate Dwayne Johnson*, Katie would come up with later.) He wore overalls that Katie could squeeze into with any three of her friends. The man's arms were wider around than her waist. He approached the two new arrivals while wiping his hands on a rag.

"Mr. Johnson, this is Ms. Spencer. She will be joining us as of Thursday."

"Hello, Mr. Johnson," Katie offered.

He stuck out his hand. It looked as if it could break every bone in her body without trying. "Nice to meet you, Ms. Spencer." His hand enveloped hers like a shark swallowing a goldfish but there was no pain. He knew his own strength, apparently.

"Mr. Johnson tends the grounds here at Greystone," Exton informed her.

"They're quite beautiful," Katie told him with a smile.

He smiled back. "Thank you, Ms. Spencer."

Call me Katie, she almost said before she remembered Ms. Palmer's warning. "You're very welcome."

They made small talk for a few more moments before Exton led her from the barn. They stopped at the top of the hill overlooking the planted rows of corn. The sun was high in the sky by then and the morning chill had vanished as if it never existed. October in New England in a nutshell.

"What do you think of our Lordships' estate?" Exton asked her.

Katie thought about it for a moment. "It's really very impressive." *That was a hell of an understatement. Good going.*

"Forgive me, Mr. Exton, but is the house and its grounds tended to by only three people? It seems like a lot of work."

"Oh, there are more. Their Lordships employ six people full-time. When they come to visit their estate, we take on more help. That would be you and a few more, not to put too fine a point on it. I've hired one already and I have more interviews scheduled for later today. Don't worry, Ms. Spencer. You will not die of loneliness during your employ."

Katie laughed, just a little. "I look forward to meeting the Morley brothers. When will they arrive?"

"Their Lordships. Never refer to them as you just did. And certainly not in their presence."

Katie blushed, first from embarrassment and then from a twinge of anger. Yes, she needed the job, and the pay was outstanding, but she wondered for the first time if she was cut out to bow and curtsey to two old men, whatever they were worth. This wasn't medieval England, and they weren't kings or princes. But there had been no anger in Exton's rebuke. He spoke to her as a teacher would to a new student. *In his own way he's trying to look out for me.* The flash of anger vanished, and she smiled again.

"My apologies."

"It's okay. Their Lordships are due to arrive late Thursday evening. They are unlikely to meet the new staff until the following day. At their advanced age they tire easily, and it is a long voyage. Therefore, I believe serving their dinner Friday evening will be your baptism of fire, as it were."

"I'll do the best I can."

"I have every confidence in you, Ms. Spencer."

"Mr. Exton, I have a question, if you don't mind."

His expression remained unchanged.

"Where do their Lordships live if not here? This is a lot of house to just sit empty most of the time."

The corner of Exton's mouth twitched in what might have been the prelude to a smile. "They were born in a small village outside London and there they spend much of their time. Their Lordships own many properties in several countries, however, and they are known to tour them all when they decide to make progress. But I suspect this visit will be of longer duration than usual. Their Lordships have business here that requires their attention." He turned to her before she could say anything more. "Now, if you will excuse me, I have other matters to attend. Your shift will begin at 3 P.M. on Thursday. Please do not be late. When you arrive come to the front door and Ms. Palmer will see to you."

"Yes, sir. It was nice to meet you, Mr. Exton." She held out her hand.

He shook it in his customary manner and escorted her back to the driveway and her car.

When she arrived at the gate it opened for her, and Katie was back onto Aldebaran Road. This time she was able to navigate the twists and turns of the road with a bit more confidence. It was fortunate, because her GPS still refused to work around here.

CHAPTER TWO

Remember When…

Dude yur not gonna
Believe where Katie
Got a job!
<u>SC</u>
<u>Brazzers?</u>
GFY! Call me asap

Spence returned his attention to the game while he waited for the call. He hadn't been able to catch the game last night so he DVRd it and avoided all news and social media so he could see for himself what was going on in the ALDS. Cole had taken a no-no into the sixth. In the span of three batters he had lost the no-hitter, the shutout, and the lead. Spence couldn't quite bring himself to be nervous. Toronto's offense had been tough all year but their pitching staff was a black hole. The Yanks would have Rizzo, Judge, and Soto in the bottom of the inning. Spence finished off his beer and walked to the kitchen to retrieve another.

His phone rang just as he sat down again. He picked it up and said, "Yo."

"So, where'd Katie get a job?"

Spence found himself disappointed with the lack of small talk. He and Scott Carpenter had not spoken in some time. Now that he had him on the phone it occurred to him they had not talked in at least four months. Spence had been hoping, apparently without knowing, for some of the old good-natured bullshit in which the two had engaged every time they got together. Spence did his best to hide the disappointment from his tone. "Greystone."

Silence on the other end for just a moment before Scott said, "You're fucking kidding me! *Denham?* Holy shit! I haven't thought about that place in years!"

That sounded like the old Scott. Spence could not suppress a smile. "Me neither. She told me about it this morning. I almost fell over."

"Does she know about that place? The devil worshippers and shit?"

Spence laughed. "I can't believe we used to believe that. But no. I didn't tell her anything about it."

"Dude, are you crazy? Why would you let her take a job there? She's gonna get killed!"

Spence rolled his eyes. If Katie had been hired at Greystone back when he was in high school his reaction would have been the same as Scott's. Back then every kid in Deacon's Landing knew about Denham, with the apparent exception of his sister. Then again Katie was in middle school at the time so her employment there was not a possibility. Spence could not point to the moment when he stopped believing in the nonsense about that road in the middle of nowhere and the people who lived there. Over time he had simply found the legend to be less and less realistic.

"No one's killing anybody," Spence replied. "According to Katie the two guys who own the house are a hundred years old. What are they gonna do, gum her to death? But there's a reason I wanted you to call me." He paused mostly for dramatic effect, picturing Scott on the other end of the line growing impatient. Spence held it for just a few seconds before he said, "I wanna go there when she's working and check the place out again."

Scott's response was instantaneous. "Get the band back together! Hell yeah!"

Spence could not help but laugh. This was precisely why Scott was his first call. If anyone was going to be down with sneaking into Denham again, it would be Scott Carpenter. They spoke for a few more minutes and hammered out some of the details. It was Scott's suggestion to meet at the old Pancakes n' Pies, the restaurant that had been their hangout back in the day. It was shuttered now but that made no difference. Its parking lot was as good a place to meet as any.

Spence was winding down the call when Scott asked, "You gonna invite Phil and Marcus?"

Spence paused. On the TV Judge was standing on second after bouncing one over the outfield wall and Soto was stepping into the batter's box. Spence had planned to call Phil next; he had been dreading the thought of telling Marcus about it. "Phil, definitely. Marcus, well, I don't know if putting those two together is a good idea."

"You think there's still bad blood?"

"Has to be," Spence acknowledged.

"Well, see what they say. Let me know what's going on."

"Will do. Talk to you later."

Spence hung up and sat back on the couch. He watched Soto take the first two pitches for called strikes. He singled on the next pitch and Judge raced home. But Spence was no longer thinking about the game. Now that Scott had given voice to what Spence had been thinking, the problem of Marcus Greer was now front and center in his head.

He watched the rest of the game before he picked up the phone and called Phil. The conversation went much as it had with Scott. Phil was agreeable to going back to Denham although he, like Spence, had stopped believing the legend.

"It'll bring back old times, that's for sure," Phil commented.

"Yeah," Spence agreed.

"You know we're not in high school anymore, right? We're not sixteen. If we get caught, we'll be arrested for trespassing."

"I thought of that. But how many times did we almost get caught back then? A lot."

"Yeah, but I'm too old to go diving into the woods every time we see a car coming."

That brought back a few memories. It was standard procedure at Denham to hide in the woods whenever they saw the headlights of an approaching car. At the time the official excuse had been that they didn't want to get caught by the devil worshippers who lived there. Even at the time, though, Spence had been somewhat skeptical as to the veracity of that claim. Yes, they had seen weird shit up there. The house with the hearse in the driveway, the clone car, the sound of drums coming from the woods. The masks on the wall in the main house took the cake, though. Spence's ex-girlfriend Michelle had seen them and freaked out, convinced of the entire urban legend in that moment. It was also the only time she had gone to Denham; she refused to ever go near the place again.

"Hopefully that won't be necessary," Spence finally said. "I'm with you on that."

After a moment of silence Phil said, "Okay, I'm in."

Spence smiled. *That's two.* "Awesome! I'll get back to you with the details when I have them."

He hung up with Phil and went to get another beer. "Diving into the woods," he said and laughed. How many times had that happened? Spence couldn't think of a single time they went to Denham where they didn't wind up in the woods at least once. His smile turned to a frown. He was already starting to regret calling anyone. The more he thought about the old crew the less he wanted to see them. He knew the conversation would consist almost entirely of *Remember when...* It wasn't that Spence disliked his old friends. It wasn't even that he had moved beyond the mentality of his high school days. He simply didn't want to be reminded of every single thing they had done, even the many times they had gone to Denham.

He also dreaded the idea of seeing Marcus again. They had been pretty close back then. But that was before Marcus had completely fucked Phil. Spence had taken Phil's side as soon as he heard about it. Scott was more diplomatic and he tried to reconcile the two. It didn't work. As far as Spence knew Marcus and Phil hadn't spoken in almost eleven years. Was he really going to tell Marcus about this? Of all his old friends Marcus was the one who most reveled in the old stories. No one was more about *Remember when...* than Marcus Greer. Spence could probably tolerate it from Scott and Phil, at least for one night. He felt Marcus would push him over the edge within fifteen minutes.

So why was the phone back in his hand?

He got Marcus's voicemail which gave him one last opportunity to hang up. He nearly did just that. In the end he said, "Marcus, Tom. Call me when you get the chance."

The next afternoon Spence sat at a table on the patio of Lucia's Italian Ristorante on Davis St. He had just ordered a sandwich (ham and cheese, keeping it simple) and a beer. He was thankful for the table umbrella above his head. It was warm for October, even hot. He was sweating already. Thankfully the beer was ice cold when the kid waiting tables brought it to him. Spence sipped his beer in the shade of the umbrella and watched the traffic on Davis St.

He heard Marcus's car before he saw it. His eyes hidden behind his mirrored sunglasses he watched as the old Gran Torino pulled into the parking lot. Even through the glare Spence could see the car's best days were behind it. Several patches of rust adorned the fenders and the hood. There were numerous dents along the body. The car used to be blue but most of the paint had been replaced with black or gray primer. Spence remembered when Marcus bought it and all the restoration work that followed. None of that was in evidence now; it looked as bad as it sounded.

Both doors opened and Spence saw Marcus and his wife Maria emerge from the old shitbox. He waved and they waved back. As they got closer Spence slid his sunglasses down his nose. *My God, they've* aged, he thought. Marcus was thirty-two, the same age as Spence, and Maria was two years their junior. Both looked as if they were pushing fifty. *What the hell happened to them?*

"Spence! How's it going?" Maria exclaimed. She mounted the steps to the patio and threw her arms around him just as he stood. Her momentum nearly carried both of them to the ground.

Spence recovered his balance in time and returned the hug. "I've been good, kid. How's about you?"

"I'm not complaining, "she replied. She cleared out of the way for her husband.

Marcus hugged him, something else Spence had forgotten about. The man was a hugger, always had been. "Bro!"

"What up, Greerbox?" They separated and Spence all but fell back into his chair. Marcus and Maria sat down opposite him. "I see you still have Blue Thunder."

Marcus glanced over his shoulder at the Gran Torino. Smoke or steam rose slowly from beneath the hood. "Yep and I always will. I'll be buried in that fucking thing."

"It looks like it's ready to be buried right now."

"Fuck off," Marcus replied and laughed. "It runs stronger now than it ever did! Rebuilt the engine and the tranny, new exhaust and suspension, new cooling system. Body's a work in progress. It'll outlast whatever you're driving!"

Spence raised his glass toward the shitbox and smiled.

"It's been so long," Maria cut in. "When was the last time we saw each other?"

Spence had been thinking about that since Katie first told him the news of her new job. "Six years, I'm pretty sure. The night we went to see Keith's band."

"At Josie's! I forgot all about that!" Marcus came close to leaping from his chair at the memory. "Was that the same night we got into that fight with the big Korean son of a bitch?"

"No, that was at Four of A Kind," Maria corrected him. "I know because I was there."

You always were, Spence thought but did not say. It had been a running joke that Marcus was not allowed to leave the house unless Maria were with him. Although there had never been any substantiated claims the rumor was she had caught him in bed with another woman. Somehow the marriage survived but Maria had not let Marcus from her sight since. Today seemed no exception.

"Right, right, Four of A Kind," Marcus agreed, nodding his head enthusiastically. "You remember the size of that fucker?"

"How could I forget? He threw me the length of the room." Spence's back ached at the memory.

"Scott was drunk off his ass that night," Marcus continued. "I think the fight started in the men's room and spilled out into the bar. But then again it was six years ago like you said, so who knows?"

Marcus paused to light two cigarettes. He handed one to Maria. "So what's up, bro? I was surprised to hear from you after so long."

Spence took a deep breath and prepared himself. He was going to have to power through his explanation and the plan to go back to Denham. If he paused long enough to take a breath Marcus would jump in and dominate the conversation with *Remember when*s… So Spence launched into the story about Katie's new job and his plan to go back to Denham to keep an eye on her. To his surprise he managed to get through the whole explanation without a single interruption. When he stopped he took a sip of his beer and waited.

The waiter emerged from the door to Spence's right with his sandwich. Spence waited for Marcus's reaction. His old friend surprised him by first taking the time to tell the kid he wanted two beers. The kid checked their IDs as he had checked Spence's and Spence almost laughed. *Not only are they old enough to drink, they look old enough to have kids old enough to drink.* In fact, they had two boys but the oldest of them couldn't be more than ten years-old.

"That's a really nice car," the kid lied. "What year is it?"

Marcus beamed with pride. "1972, m'man."

The kid whistled through his teeth. "Man, that's awesome. Are you the original owner?"

Spence spit out his beer. Maria laughed.

Marcus's mouth disappeared into a thin line. "Just get the beers, man."

"Right away," the kid replied, seemingly unaware of the cause of Marcus's sudden change in tone.

After the waiter had once more disappeared Marcus placed his elbows on the table. "I'm in." It was his only comment.

Spence blinked. "That's it? 'I'm in'?" He waited for the other shoe to drop. He had prepared himself as best he could for the nostalgia blast Marcus was sure to hit him with, but it did not seem to be coming.

"Yeah, I'm in," Marcus confirmed. "Why? Were you expecting me so say no? I *loved* going to that place. There and Old Lichgate were my two favorite places on Earth. I've thought about going back for years. I just didn't think anyone else would want to. So, yeah, I'm in."

"*We're* in," Maria added. She put out her cigarette in the ashtray and squeezed her husband's hand. "I'd like to see that place, too."

This, at least, Spence expected. It was no longer possible to get Marcus without getting Maria as well. He had allowed for that, had even warned Scott it was likely to happen when he texted his friend after the call with Phil. Spence realized he was wound up, still anticipating a barrage of *Remember whens…* from

Marcus that now seemed destined to never occur. He relaxed his shoulders and took a bite of his sandwich.

"I take it Phil's going?" Marcus asked as Spence reached for his beer.

Spence's hand froze an inch from his glass. He had anticipated this, as well. It was no secret Spence had taken Phil's side. Frankly, he didn't see how anyone could do otherwise. Still he dreaded getting too much into it.

"Yeah. I talked to him yesterday."

The waiter appeared and placed a beer in front of Marcus and another in front of Maria. "Would you like anything else?"

Maria smiled at the kid and said, "No, thanks, we're good."

"I'll have another," Spence told him, holding up his nearly empty glass.

"I'll be right back," the kid replied and vanished again.

"Cool," Marcus said. "I'd really like to bury the hatchet. It's been, what, ten or eleven years?"

"The carnival, yeah," Spence replied. He had spent enough time in the last twenty-four hours thinking about that fucking carnival. He certainly did not want to rehash it now. "Look, I know he's still pissed. But who knows? Maybe you two *can* work it out." It seemed unlikely to Spence. The only hatchet Phil would bury was likely to be in Marcus's head. Then again, they had all been very close once. Anything was possible in a world where Spence's little sister had been hired at Greystone fucking Manor.

They spent the rest of their time at Lucia's reminiscing, Spence's least favorite activity, but at least the conversation never gravitated toward Denham. Considering Marcus's statement about always wanting to go back, Spence was surprised, but pleasantly so. Marcus even brought up their old high school principal, Mr. McAdams. Spence hadn't thought of that particular bane of his existence since they all graduated. *The things this guy remembers. So much for weed wreaking havoc on the brain cells.* Marcus and Maria had one more beer apiece and smoked several more cigarettes. Spence stopped at his third beer.

When it was time to go the Gran Torino sputtered but started and Spence waved to them as they pulled out of the parking lot. Marcus gunned the engine and held his raised fist outside the driver's window. *Just like he did every time he left somewhere*, Spence remembered. He had vivid memories of Marcus doing the same thing—with the same car—in high school. *Christ, some things never change.*

He had his old Denham crew, or, at least, as much of it as he could assemble. Glen and Vic had long since moved out of state and Johnny D had vanished off the face of the earth. Spence had left Facebook messages with Glen and Vic with the news and had received a quick reply. *Fucking Greystone!* Vic had said. *Don't let the devil worshippers get your sister!* Spence assured him Katie would be perfectly safe. Glen asked for photos and Spence said he would try to remember to take some.

Johnny D was just...gone. No one knew where he had moved or even when. Unless he popped up on social media (or showed up at someone's house) there was no way to contact him. Spence would need to be content with the group he had. And he was. Even Maria was okay with him.

He walked to his Pathfinder and started for home.

CHAPTER THREE

The Gates of Hell

Katie emerged from the bathroom and paused in the doorway. Ms. Palmer stood a few feet in front of her. The younger woman's eyes started at Katie's feet and made their way slowly north. She lingered in several places, several *key* places, Katie realized. *What are the chances she's checking me out?* But no. Ms. Palmer had given no sign that she was the least bit interested in Katie Spencer as anything more than an employee she would need to train to the high standards of Greystone Manor. Still, her eyes lingered…

"Presentable," Ms. Palmer proclaimed at last. "This way, please."

Katie fell into step behind her new boss. Her shoes were brand new and tight. She would need a foot massage after this. They headed down the corridor of the third floor toward the stairs. She was excited, she had to admit. Serving meals to two very old wealthy men was hardly her dream job but the mansion itself was quite a place to work. It was also a lot to memorize. If not for Ms. Palmer's presence Katie might have already gotten lost. Greystone Manor contained so many side corridors and small, hidden nooks that Katie feared it would not be long before she found herself wandering the halls searching for a specific room in which she had duties. She tried committing the paintings on the walls to memory. The staff bathroom she had just used (one of many, Ms. Palmer informed her) was next to the portrait of Henry VII. She could start by remembering that.

Ms. Palmer stopped abruptly in front of another door. Katie had to pull up to avoid colliding with her. Her boss faced the closed door with her hands folded in front of her. Katie mimicked her posture.

A moment later the door opened. A girl younger than Ms. Palmer and dressed identical to Katie emerged into the hallway. The new arrival glanced nervously at the two women in front of her. Ms. Palmer examined the girl in the same way she looked over Katie.

"Presentable. This way, girls."

The new girl breathed a sigh of relief and some of the tension in her shoulders released. She took her place beside Katie and the two new employees followed their boss down to the first floor.

Ms. Palmer led them through more rooms and corridors until they emerged into the kitchen. On the far side of the ridiculously large room a woman in a black chef's outfit stood over a large sink.

"Ms. Arnold."

The woman turned. She was older and rounder than anyone Katie had met thus far. She held a dishrag in one hand and a dinner plate in the other. Her lips smiled at the three intruders, but the gesture failed to reach her small, dark eyes. "Ms. Palmer," she replied in a thick British accent.

Ms. Palmer led Katie and the new girl across the kitchen until they stood before the chef. "This is Ms. Spencer and Ms. Regan. They will be serving their Lordships. Please show them around your domain and send for me when they are ready."

Ms. Arnold's eyes moved from Katie to Ms. Regan and back again before she treated Ms. Palmer to an unpleasant smile. "Very good, Ms. Palmer."

Ms. Palmer turned on her heel and exited the kitchen.

Katie watched her go and turned her eyes to Ms. Arnold. She smiled.

"I give this tour one time and one time only so pay attention. I am not here to hold your hand. If you need someone for that I suggest Mr. Exton or Ms. Palmer. Understood?" Katie nodded. So did the girl beside her.

Ms. Arnold returned the gesture. She proceeded to walk them around the kitchen, pointing out various stations and their function. She ended each description with the statement, "You won't have to deal with this yourself. I'll do it." The tour continued until they reached the large, long counter on the far side of the room opposite the door through which they had entered. "This is where most of your attention will be focused. Anytime you see a dish sitting here it is ready to be taken to their Lordships. Do so at once. Any questions?"

Katie shook her head. It seemed pretty easy to remember. She was grateful to learn that not everything in the kitchen was her responsibility. She felt she could spend an entire shift in here just wiping down surfaces—not that any appeared dirty. The kitchen, like the rest of the mansion, was spotless..

Ms. Regan asked, "Will we be doing any cooking for their Lordships?"

Ms. Arnold scowled. She leaned in close to the new employees. "No one—and I mean *no one*—but me prepares meals for their Lordships. You'll be serving them and assisting with cleaning the dishes. That's why you're here. Perhaps that wasn't made clear to you until now."

Ms. Regan shrunk back a little. Her eyes went to her feet. "Ma'am," she replied.

There's always one, Katie thought. Exton had seemed nice enough. Johnson was even more so. Palmer was stiff and formal, but she had not said or done anything that raised any alarm bells. Arnold, on the other hand… Katie had dealt with asshole supervisors before. She felt confident she could handle this one. She hoped Ms. Regan could, as well.

Ms. Arnold seemed pleased with the girl's response. She led them to an empty corner of the kitchen next to an exterior door. She turned to them expectantly. Katie waited. So did Ms. Regan.

The three women stood near the empty corner, all seemingly unwilling to be the first to speak.

It was Ms. Arnold who broke the silence. "You'll be bringing the meals to the dining hall through here." She placed one meaty hand on the wall to their side and pushed. The door was hidden so well Katie had no idea of its existence until that moment. She started. So did Ms. Regan. Ms. Arnold did not bother to cover up her expression of smug satisfaction. "I expect my assistants to be more observant in the future," she told them. "Mr. Exton and Ms. Palmer insist upon it. How else will you know how best to serve their Lordships?"

Katie was still looking at the hidden door. She had stood no more than three feet from it and had still failed to notice it. She wondered how many others she had walked past or stood next to while oblivious to its presence. For a brief moment she thought maybe Ms. Arnold was correct; she would need to be more observant. "Yes, Ms. Arnold." She needed this job.

Ms. Arnold stepped aside and extended her arm toward the door. "Follow it to the dining hall so you'll know the way."

Katie peered inside. The passage was narrow but not claustrophobic. The inner wall was a combination of old sheetrock and even older stone; the outside wall was ancient stone and mortar. Lightbulbs had been strung along the ceiling at uneven intervals but at least they provided enough light. No fancy wall sconces in here, Katie noted.

She stepped inside. Ms. Regan stayed a few steps behind her. The light from the kitchen vanished after a few feet and the girls were left with the ceiling lights to guide their way. Katie walked slowly, her footsteps echoing in the small, enclosed space. The floor alternated between old planks of wood and patches of stone. The planks creaked a bit when both she and Ms. Regan stepped on the same one at the same time.

"I wonder what's under here," Ms. Regan whispered.

"The basement, maybe. Who knows? Maybe nothing at all," Katie whispered back.

"In this place I wouldn't be surprised if it was the gates of hell."

Katie suppressed a laugh. She didn't know if Ms. Arnold was still listening back inside the kitchen but she didn't want to take the chance of being scolded again. Best to press on to the dining hall.

"There's something ahead on the right," Ms. Regan told her a few moments later.

Katie could see it, a square of diffused light on the inner wall. The two girls approached and stopped in front of it. They were looking into the drawing room Katie had seen during Mr. Exton's tour. The square held some kind of vague image, as if someone had traced patterns and colors into it long ago.

"It's a painting," Ms. Regan announced, her voice still a whisper.

Katie reached out her hand but pulled it back before she made contact. "It's one of the paintings on the wall," she whispered back. She turned to Ms. Regan. "It's like a two-way mirror, only it's a painting. Jesus, I looked right at this when Mr. Exton was showing me around. I had no idea."

"I think that *is* the idea," the girl said. "I bet there are more like this. Someone could come back here and spy on people and they'd never know it."

"Okay, that's just creepy." Katie's voice was still a whisper, but she didn't particularly care if Ms. Arnold heard her.

"Yeah it is," Ms. Regan agreed.

They left the two-way painting behind and continued on their way. The next one they came across looked into the mask room. The girls paused only briefly before pressing on. It took two more such paintings before they arrived at the dining hall. Unlike the previous two-way paintings, this one had the added bonus of a small shelf that Katie imagined would hold a glass or mug for the watcher. *Spying must be thirsty work*, she thought. She also found a stud on the stone portion of the wall. Katie pressed it.

The secret corridor was flooded with light as the wall panel opened into the dining hall. Katie and Ms. Regan stepped through. The long, elegant table was barren except for two elaborate silver candleholders placed in the center. Two high-backed chairs, one on either end, accompanied the table. Several more such chairs were stacked in a corner.

Katie turned and regarded the painting through which they had viewed the room. It was of a man on horseback leading a pack of hounds on a hunt. Katie stepped closer, trying to penetrate the painting to the space on the other side. She could see nothing but the man and his canine hunting party. "Man, this is so weird," she told her companion. "I can't see through this at all."

Ms. Regan appeared next to her. After a moment she answered, "Me, neither. Kinda gives me the creeps now that I know about it."

"Yeah. Come on, let's get back to the kitchen." Once they were both inside the passageway Katie pressed the stud again and the no-longer-secret door closed. She led the way back to the kitchen and their unpleasant host.

Ms. Arnold was slicing the thickest steak Katie had ever seen on a cutting board on one of the center islands. "Get lost?" she asked. Her tone was conversational if not pleasant. Slice. Slice. Slice.

"We found it okay," Ms. Regan replied.

Ms. Arnold nodded. "Ms. Palmer was here a few minutes ago. She said you can take thirty minutes for yourselves before she wants to see you in the drawing room." She never took her eyes from her task nor did she pause. The blade sliced clean through the meat and some blood pooled around it on the cutting board.

Katie swallowed. "Thank you, Ms. Arnold."

The chef did not reply. Slice. Slice. Slice.

Ms. Regan tugged on Katie's sleeve and the two girls headed for the door.

They walked through several rooms until they found the foyer and the front door. The outside air greeted them, and Katie took a deep breath. The sun warmed her face and hands (the only skin left exposed by her uniform) and Katie stood for a moment and let it wash over her. After the dark and damp of the hidden passage the sun and clean air were most welcome. Katie did not know how long she stood in that spot and she did not care.

"Come on, this way," Ms. Regan told her.

Katie opened her eyes and saw her new companion heading toward the side of the house. She stopped near a door although Katie had no idea where in the house the door led. Ms. Regan sat on the steps and fished in her pocket. She found a cigarette and her lighter. "You want one?"

"Nah, never got into it," Katie replied.

Ms. Regan nodded to an old coffee can on the side of the steps. Katie saw it was full of cigarette butts. "Someone takes their smoke breaks out here. I saw it when Mr. Exton was showing me the grounds." She lit up and took a deep drag. "I'm Amanda."

"Katie. Nice to meet you."

"Nice to know someone's first name around here," Amanda replied.

Katie could only nod. "Yeah, they're very formal."

"What do you think of the staff? I mean, I've only met Exton, Palmer, and Johnson so far. Oh, and our friend in the kitchen, of course."

Katie shrugged. "Mr. Johnson seemed pretty friendly. The jury's still out on the rest. Oh, and I saw a girl here the other day when I interviewed. I think she was hired, too. It's the house that fascinates me, though. I can't believe how big it is. Every time I think I've reached the end of a corridor it branches off in a different direction. It's like it's never-ending."

"And that secret passage," Amanda added. "I've never seen anything like that outside of a movie."

"Yeah, this is some Bela Lugosi shit."

"Some what?"

Katie smiled "I am old. Never mind."

Amanda glanced at her watch and lit another cigarette. "We still have some time left. Where are you from?"

"Here. Deacon's. You?"

"West Philly represent!" Amanda thumped her chest twice.

Katie laughed. "Never been. Why are you here? I mean, do you live here now? Moved for family or something?"

Amanda flicked ashes and shook her head. "No family to speak of. Have a mom I haven't seen since I was sixteen. My dad is God-knows-where. It's just little old me. Saw the ad online for a housekeeper here. Thought I'd give it a go."

"No jobs closer to Philadelphia?"

"I'm trying to see the world."

Katie laughed again. "So, you came here? Not Venice, not Tokyo. Deacon's fucking Landing, Connecticut?"

Amanda laughed as well. "It's a place, ain't it?"

"Only in the broadest sense," Katie replied.

Amanda sat and smoked in silence for a few moments before she asked, "How about you? Family?"

"No kids if that's what you're asking. Not yet, anyway. My mother passed away three years ago. My father skipped out when I was two. It's just me and my brother, Tom."

Katie waited for a hint of recognition in Amanda Regan's eyes. Everyone knew Tom Spencer. His name had once been a fixture in the police blotter. But it seemed his fame, or infamy, did not extend past the borders of Deacon's Landing. Amanda Regan did not react at all to the name. "I told Exton I don't talk to my brother but that's not exactly true. Tom has a bit of a reputation in town. So, I kinda…lied on my resumé and said I didn't have family. I know, it was a shitty thing to do. I still feel guilty about it. But Exton found out anyway and he still hired me so there's that. And I did tell Tom about this job."

"Family's tough," Amanda replied. "And I'm sorry about your mom, too."

"I'm still getting used to that," Katie told her. "But thanks."

Amanda checked her watch again. "It's about that time." She stood and tossed the cigarette butt into the coffee can. "Shall we?"

"We shall," Katie replied. They walked back to the front of the house and reentered Greystone Manor.

Ms. Palmer awaited them in the drawing room. She stood in front of one of the fireplaces and chatted with Mr. Exton. They noted the new arrivals. Katie and Amanda stood near the doorway and waited for the conversation to end. It did a few moments later and Mr. Exton headed for the door. He nodded as he passed them. "Ladies."

"Mr. Exton," the girls said together. Ms. Palmer approached them, and Katie and Amanda turned their eyes to her.

"Ms. Arnold showed you the passage for the servants."

Both girls nodded but it was Amanda who spoke. "Yes, ma'am."

"You'll be expected to enter the dining hall through there unless their Lordships say otherwise. They are likely to entertain guests during their stay with us. It is unlikely but not impossible to happen the first night, but it is almost certain to occur at some point. Perhaps many nights depending upon their business so you will make several trips via the servants' passage. Be aware."

"Yes, ma'am," they answered in unison.

"Tonight Mr. Exton and I shall have dinner in the dining hall. You may consider this a dress rehearsal for tomorrow night when you will serve their Lordships. Dinner will be served promptly at eight. Do you have any questions?"

"No, Ms. Palmer," Katie replied.

"Ms. Palmer, will we be here to greet their Lordships when they arrive from the airport?"

Ms. Palmer looked Amanda up and down, much the same way she had examined both girls in their new uniforms. "No," she said after a moment. "It is likely to be very early tomorrow morning. I would hope you would be home in bed fast asleep when their Lordships arrive. You will need your rest for tomorrow night."

Amanda failed to hide the disappointment from her voice. Or perhaps she did not try. "Yes, Ms. Palmer."

Ms. Palmer nodded. "Prepare the table for Mr. Exton and me, please."

"Yes, ma'am," Amanda said for both of them.

The girls headed for the door.

"Oh, and Ms. Regan?" The girls stopped and turned. Ms. Palmer withdrew a small white cylinder from her pocket and tossed it to Amanda. "Their Lordships do not smoke, nor do they enjoy the smell. Use that afterward. It works." The corners of her mouth drew back ever so slightly in what might have been a smile.

Amanda regarded the small capsule of perfume in her hand. She clearly made no attempt to hide her smile that time. "Yes, Ms. Palmer."

Katie and Amanda headed for the kitchen. They made it perhaps halfway before the laughter took them.

CHAPTER FOUR

Taking Two Cars

Spence knew when Marcus pulled up outside his apartment. The sound of the Gran Torino was unmistakable and unmissable. Somehow, even above the sound of the old V8 beast, Spence could hear Saliva's *Click Click Boom* blaring from the speakers. Spence froze, his hand halfway to picking up his leather jacket on the back of the kitchen chair. He had forgotten about that old song, had not heard it probably since the last time Marcus had pulled up to his house. It was what Marcus referred to as his *arrival song*. He had it cued in the cd player he hardwired below the dash.

All at once Spence was back in high school, rushing out the door to hang with his crew on a Friday night. Marcus's ride was not a large car, but they were usually able to stuff their whole group into its innards. Then they were off to the Eight Ball Arcade (closed two months before their high school graduation), or to cause mischief at Old Lichgate Cemetery out on Route Six. And sometimes they would spend the night diving into the woods to avoid approaching cars at Denham while sneaking up to Greystone for a peek through the windows.

Spence put on his jacket and locked the door behind him. When he got close enough to the car Maria stepped out and pulled the front seat forward so he could get inside.

"Hey, Tom," she said by way of greeting.

"Hey back," he replied. The smell of old leather and old (and new) cigarette smoke filled his nostrils. The music was loud and his seat vibrated with every beat. "Damn, man, turn that shit down, will ya?"

Marcus, sitting behind the wheel, half-turned and flashed a smile at Spence. "If it's too loud..."

"You're too old," Spence finished for him. He had to shout to be heard. "Yeah, I know. I guess I'm old then because it's way too fucking loud back here." Marcus turned the volume knob and the assault on Spence's ears eased up a bit. "Thank you," he shouted, then smiled at his too-loud response.

"Old bastard," Marcus said with a laugh.

Maria returned to the passenger seat and closed the car door. Marcus slammed his foot on the gas pedal and the Gran Torino responded instantly. Spence was thrown back in the seat and that brought back a lot of memories, too. The old muscle car's interior was as worn and pitted as its body, perhaps even more so. Still, Spence had to admit he had missed this car and its driver.

"Where we meeting everybody?" Marcus asked as he took the turn onto Archer Street at much too high a rate of speed. The Gran Torino's tires squealed, and Spence was tossed across the seat.

"Old Colonial," he replied when he was able to steady himself. *Christ, he hasn't changed at all. He's still acting like we're seventeen and cruising the Landing for chicks. Next he'll probably want to egg someone's house.*

"Old Colonial, got it."

Maria lit a cigarette and turned to look at the back seat passenger. "Who are we meeting? God, I haven't seen the gang in years."

"Scott and Phil," Spence replied. He watched Marcus for a reaction to the latter's name but saw nothing. *He probably thinks everything's good with them. Just don't say anything stupid. Just don't say anything stupid. Just don't say anything stupid.* It would be Spence's mantra for the evening. He had been reciting it in his head all day.

"Just tell him to keep his fucking mouth shut," Phil had told him on the phone a few hours ago. Spence had come clean and informed Phil that Marcus and his wife would be joining them. "I don't wanna be reminded of how he fucking left me for the cops."

"I'll tell him," Spence had assured him.

"And I don't want to hear any of that commie bullshit, either. It wasn't funny then and it ain't funny now."

"Will do."

Phil listed a few more conditions that would need to be met in order for him not to stomp on Marcus's head. Spence agreed to them in turn. He even assured his friend they would have a good time tonight. Phil replied with his customary, "Uh huh," and hung up.

Now Spence sat in the backseat and tried to come up with a way to ease Marcus into that conversation.

Maria saved him the trouble. "Don't say anything to piss him off," she told her husband. "You two haven't seen each other in how many years? Let's not start a fight over anything that happened in the past."

Marcus nodded. "Don't worry, I'm cool. That commie prick loves me. You'll see."

Spence's relief at the first part of Marcus's statement was replaced by dread at the second. He repeated his mantra a dozen more times.

The Old Colonial had not changed much in the past ten years. In point of fact it probably had not changed much in the past seventy. The diner's exterior evoked the soda shops of the 1950s that appeared in every teen movie of the time. Back in high school Spence had always wanted a waitress on roller skates to come out and take his order. If indeed that had ever been the case in the diner's existence those days were very much over by the time Spence and his friends started to frequent the place. It still appeared rundown. The neon sign winked at them and made his eyes hurt. Spence had to look away.

Maria exited the car and pulled the seat forward for him. Marcus revved the engine one last time for good measure as he always did and then killed it. His door creaked when he opened it.

"The fucking Old Colonial," Marcus said with admiration in his voice. "Remember we used to be here all night? What was that waitress's name? The cute one with the blonde hair and the big ass?"

Spence could picture her right away. The poor woman always seemed to draw the short straw and had to wait on them no matter where they sat. They were apt to give her a hard time, especially Scott and Marcus, demanding food be sent back, asking for more napkins, a different ketchup bottle, her phone number. Scott actually left the woman a joint one time instead of cash for a tip. Spence could just about see her nametag in his memory, but it eluded him. He shrugged. "I know the one you mean. Damned if I can remember her name, though."

Maria smacked her husband's arm. "'The *cute* one?'"

"Ow! She was before your time, babe."

"She better be," Maria informed him.

The trio mounted the steps and Marcus held the door for Maria and Spence. The Old Colonial's interior matched its exterior. The counter, the tables, the booths and chairs, everything had seen better days. It was identical to the place in Spence's memories, or nearly so. There was no haze of cigarette smoke hanging in the air. The statewide smoking ban had seen to that, a fact for which Spence was grateful. It had always been the one drawback to hanging here back in the day. Now that he was not forced to peer through a haze of smoke, he found it easier to locate Scott and Phil.

They sat at a booth in the corner with a third person whose back was to him. Spence pointed to them and led Marcus and Maria to the table. The third man at the table was big, *very* big. Spence ran through his mental rolodex but failed to come up with anyone they knew who fit the description of this stranger. He wore a short sleeve shirt, and every square inch of his arms was covered with ink. *Christ, Phil didn't bring backup, did he?* Spence couldn't imagine Marcus—or any of them—lasting more than a few seconds against the mystery man.

At their approach Scott waved and Phil grimaced when he saw Marcus. The third man turned to look at them and Spence saw it was Phil's brother, Keith. *When did he get out?* Spence wondered. He hadn't seen the younger Volokhov in years. Keith had been a rather annoying staple of their youth. The pain-in-the-ass little brother who never left them alone and threatened to tell on them if he witnessed them doing anything wrong. Phil once had to bribe the little shit to keep his mouth shut when he caught them smoking weed in Phil's backyard. That skinny little prick was neither skinny nor little anymore. Spence hoped he wasn't still a prick, too.

Keith's presence could complicate things for Marcus. It was hardly a secret he despised the man for what happened between Marcus and his brother. Spence could not hope to successfully stop the younger man if he got it into his head to even the score on his brother's behalf. Keith was simply too big; it would take all of them to hold him back, and even then…

"Wassup, motherfuckers?" Scott called and drew a disapproving look from the older couple at the next table.

"Hey, guys," Marcus said by way of greeting. He slapped hands with Scott and looked like he was about to do the same with Phil before he apparently thought better of it. He stepped aside so Maria could sit first and slid into the spot next to her. Keith moved over enough for Spence to take the spot next to him.

"How you been, man?" Spence asked Keith Volokhov. "How's the Navy treating you?"

"Four and out," Keith replied. "What does that tell you?"

Spence laughed. So far so good. Keith had yet to even look in Marcus's direction. He eyed Phil on the other side of the table. Whether by design or accident Marcus had allowed Maria to sit first, placing someone between himself and Phil. It was a smart move if done intentionally. Spence doubted they would actually mix it up, and probably not inside the diner, but it was still a smart move.

"Phil, you commie fuck! What's up!"

Spence cringed. So much for *Just don't say anything stupid.* He placed his hands on the table and prepared to reach across and try to separate the two men before punches could be thrown. To his surprise Phil simply smiled and replied, "Not much, you kraut bastard. How's things?" Phil glanced across the table at Spence. His eyes said, *I told you. I fucking told you. This night is not going to end well.*

The waitress appeared and took their order. It was not the cute blonde with the big ass. Spence could see the disappointment in Marcus's eyes. It did not linger there long, though; Marcus eyed the waitress when she retreated to the kitchen with their order. Maria, engaged with Phil, failed to notice, which probably saved her husband another slug to the arm.

It *was* typical Marcus, though. In his world everything stayed the same. So of course the waitress they had tormented back in high school still worked at the Old Colonial. Spence didn't doubt for one second Marcus planned further torments if their old waitress had presented herself. *Hopefully she's long gone from here*, Spence thought. *Living it up somewhere warm where the drinks keep coming and she doesn't have to deal with assholes like us.*

Marcus and Scott flipped through the pages of the table jukebox and derided the lack of anything worth playing. Spence was grateful that Marcus seemed to be leaving Phil to himself. Phil, for his part, talked with Maria and Spence and Keith. He seemed content not to throttle Marcus, at least for the moment.

By the time the waitress brought their food the conversation had turned to Denham. *Remember When*s… were flying around the table and all the greatest hits were playing.

"What's the clone car?" Maria asked when Scott mentioned it.

"Oh, man." Scott leaned back in the booth and ran a hand through his hair. He looked at Phil. "Who was driving that night? You?"

Phil shook his head. "Glen."

Scott's eyes widened and he smiled. "That's right! He had that old Camaro. What the hell did he call it? He had a name for it."

"I don't remember," Phil admitted.

"Wasn't it *Love Machine*? No, wait. War *Machine*! That was it. Fucking *War Machine*!"

Spence was nodding and smiling himself. "He always blasted that KISS song *War Machine*, too. It could be five degrees outside and he'd have the windows down just cruising around with that song blasting. God, I forgot all about that!"

"And I'd be in the back seat freezing my nuts off," Scott added.

"God *damn*, man," Phil added. "The things we remember."

Scott returned his attention to Maria. "We're in Glen's Camaro and we didn't walk down the street that time, we drove. We didn't do that often because the road is so narrow that if another car came in you could get boxed in pretty efficiently. But this time, I don't remember why, we drove."

"Middle of the fucking night and we see another car coming up behind us," Phil added. When Maria gave him a quizzical look he said, "A long stretch of that road is a straightaway. At night you can see headlights a good half mile away. So Glen got to the widened part of the road where it becomes dirt and turned around."

"Okay." Maria took a sip of her beer and waited.

"As the two cars passed each other," Scott continued, "we looked inside. There were like five guys in that car and they all looked the same. Dressed the same, same haircut, same glasses, fucking same everything. We immediately dubbed it the *clone car.*"

"But Johnny D didn't see them and didn't believe us," Spence added. "So when Glen saw they were turning around like they were gonna follow us, Johnny D wanted to get out and see for himself. So the asshole jumped in the woods and got a good look when they drove past."

"No shit." Maria looked both fascinated and nervous.

"Hand to God," Scott said. "So those assholes started chasing us. I don't know what kind of car they had but it wasn't anywhere near as fast as the *War Machine.* We lost them on the back roads. But we got pretty lost ourselves. To this day I have no idea where we ended up. So end of story, right?"

Maria shrugged. "I guess?"

"Well, we had to go back and find Johnny D."

Maria's eyes widened. "Oh my God! I forgot about him!"

Spence's smile matched Scott's and Phil's. Now that someone was telling the story aloud the memories were flooding back.

"This time we parked on the opposite side of Route 26, like we usually did when we went there. Glen had a shitload of things in his trunk you could use as weapons. Crowbars, baseball bats, shit like that. We loaded up and walked down the road to find Johnny D."

"Except *this* pussy stayed in the car!" Spence pointed to Marcus.

Marcus looked at his wife and shrugged his shoulders. "I was high as fuck that night. I barely remember it. What was I gonna do besides fall into the woods and drool?"

Even Phil was smiling. "You were fucking *baked* that night."

"Hell yeah I was." Marcus laughed and looked like he might try to high-five Phil. At the last minute he changed his mind and sat back in the booth.

"So, anyway, we go walking down the road, and I'm nervous as shit about the clone car coming back," Scott continued. "But we found Johnny D and we tossed him a crowbar and we got the fuck out of there."

"Do you remember what he said?" Spence asked. When no one did he said, "Johnny D told us he heard drums coming from the woods somewhere behind him."

Scott nearly leaped from the seat. "Holy shit, that's right! I forgot about that."

"Drums?" Maria was clearly confused. "Like Tommy Lee?"

"Like voodoo shit," Scott said.

Spence shrugged. "That's what he said, anyway. Johnny D wasn't known for his bullshit. At the time I certainly believed him. I think I still do."

"Jesus," Maria remarked. "And you idiots kept going back after that?"

Scott shrugged. Phil took a sip of his beer and said, "It was something to do. It's not like the Landing was an exciting place even back then. After the Eight Ball closed down what were we gonna do? Go hang at the Waterbury mall? That place was a ghost town."

"Oh, I don't know. Maybe hang somewhere where you don't get chased by clones."

Everyone laughed.

"Okay, I need a cigarette after that." Maria stood and waited for Marcus to let her out of the booth.

"Me, too," Marcus added.

Scott raised his hand. "Same."

A moment later they were outside, and Spence was left with the Volokhov brothers. He drummed his fingers on the tabletop and waited. Phil did not keep him waiting long.

"God, he's still an asshole," Phil said at last.

"Got that right," Keith added.

"He's acting like nothing happened," Phil continued. "Did he fucking forget about the carnival?"

"No one anywhere has forgotten about the carnival," Spence replied. "Look, I'm not in his head, but it looks like he doesn't know how to broach the subject. I think he wants to apologize for what happened but he's not sure how."

"Then he can figure it out," Phil replied. "If he's waiting for me to make the first move, he's gonna go home very fucking disappointed."

"Fucking A," Keith added helpfully.

Spence shrugged his shoulders. "Let me talk to him. I'm sure we can work this out."

Phil sat back and crossed his arms. "Don't count on it, Spence."

Marcus, Maria, and Scott returned a few minutes later. The conversation returned to Denham and a few more tales were related. The stories lasted long enough for another round of beers before the manager started giving them the stink eye. They asked for the check and paid it and left a decent tip. Marcus even managed to tell the waitress, "Have a nice night," instead of something that could be legally construed as sexual harassment. This was no doubt due to the presence of his wife standing next to him.

"We all going up in my car?" Marcus asked when they reached the parking lot.

Phil and Keith regarded the beat-up Gran Torino and Spence knew right away they would be taking two cars to Denham.

"I'll take my car," Phil told Marcus.

"I'm with you," Keith said.

"Yeah, I'll stick with Phil's Equinox," Scott added. "I don't want Spence getting any ideas with me in the backseat."

"Hey, that only happened once," Spence said, "and that was in '09 and I'd been drinking."

They laughed like the old friends they were. Spence returned to the Gran Torino's backseat, and he watched Scott and Keith step into Phil's black SUV.

"We'll follow you," Phil called to them before he got into the driver's seat.

"Keep up, motherfuckers!" Marcus waved to him and fired up the big block V8. He revved the engine a few times and waited until he saw Phil's headlights come to life. Then he mashed the gap pedal and the Gran Torino fishtailed out of the parking lot.

Spence felt his dinner start to rise and he squashed it back down. He regretted not joining Phil who was only now pulling out of the Old Colonial's parking lot at a much more reasonable pace.

"You do remember how to get there, right?" he leaned forward and asked.

"Look who you're asking," Marcus replied. He shoved the CD into the player beneath the dash and cranked up the volume and Saliva was thundering in Spence's ears.

It was going to be a long ride.

CHAPTER FIVE

Around the time Marcus was pulling into the Old Colonial's parking lot Katie stepped out of her car and locked the door. She saw Mr. Johnson some distance away leaning against the open doorway to the barn, cleaning something with a rag. He smiled and waved to her. "Good evening, Ms. Spencer."

Katie waved back. "Hi, Mr. Johnson."

"Big night for you."

"I suppose so. I have to admit I'm a little nervous."

Mr. Johnson's smile widened. "You'll do great!"

Katie returned the smile. "Thanks. I hope so."

He waved again and disappeared into the barn.

Katie walked around the side of the house to the door and the steps with the hidden coffee can. She rang the bell and waited. A moment later the door swung open and Ms. Palmer stood on the other side of the threshold.

"Good evening, Ms. Spencer," she said by way of greeting.

"And to you, Ms. Palmer," Katie replied. Her boss neither spoke again nor moved. *Is she expecting me to curtsey?* Katie waited in silence while Ms. Palmer looked her over again.

After an uncomfortable moment Ms. Palmer stepped aside and Katie entered Greystone Manor through the servant's door as ordered. Ms. Palmer closed the door behind her and turned the lock. "This way, Ms. Spencer."

Katie followed her boss through the maze of corridors and up to the second floor. Ms. Palmer paused to wipe a speck of dust from a small round table in the hallway before continuing to the third floor. Ms. Palmer stopped before the door to the changing room and opened it for her. "Your uniform is cleaned and pressed and ready."

"Thank you, Ms. Palmer." Katie stepped inside the room and the younger woman closed the door behind her. Katie regarded the uniform for a moment before changing into it. Once dressed she emerged back into the hallway. Amanda Regan had joined them, dressed identical to the other two women. "Hi, Ms. Regan."

"Hello to you, Ms. Spencer," Amanda replied with a nervous smile.

"Ladies, this way." Ms. Palmer led them back the way they had come. "You will assist Ms. Arnold with food preparation until eight o'clock, at which time their Lordships will be seated for dinner."

"Yes, ma'am," both women said in unison.

Ms. Palmer left them with Ms. Arnold and departed. The two new staff members of Greystone Manor waited silently for the chef to acknowledge them. It took some time; Ms. Arnold's attention was focused entirely on the largest piece of beef Katie had ever seen. It was sprinkled with spices Katie could not identify but she had to admit, even in its current undercooked state it looked delicious.

Finally, Ms. Arnold turned to them. "Why are you standing there like two statues? You're even worse than the two new servants on the day shift. Get to work." She indicated a row of platters sitting atop the far counter. "Fix those up for their Lordships and be quick about it."

Katie glanced at Amanda's watch. 6:40 P.M. There seemed plenty of time for meal prep. What was the older woman's rush? Instead of questioning Katie said, simply, "Yes, Ms. Arnold." The two newest employees got to work.

The time got away from them. When the platters were covered with finger foods—enough for twenty people, in Katie's opinion—the time on Amanda's watch read 7:37. Katie turned to Ms. Arnold who was taking the large slab of beef from the oven. "We're ready, Ms. Arnold."

The chef inspected the dinner before she turned her attention to the platters. Her eyes paused on each in turn until she seemed satisfied. "You have ten minutes. Then you'll begin service."

Katie needed to pee in the worst way. She had had nothing to drink but some sips of water so it was most likely nerves. She excused herself and hunted for one of the staff bathrooms. She returned to the kitchen a few moments later. Ms. Arnold seemed uninterested in small talk so Katie simply stood by the counter and waited. Amanda reentered the kitchen a few minutes later smelling like perfume. She took her place next to Katie.

Ms. Arnold consulted the clock on the wall and nodded to the girls. "Begin."

Katie and Amanda began.

****

Marcus put the Gran Torino in park and killed the engine. The music thundering in Spence's ears ceased all at once. He rubbed his ears until he felt better. The CD changer beneath the dash apparently contained Metallica, Godsmack, Avenged Sevenfold, and Korn in addition to Saliva. Spence tried a few times to get Marcus to lower the volume but his old friend either didn't hear him or pretended not to. When they got closer to Denham Marcus queued up his arrival song. Birds scattered from the trees as they raced along the narrow streets on the outskirts of Deacon's Landing. Now, with the Gran Torino parked on the other side of Aldebaran Road, all was silent again.

Spence tapped Maria on the shoulder and she opened the door for him. He stepped out of the car and leaned on it. His meager supper and the beers from the Old Colonial were threatening a revolt. It took him several moments to put down the insurrection. By the time he succeeded Phil's Equinox was making the turn onto the cross street.

"You look a little green, Spence," Phil remarked as he drove past.

Spence flipped him off.

Phil laughed and turned the Equinox and parked behind Marcus.

Marcus and Maria stepped out of their car and lit cigarettes. They approached the idling Equinox. "We going in yet?" Marcus asked.

Spence looked at the sky. "It ain't quite dark enough yet. Are you high?"

"I'm about to be," Marcus replied. From his pack of Marlboros he pulled a joint and fired it up. After a couple hits he passed it to his wife.

"It'll be dark enough in a few," Scott announced as he extricated himself from the SUV's backseat. He accepted the joint from Maria. "Especially with all the trees around here. I say we chill until then. I've never been here in the daytime."

"I bet no one has," Phil added. "I'm with Carpenter. We wait until it gets a little darker."

"I'm down with that," Spence told them. In truth he wouldn't have minded setting off now. Yes, they would be seen easily by anyone who happened to look out a window. And any cars that came along would also spot them. But he wanted to see his sister. Spence did not believe in the backstory about devil worshippers and all that nonsense, not anymore, but he had seen enough at Denham to make him a bit uneasy with the idea of Katie working there, and at the main house, no less. But Scott and Phil were right. It was always better to wait until dark. Spence eyed the sky and waited.

****

Katie balanced four platters. The passageway from the kitchen to the dining hall was narrow and marginally lit but she managed to traverse the distance without dropping anything. Behind her she could hear Amanda keeping pace.

They were retracing the path they had navigated the night before. Their practice run serving dinner to Exton and Palmer had gone well enough. Neither woman had dropped anything. Both their bosses had some tips for them to improve their level of service for when the Lords Morley were present but both she and Amanda Regan had escaped the practice run with their jobs and egos intact. Now, of course, it was time for the real deal.

"Almost there," Katie announced unnecessarily. "How you doing back there?"

"Just peachy," came the reply. "Except that I'm dressed like the maid in a porno." A pause. "Not that I would know about such things."

Katie laughed. "Of course not," she agreed.

"I wonder if they're into younger women. Bow-chicka-bow-wow."

Katie had to stop herself from laughing because she was close to losing one of the platters. She righted it and kept moving. *I seriously doubt they're into anything. They looked ancient in those portraits and I got the impression they were painted a long time ago. We'll probably have to wipe their chins after every bite. We might have to feed them, too.* What she said was, "Don't count on it."

Katie paused at the painting and looked inside the dining hall. Dozens of candles were lit, the large crystal chandelier above the center of the table was blazing light, a fire was crackling merrily away in the fireplace. Exton stood near the table, a white towel draped over his arm. He stood stiffly as if he were a Marine standing in the presence of his general. His eyes were fixed on the hidden door but they seemed to penetrate it and find Katie.

At either end of the table sat the Lords of Greystone. Katie could not see them from this angle, only withered arms draped upon the armrests of the high-back chairs. She swallowed. Her heart started thumping and the sound of her own breathing filled her ears. *Why am I suddenly so nervous? They're two old men, two very old men. Nothing more. Calm down, idiot.* She had to pee again.

"We're here. Ready?"

"Yep," Amanda replied.

Katie pushed on the hidden door in front of her and the dining hall light spilled into the passageway. The temperature in the dining hall struck her and she nearly lost all four platters. It was at least twenty-five degrees warmer than in the passageway. The heat from the candles and the fireplace seemed to bake the skin on her face and hands. She gasped but managed to retain control of the platters. She turned quickly to warn Amanda but the other woman saw her reaction and had time to prepare herself. Amanda's smile remained in place.

"*Hors d'oeuvres*, my Lordships," Exton announced.

Two pairs of very old eyes moved in the direction of the two new arrivals.

Katie's feet grew roots into the hardwood. Her muscles locked up and her breath caught in her throat. Her eyes were fixed on the ancient man in the chair closest to her. William or Arthur Morley leaned forward a few inches and regarded her. His eyes were deep set and pale blue, nearly white. His face was a roadmap of creases and wrinkles. A few wisps of white hair survived upon his spotted scalp but most of their brethren had long since departed. Thin pale pink lips spread in what might have been an attempt at a smile. He raised one hand a few inches from the armrest and gestured her closer. Katie's muscles disobeyed him and she remained in place.

Amanda Regan apparently suffered no such rebellion. She stepped around Katie and approached the table. "My Lordships," she said. She placed her platters on the table and curtsied.

"Let me look at you," William/Arthur told her. His voice was little more than a whisper but it still sounded like sandpaper scraping old wood. His accent was pronounced but Katie could not place it. The ancient man did not sound English. Scottish, perhaps? Irish? "Yes, pretty indeed. You can still pick them, Exton."

Exton bowed his head. "Your Lordship is too kind."

"And you?" called the twin at the opposite end of the table.

Katie's eyes moved in that direction. Arthur/William squinted at her. Katie managed to open her mouth but not to speak. Her vocal chords had joined the rebellion begun by her muscles.

"Are you mute, girl?" Arthur/William asked. Unlike his brother this one seemed to have no problem speaking above a whisper. His tone was identical to his twin's. "Say something."

Katie stammered. *You're blowing it, bitch. Say something before Exton decides he's made a mistake and fires your ass right now.* Her lips quivered. It felt like hours before she regained enough control to squeak out, "My Lordships."

"Not a mute after all," Arthur/William announced to the room. "Come closer. My eyes aren't what they used to be."

Katie doubted that. Despite the age of the man in the expensive tuxedo his eyes seemed to work just fine. They burned their way into hers even at a distance. Katie's feet ended their uprising and began moving in the direction of Arthur/William. She found she could not stop herself. The platters felt as if they weighed one ton each. Her arms ached under the burden, but she could not course-correct and place them on the table. She finally came to a stop before the withered Lord of Greystone. In her amped up state she felt suddenly cold, as if the warmth of the room had vanished in the space of a single heartbeat.

The old man's eyes moved across every inch of her body and Katie felt as if spiders were crawling along her skin. After a few moments he sat back in his chair. "Yes, very well done, Exton. My compliments. Well, don't just stand there, girl. Serve the *hors d'oeuvres.*"

Katie placed all four platters on the table in front of Arthur/William. She somehow managed to do it without spilling anything. Relieved of the weight Katie wanted to breathe a long sigh. She found she could barely breathe at all. The old man's eyes returned to her as she spooned some of the meats and cheeses onto his plate.

"That will be enough," the old man informed her.

Katie stepped back quickly. Was her breath frosting the air? No, of course not. It was stiflingly hot in the dining hall. So why was she shivering? *Christ Almighty, get a grip. What the hell is wrong with you?* She was at a complete loss.

"Arthur, stop torturing the poor girl," Lord William intoned from the other end of the table. His voice was still barely above a whisper yet Katie had no trouble hearing him. "She's nervous enough as i'tis." He inclined his head at Katie. "Don't mind him, my dear. I'm afraid my brother has become somewhat cantankerous in his dotage."

"Leave it be," Lord Arthur growled at his twin.

"More cheese, My Lord?" Amanda shot a look at Katie—*Are you okay?*—as she placed more of the colored cubes onto William Morley's plate.

"Yes, my dear, thank you," Lord William replied.

Katie was slow to recover control of her limbs but she at last felt she had a handle on herself. She controlled the chill in her bones as best she could and managed to get through the service without spilling anything or shaking enough to draw attention. After what felt like hours Exton raised his arm and snapped his fingers. Amanda picked up all four platters before Lord William. She added the plate from which he sampled the *hors d'oeuvres* and headed for the door to the passage. She paused and waited for Katie.

Katie did a reasonable imitation of her fellow server. She even managed a smile. Lord Arthur returned it; his thin almost-white lips pulled back from his yellow teeth. Katie licked her lips and swallowed and joined Amanda at the door. Exton nodded at them and they disappeared into the passage.

The air was cool but Katie felt much warmer. She leaned against the cold stone of the outer wall and now she had enough air in her lungs for that long sigh.

"Jesus Christ, are you okay?" Amanda asked, her voice low. "What happened?"

Katie took a few more deep breaths. She shook her head. "I don't know. I really don't."

Amanda leaned in closer. "Are you gonna be all right?"

Katie eyed her. "Yeah." She stood up straight. The strength had finally returned to her limbs. "I'll be fine." She headed for the kitchen. Amanda had to rush to follow.

"You can put all the leftovers onto one platter," Ms. Arnold informed them when they returned to the kitchen. "I give them to the neighbors' dogs. Then put the others in the sink over there. No, the one next to it. That's it. You can wash them after their Lordships finish with dinner."

Katie and Amanda did as they were told. *Looks like the dogs are going to eat better then I will tonight*, Katie thought. She had a feeling Amanda felt the same.

She felt herself again but her mind returned to Arthur Morley. There was no reason for her reaction to the old man. He had ogled her, yes, but that was hardly the first time she had that kind of experience. Then what? She couldn't put her finger on it. Amanda seemed none the worse for wear for her experience with Lord William. *Just get it together. This is a temp job, nothing more. Make enough cash to get out of the Landing and you can forget all about the old man and Exton and Palmer and all the others. Six weeks. Come on. You can do six weeks standing on your head if you have to. Eyes on the prize, Spencer.*

Katie finished placing the platters into the sink. She stood next to Amanda and waited for Ms. Arnold to inform them when dinner was ready to be served.

CHAPTER SIX

Denham Lore

It was probably Spence's imagination, but it seemed to take an interminably long time for the sky to get dark enough. He and his five friends sat on the cars and joked about old times and brought up a number of *Remember When*s… and all he wanted to do was start down the road toward Greystone. Spence had come close to telling them to quiet down a number of times. At first it was because one simply did not make a lot of noise at Denham. The last thing you ever wanted to do here was draw attention to your presence. It was ludicrous, of course. There were no devil worshippers here. No one was going to grab them and crucify them upside-down or sacrifice them to Lucifer. *No, but they can call the cops. It might take them a while to get out here, but they'll come when these rich people call. And we're a bunch of thirty-something assholes trespassing on private property. That'll look good in tomorrow's paper.* And Marcus, Maria, and Scott could all be charged with public intoxication on top of it. Nothing that would set the world on fire and get them on the evening news, but an arrest was an arrest. Spence would prefer to end the night in his own bed instead of in a cell at the new Deacon's Landing Police Headquarters.

Spence's eyes kept returning to the house on the corner. It was an outlier; there were no other houses anywhere near the start of the dead-end road. He often wondered, back in the day, about whoever lived there. Were they part of the cult, too, or just someone who wanted to live away from town? Did they know about their devil worshipping neighbors? Did they sleep with all the lights on? Christ, he had been so stupid back then. Now that he thought about it, he had never seen lights on in the first house. The only evidence it was inhabited came from the expensive cars that took up space in the driveway.

Now he eyed the house for a different reason. If they made too much noise the inhabitants might call the cops to report on the hooligans loitering across the way. As always, Spence could see no sign the house was inhabited except for the BMW in the driveway.

Maria stopped fooling with her phone. "No signal out here. I was gonna do a live stream on Facebook. So much for that."

"Yeah, there are no cell towers out here," Scott informed her. "Back in the day we tried just about every square inch of this place trying to get a signal and we never did. Total blackout zone."

"Rich assholes don't want their scenery ruined by cell towers," Marcus added.

"I really wanted to do a live feed." Maria's disappointment was obvious. She slipped the phone into her back pocket and lit another cigarette.

Phil was standing by his Equinox and relating the story of when he, Marcus, and Vic had gotten lost in the fields across from the main house. Spence had heard the story a thousand times, at least. They had been drunk and somehow wandered so far away from Denham they had to sit in a field while Vic drew a crude map in the dirt to figure out their position. They eventually came out somewhere in Waterbury where they found an old pay phone and Maria belly-laughed and teased her husband.

At least Phil isn't taking a swing at Marcus. Maybe we'll get through tonight without any punches being thrown. He hoped so. It was his idea to get the crew back together. The last thing he wanted was any more bad blood coming to the surface. For the first time in years they were all together, minus the three who had left the Landing behind. It would be unfortunate if an old grudge reared its ugly head and spoiled the reunion.

"Is it dark enough yet?" Keith asked. His body language and refusal to even look in Marcus's direction told Spence there was still a real possibility of trouble. Spence could just about read Keith's mind. *Maybe my brother's okay with what you did but I'm not. Step out of line in any way and I'll dent your skull.* "I mean, Christ, we've been here almost an hour. Shit or get off the pot."

"Yeah, it's dark enough," his brother told him. Phil hopped off the hood of his Equinox. "You guys ready?"

Spence was more than ready. He stepped away from the Gran Torino and started for Aldebaran Road.

"Hang on a sec," Marcus replied. He took out his keys and opened the Ford's trunk. "I have some presents for you motherfuckers." He rummaged around the trunk and tossed something to Spence.

Spence caught the crowbar and regarded it. "I'm not taking this. Are you nuts? We can't have anything that could be used as a weapon."

Marcus looked at him as if he had two heads. "What are you talking about? We always go in there armed to the teeth."

"Not a chance." Spence handed the crowbar back to its owner. "Think about it. If someone calls the cops and we get caught here, it's trespassing. If we're carrying anything that could be used as a weapon, that's a whole different story. Fuck that."

"Yeah, he's right," Scott said.

"Are you guys serious?" Marcus clearly could not believe his ears.

"As a heart attack," Spence told him.

Marcus looked for help from Phil and Keith. Both brothers folded their arms across their chest. Phil shook his head. "No way, man. I'm not getting arrested for threatening. Leave that shit in the trunk and hope they don't search it later."

Marcus shook his head. "Bunch of fucking pansies around here." He tossed the crowbar back into the trunk. It landed with a loud *clang* that resonated at the base of Spence's spine and then bounced off the spare tire. It sailed out of the truck and hit the ground with another *clang*.

"Maybe you should just keep your fucking mouth shut," Keith informed him.

Here we go. Spence positioned himself between Marcus and Keith. The younger Volokhov had not yet moved closer to Marcus but it seemed he might. It would take all of them to hold him back, and even then…

"Hey, fuck you!" Marcus shouted at him.

Maria and Spence moved immediately to pull Marcus back. Phil and Scott did the same to Keith.

Keith stabbed a finger in Marcus's direction. "Come over here and say that you scumbag fuck! After what you did to my brother you're lucky I haven't smacked the fuck out of you already!"

Marcus tried to reply but Spence had his hand clamped over his friend's mouth. Maria was shouting for them to stop. Phil had a hand on his brother's chest and told him to calm down.

"You're okay with what he did?" Keith asked his brother. "He fucking left you for the cops. Now he's Mister Big Balls talking shit and making out like it never happened. Yeah, fuck you, Greer!"

Phil and Scott appeared to have Keith under control. Spence returned his attention to Marcus. He was breathing heavily and his face was bright red but his struggles had ceased. He pulled free from Spence and Maria took him aside and did her best to calm him.

Spence crossed the distance to the other group. He leaned in close to Keith. "Listen, man, no one's excusing what happened at the carnival. No one's forgetting about it, either. Can we just get through tonight without any punches being thrown? Please?"

Keith's eyes moved from Marcus to Spence. He was still angry, livid, in fact, but there was no malice directed in Spence's direction. He took a long breath. "Fine. As long as he keeps his mouth shut. You'd better tell him that, too. Not a fucking word to me or my brother, Spence."

"I'll tell him."

Spence rejoined Marcus and Maria. "We cool?"

Marcus seemed less angry than surprised and hurt. Maria lit another cigarette and handed it to her husband. Marcus took a long, slow pull on it. "What's his fucking problem, man? We always go in there armed. And talking shit like that, he's lucky you guys got between us."

I think you might have that backwards, Spence thought. *If you're lucky all of us might have been able to keep him off you.* What he said was, "He's cool if you are. Just ignore them, okay? No comments, no threats, just pretend they're not here."

Marcus smoked and nodded. "Yeah, whatever."

Spence picked up the crowbar and hefted it before he returned it to the Gran Torino's trunk. "We can't bring any shit like this. We're not seventeen anymore. You really want to spend the night in jail?"

"He's right, babe," Maria added. "It's not worth it."

Marcus looked into the open trunk and its myriad contents. "You're gonna regret this if we run into trouble."

Spence smacked Marcus's face gently. "When did that ever happen?" Marcus smiled and Spence returned it. "That's better." He looked over his shoulder. Keith appeared calm, as did his brother. Scott was absentmindedly kicking the Equinox's tires. "We ready?"

"About time," Keith responded and started for Aldebaran Road. The others had to rush to catch up.

Spence watched the first house like a hawk. He saw no sign of movement, heard nothing from within. He caught the telltale red flashing light from within the beamer, notifying would-be troublemakers that the thing was alarmed. That was it. It took only a moment for the group to move past the house.

The trees were thick right from the start. Their branches met high above the road and intertwined, cutting off the last remnants of dusk. They heard nothing but their own muffled footfalls; there were never any night sounds at Denham. Spence had forgotten that odd fact until this moment. No crickets, no mosquitos, no coyotes, no anything. They were too far from anything resembling civilization so there was no road noise, either. Spence thought it was this phenomenon more than anything else that caused them to speak in whispers whenever they ventured here back in the day. They may have told themselves it was because their mission required stealth, but he felt now that was untrue. Something about this place made silence almost instinctive.

Marcus had fired up another joint and he was sharing it with Maria and Scott. They laughed at something Scott whispered but even their laughter was subdued. Maria, this being her first time, seemed to understand the need for quiet. As had everyone else who ever came here, Spence was willing to bet.

"Why is it called *Denham*?" she had asked in the car on the way here from the Old Colonial.

Spence shrugged. The origins of the name were lost, he told her. It had always been called Denham as far as Spence knew. He remembered Vic's father saying something to the effect of, "That place is still a thing? We used to go there when *I* was in school, for Christ's sake," one night when Marcus let slip where they were headed. Vic's father had not seemed concerned about their destination—he had probably outgrown the legend just as Spence now had—but it confirmed the name was in use going back to at least the 1970s.

The first driveway they came across was on their right. Two modest stone pillars stood sentry on either side. The driveway turned to the right perhaps fifty feet into the woods; the house to which it led was not visible in the darkness. Spence paused to listen but heard nothing but the muted laughter of his friends. He continued walking.

It was at the third driveway, this one on the left, that Marcus paused. "Hey Spence," he whispered, "wasn't this the one with the hearse? I can't remember."

Spence couldn't, either. One night long ago they had gotten brave enough to walk up one of the driveways. The house they found was large but not in the same league as Greystone. Parked in front of the three-car garage was a hearse. It instantly became part of Denham lore. The devil worshippers, they reasoned, needed a way to dispose of the bodies of their human sacrifices. What better way than a hearse? Spence had to smile at their teenage stupidity. "I don't know," he whispered back. "It might be. I don't remember."

"Should we check it out?" Scott asked. He was clearly high as a kite.

"I want to see it," Maria told them, obviously as high as Scott. She started in the direction of the driveway. She paused, pulled her phone from her back pocket. "I can grab some pictures, too!"

"Terrible idea," Phil told her. "That flash will draw attention. Shit, just having it on right now is like sending up a flare. I'd keep that thing off if I were you."

Maria frowned. "I guess you're right. Oh, and if anyone's interested, I still can't get a signal."

"I wouldn't mind seeing that shit, myself." Keith had materialized next to Spence. "A house with a hearse? Cool."

Spence jumped, completely unaware of Keith's presence until he spoke. Spence frowned. "This ain't why we're here. We're supposed to be checking on my sister."

Keith clapped him on the shoulder. "It'll take five minutes. I'm sure your sister will be just fine." He followed Maria, Marcus, and Scott into the driveway.

Spence turned to Phil. The other man shrugged. "I've seen it. I don't need to see it again. And these idiots are wrong, anyway. It's two more driveways up. And it's on the right side."

"Don't tell them."

Phil made the motion of zipping his lips closed.

Spence joined Phil in the middle of the road. He looked both ways but saw no headlights from either direction. "Keith's cool, right? Should I be worried he'll do something to Marcus?"

"Nah," Phil replied. "I told him if anyone was gonna punch the shit out of Marcus it'll be me. Don't worry, I don't plan on it. Not here, anyway."

Spence returned his attention to the driveway. He could no longer see his friends, could, in fact, see nothing beyond a few feet into the property. He stood next to Phil and waited.

It was a bit longer than five minutes before they returned to the road.

"I don't think it was this house," Scott announced. "It didn't look familiar at all. No hearse, either."

"You guys are so full of shit," Keith said when he rejoined his brother and Spence. "I can't believe I fell for that. Fucking hearse." He laughed a bit too loudly.

"No, dude, for real, there really was," Scott protested. "Motherfuckers owned a hearse. I swear. It must be another house."

"Uh huh." Keith was clearly still skeptical.

Spence was relieved to see Marcus looked none the worse for his side quest to the house. Maybe Phil was right about his brother. "Find it on the way back," Spence said. "Let's hit Greystone." He resumed the march up Aldebaran. He was satisfied when he saw the others fall into step behind him.

Perhaps ten minutes later they came across one of the named houses. "*Night Song*," Maria read for the group. "That is such a cool name! Can we see the house?" She directed her question to her husband. Marcus shrugged.

"Later," Spence told her. They had already wasted enough time, in his opinion.

Maria appeared disappointed but she did not press the issue. She returned her hand to her husband's and fell into step beside him.

They walked mostly in silence until they reached the turnaround where the blacktop ended and the dirt road began. Here they paused, as they always used to. The tree limbs overhead blotted out the night sky. Their yellowing leaves rustled in the soft breeze but the area was otherwise silent.

"We're about halfway to Greystone—"

"Car!" Phil hissed.

Spence whipped his head around. The headlights were small in the distance but overly bright to his darkness-adjusted eyes. It had come from the direction of Route 26 and it was moving entirely too fast for the width of the road.

"Woods!" Marcus whispered as loudly as he dared.

Spence bolted to the left and crashed into the underbrush. Marcus and Maria landed beside him. The others he could not see. "Keep your head down and don't make a sound." He didn't know if he was advising Maria or warning Marcus. Most likely it was both.

For several long moments the sound of the car's engine grew louder. *He's flying*, Spence thought. *What the hell is wrong with him? He's gonna wind up in the woods right on top of us.*

The car did not crash into the woods. It did, however, screech to a stop at the blacktop/dirt boarder. Dust billowed around the vehicle, the slight breeze doing little to disperse it. Spence could not guess at the make or model, it was simply too dark. It was old; the silhouette of the car's body told him that much. It was a muscle car, probably from the 60s or 70s. Beyond that Spence could not begin to guess.

"Oh shit oh shit oh shit," Maria whispered. Her eyes were wide and scared and fixed on the car that idled fifteen feet from where she lay. "How do they—" Marcus placed a finger over her lips. Maria got the message.

Spence licked his lips. *Could they have seen us? No, no fucking way. They were way too far off.* Right on the heels of that, *Then why did they stop right here, dickhead?* Spence swallowed. If the car's doors opened, if whoever was in there approached them… What? What was he going to do? Oddly, in all the times they had come to Denham, that question had never presented itself. It was just a given that whoever it was would keep on driving. Spence and his crew were too quick to be seen diving into the woods. Never had a car simply stopped where they hid. *Jesus, Marcus was right after all. We* do *need weapons.*

The driver took their foot off the brake pedal and gunned the engine again. The car tore off up the dirt road leaving another cloud in its wake.

Spence released a breath and heard Marcus and Maria do the same. Maria started to stand but Spence placed a hand on her arm and shook his head. "Not yet." He craned his neck but could see nothing. The car was gone. "Stay." He rose to his knees and then his feet. Spence approached the road, still straining to see any sign of the car. He saw nothing but darkness. The sound of the car's engine was still audible, but it was receding rapidly. His eyes still on the road leading to Greystone, he motioned for Marcus and Maria to join him.

"That was fucking freaky," Scott exclaimed when he emerged from the woods on the opposite side of the road. "Did you see that shit? It was like the dude knew where we were!"

"That was fucking weird, yeah," Spence replied.

"Never saw that shit before," Phil added. "He must have seen us. We're getting old, Spence. We used to be faster."

I don't think he did see us. I don't know how he knew we were there, but he didn't see us dive into the woods. What he said was, "I guess."

"I don't know about this." Maria's voice was soft and unsteady. Her eyes were wide. "Maybe we should just get outta here. Go have a drink someplace. A lot of drinks." Her eyes darted between both ends of the road.

Spence was reminded of everyone he had ever introduced to Denham. Some were curious, some liked the idea of the "danger," even if it was completely made up. Some talked with brass balls. In the end, every single one of them had lost some or all their nerve and wanted to get back to town as quickly as possible. Maria Greer was only the latest in a long line of these.

"We'll be okay, honey," Marcus told her. "That was freaky, but I told you we saw a lot of weird shit up here. That's just one more for the list."

"It's like the guy knew we were there," she said to her husband before her eyes fell on the rest of the group. "So? Are we getting out of here?"

"You can go," Spence told her and Marcus. "If you want to, I mean. I'll ride back with Phil."

"We'll be fine," Marcus said. He squeezed Maria's hand. "Right, babe?"

"Yeah." She sounded entirely unconvinced.

They started up the road again. Spence's eyes were glued to the darkness ahead. There was only one house after the blacktop/dirt boundary, only one destination for the car. If they were coming back this way Spence wanted plenty of warning. As it turned out he was looking in the wrong direction.

CHAPTER SEVEN

New Blood

Katie's feet were starting to ache. It was the damned shoes. They were too narrow for her feet and they crowded her toes. She would have liked to take them off even if only for a few minutes but she doubted Mr. Exton or, worse, Ms. Palmer would take kindly if they caught her. It had been the same way during their practice run the night before. She served dinner to Ms. Palmer while Amanda saw to Mr. Exton. Katie's feet began barking at her before they got to the second course. By the time her shift was over she was almost limping. She had no choice but to inform Palmer. The woman promised to secure new shoes for her. She hadn't lied; these were definitely not the same pair she wore the night before. They simply felt no different. Katie shifted her feet and tried not to draw attention to herself.

She stood five steps behind Lord Arthur Morley. The old man remained in his dining room chair and ate from his half of the giant slab of beef Ms. Arnold prepared for him and his brother. *How the hell can anyone eat that much? I could live for a week on that steak.* Lord William had likewise remained in his chair and Amanda Regan stood at the station five steps behind him. Amanda for her part seemed to be weathering her wardrobe better than Katie. The young woman gave no outward sign of discomfort.

Katie did not know she was hungry until she smelled the beef. There were spices baked in that she could not identify but god *damn*, it smelled good. Her stomach growled and she hoped no one heard it.

Mr. Exton stood near the door, hands behind his back at parade rest, his back stiff and straight. He had not spoken since he ordered the girls to serve the wine. The bottle was encased completely in an elaborate, intricately crafted metal sheath. Katie had no idea of the brand, but it must have been beyond expensive; the smell alone made her lightheaded.

She shifted her feet again and cursed Ms. Palmer for these ridiculous shoes. She doubted either Lord Morley had so much as glanced at her feet. She could have been wearing her Reeboks for all they knew.

Dinner proceeded apace with neither Morley brother speaking or even acknowledging anyone in the room. They sipped their expensive wine and ate the rarest cut of beef Katie had ever seen—*Christ, this thing is still mooing*, she had thought when Ms. Arnold presented her and Amanda with the large platter—pausing only to hold up an empty wine glass to be filled once more. Katie and Amanda waited on their employers dutifully and silently.

When the brothers had at last finished their meal they sat back in their chairs and sipped their wine. They waved in unison for the girls to collect their plates and cutlery. Katie and Amanda did as they were expected. The walk back to the kitchen was uncomfortable. Katie thought she might be starting to limp because of the goddamned shoes.

When at last she emerged into the kitchen, Amanda on her heels, she saw what she took to be an auto mechanic or perhaps someone who worked the grounds of the estate whom she had yet to meet. The young man leaned against the far counter, a rather large beer bottle in one hand. His hair was dirty and not quite shoulder length. His clothes were likewise stained with all manner of fluids Katie could not begin to name. His hands were covered with dirt or grease. He smiled when the two women entered the room.

"New blood!" he exclaimed with a look at Ms. Arnold. "You didn't tell me you had new hires."

Ms. Arnold ignored him. "You know where the platters go, ladies."

Amanda acknowledged she did, and Katie followed her to the appropriate sink. It was only a few feet away from the dirty young man. Katie stole glances at him as she tended to the platter.

"Aren't you gonna introduce me, Victoria?" the young man asked. His tone was both playful and aggressive.

"No, I am not." Ms. Arnold continued seeing to several platters full of finger foods.

The young man grinned his yellow-tooth grin and laughed. "She's so stolid," he remarked to Katie and Amanda. He thrust his hand in front of Katie. "Martin Jacoby. Pleased ta meet ya."

Katie regarded the hand. Even with her white gloves on she had no wish to touch the man or be touched by him. She swallowed, thought of Christmas, and took the offered hand. "Katie Spencer. Nice to meet you, Mr. Jacoby."

"Mr. Jacoby? Jesus Christ. If you call me that again I'll have to tell my dear old uncles to fire you. The name's Martin." He smiled again. His voice made Katie think of maggots.

"Martin," she said.

"And you?" He extended his hand in Amanda's direction.

"Amanda Regan, Martin. It's very nice to meet you."

"It *is* nice to meet me!" He took a long swig of his beer and belched. "How long have you been here at old Greystone?"

Katie waited for Amanda to reply but the other woman had returned her attention to rinsing her platter. Katie wanted to throttle her. "Hired the other day but this is really our first on the job."

"Ah. Well, you'll hate it here, don't worry." When Katie made no reply he placed his hand on her shoulder and leaned a little closer. "It's a joke, babe, just a joke. You gotta lighten up a little." His breath was an even mix of beer and cigarettes and weed. He leaned in even closer and lowered his voice. "If you two wanna party later when the two geezers go to their coffins just gimme a nod. I gotcha covered." He winked.

Katie did her best to smile. She could not tell if she succeeded. The double assault of the man's hand on her shoulder and the stink of his breath made her head spin. "Thanks, Martin. We'll definitely keep that in mind."

He opened his mouth to say more.

"That'll be enough of that," Ms. Arnold said sternly from across the room. "These two have duties to perform, which is more than I can say for you, Martin Jacoby. Leave them be."

Never was Katie more grateful for Ms. Arnold than at that moment. She might have kissed the woman if she were not on the other side of the cavernous kitchen.

Jacoby retreated a step. "Yes, *Victoria*. Whatever you say, *Victoria*." He glanced at Katie and Amanda. "She hates being addressed by her first name. It's a Greystone thing."

"*Now*, Mr. Jacoby." Ms. Arnold tilted her head in the direction of the nearest door.

Jacoby took another step away from Katie. He mouthed the word *Later* and strolled from the room, guzzling from the bottle.

Katie exhaled. She resisted the urge to brush off her shoulder when she saw Ms. Arnold's lips twisted in a scowl. She returned her attention to her platter.

"That was fucking gross," Amanda whispered.

"You have no idea," Katie agreed.

They finished rinsing the platters and waited while Ms. Arnold tended to the others. Katie counted twelve platters all told. From what she could see they were filled with everything from meats and cheeses to fruits to cocktail shrimp. *How much can two old men possibly eat?* Katie wondered. Ms. Arnold looked as if she were preparing for a large party.

"Take these to the mask room," Ms. Arnold said at last. "Place them wherever you can but always keep one with you to serve anyone who might be nearby."

"Um, Ms. Arnold, are there more people coming?" Amanda asked.

The old woman regarded them without patience. "Oh, yes. The neighbors like to pay their respects whenever their Lordships return to Greystone. Since it has been some time since they were last here, I expect a full house."

It would have been nice to know that, Katie thought but did not say. "Yes, Ms. Arnold." Her feet, which had forgotten their pain when Martin Jacoby introduced himself, remembered with a vengeance. Both were throbbing now. Katie winced when she crossed the kitchen to take up the first two platters.

"When you've brought them all to the mask room, I suspect you'll have anywhere from ten to twenty minutes before the neighbors begin to arrive. You may spend that time as you see fit."

"Thank you, Ms. Arnold," Amanda told her. She picked up two platters and followed Katie out of the kitchen.

It took three trips apiece before all the platters were arranged in the mask room. Katie feared running into Martin Jacoby again but the Morleys' nephew failed to present himself. That was just fine with her. If she was very lucky she might not see him again the rest of the night. Katie was tempted to plop herself down onto one of the sofas and tear her fucking shoes off, Palmer and Exton be damned. But no. *Six weeks*, she told herself. *Six weeks and out of here forever. You can do this.* She almost believed herself.

"Okay, I'm dying for a cigarette," Amanda announced. "Join me?"

The thought of being outside—where she could get her feet out of these torture devices—made her smile. She took Amanda's hand in hers and said, "God, yes!" Amanda seemed perplexed at her reaction. She laughed and led the way to the servants' entrance.

Katie thought she had never felt relief as much as she did the moment she wrenched the shoes off her feet. She closed her eyes and tilted her head back. The cool night air filled her lungs and felt wonderful on her skin. "Oh. My. God." She took a deep breath, exhaled slowly. "Holy shit that feels good."

Amanda smoked and laughed. She held the cigarette out to her. "I always smoke after an orgasm. You?"

Katie could not help but laugh. "It's not quite *that* good but it's close." She bent forward and rubbed her feet. "I don't know if they're too small or they just suck. Either way I think I have to tell Ms. Palmer I need different shoes. Again."

"Yeah, Palmer." Amanda exhaled smoke toward the sky. "Did she tell you there was a party tonight?"

Katie shook her head. "Nope. Not a word. Exton didn't, either. And I'm pretty sure she told me there wouldn't be a party on the first night. I guess plans changed."

"Think your feet are gonna hold up?"

Katie continued rubbing them. She counted three blisters so far. "No, but they'll have to, won't they?"

"Soak the shit out of them when you get home."

"That's what I did last night."

They spent the next several moments in silence. Katie rubbed her feet (four blisters now) and Amanda went to work on her second cigarette. By the time she had finished it they heard voices coming from the driveway. Katie wanted to get up but the thought of putting on her shoes again forced her to abandon the idea. Amanda walked to the edge of the house and peeked around the corner. After a moment she returned.

"People are showing up. They're walking so I assume they're the neighbors. I couldn't tell how many but it looked like a lot."

"Greeeaaat." Katie gritted her teeth and forced the shoes onto her feet once more. She held out a hand and Amanda pulled her upright.

Amanda took the bottle of perfume from her pocket and spritzed herself a few times. "Ready?"

"After you." Katie opened the door and followed Amanda into the house.

CHAPTER EIGHT

One Last Round

The car had freaked him out more than he thought. Spence had been through it a hundred times before. Everyone who ever ventured down Aldebaran Road knew to take cover when they saw headlights approaching. But no car had ever stopped before, let alone directly in front of their hiding spot in the woods. He had run through the sequence in his head a dozen times. There was no way the driver could have seen them. No one had lingered on the road after Phil hissed his warning. They had gone into the woods far enough not to be seen from the road. So how had he known? *Maybe the people who live here have a sixth sense about it by now. God knows how many decades Landing kids have been coming here.* Spence shook his head. It had to be something else. Maybe someone *had* lagged behind just long enough for the driver to catch a glimpse of them. But still…

Spence had his eyes glued to the dark road ahead of them. So far the mystery car had not come back this way. And it was loud enough that it wouldn't be able to sneak up on them. It had to be someone who lived at Greystone, there was no other explanation. He started to relax. For the first time since the car Spence chanced a look over his shoulder. He couldn't allow himself to be so focused on the way ahead that he neglected to watch out for other cars coming up behind them.

At first he thought the light was coming from another car. It took his brain a moment to recognize this could not be so. The light was weak and bobbed up and down and left and right. "Flashlight!" He almost shouted it and gave away the game. As it was he feared he was still too loud.

His friends stopped and turned and bolted into the woods again. This time Spence wound up on the right side of the road next to Keith and Phil. They were too close to the road. They had known instinctively not to go in farther; they had made enough noise already when they crashed into the underbrush. But they were no more than six or seven feet inside the woods. If the person with the flashlight swept it in their direction there is no way they wouldn't be seen.

Spence thought back to all the times he and his friends had been here. Not once had they ever encountered someone on foot. In point of fact, aside from the incident with the clone car, they had never actually seen another person here, resident or otherwise. The possibility had somehow never occurred to him. *Stupid, stupid, stupid. Now what, asshole?* He answered himself. *If it comes down to it there are five of us plus Maria. Hopefully whoever this is won't even know we're here.*

The person holding the flashlight approached. Spence could see nothing more than a dark shape at the end of the beam of light. He held his breath. The person was followed by another, then a third. Spence leaned forward as far as he dared, his eyes wide and nervous. An entire procession followed the person lighting their way. Spence lost count quickly but he estimated fifteen to twenty all told. *So much for there being five of us…*

The new arrivals walked slowly and silently and steadily and they did not pause. After the incident with the old muscle car part of him expected these people to stop and turn in their direction. They did not. The march continued toward Greystone Manor.

After the last person passed Spence stayed put. To his relief so did Phil and Keith. No one spoke, not even to whisper. They were of one mind: *What if there are stragglers?* Spence waited another few moments before he quietly pushed himself to his feet. He motioned for Phil and Keith to stay down. They nodded their agreement. Spence took a single step toward the road. Dead leaves crunched beneath his sneakers. He winced at the noise, which sounded as loud as Marcus's stereo in the total silence around them. His eyes darted in both directions. He saw nothing. Two more strides brought him to the edge of the road. He looked again. No one presented themselves. Spence let out a long, loud breath and his shoulders sagged.

Phil and Keith emerged from behind him. After another moment the rest of the group joined them from the opposite side of the road. Spence's eyes darted both ways again and continued to sweep the area around them.

"Okay, fuck this." The fear was evident in Scott's voice. "Let's get the fuck out of here."

"Seconded." Maria raised her hand.

"Yeah, that was too much for me," Marcus added.

"Yeah, it figures you'd wanna bail," Keith whispered.

Scott had the presence of mind to step between Marcus and Keith. It was a good thing; Spence's feet felt nailed to the ground.

"You saw that shit, right?" Marcus whispered back. He seemed utterly uninterested in responding to Keith's taunt. "I mean, what the fuck *was* that?"

Keith turned to Spence. "Your sister said the owners of this house were coming home, right? Maybe they're throwing a block party. Who the fuck knows?"

"That's a party I can do without," Marcus answered.

Keith took a step closer to Marcus. Scott stepped forward and put his hands up. "Be cool, man. This is the last place we need any trouble."

Spence finally took his eyes from the road and regarded Keith. "He's right. We start making noise they might come running. There are a lot more of them than there are of us."

Phil placed his hand on Keith's shoulder. "Be cool, bro."

Keith apparently saw the wisdom in their advice. He backed down.

"What do you think, Spence?" Phil asked. "It's your show."

"You guys can go." His voice was flat. "I'm going to check on my sister." He started toward Greystone.

"Hold on," Maria whispered. "Those people are between us and the house. Shouldn't we, I don't know, give them a little more time to get there?"

"There's an open field up ahead on the left," Phil told her. "They use it to grow corn and shit. We can cut through it. It leads right up to the main house."

"The cornfield!" Scott proclaimed. "I forgot all about that. Remember that night we were running down the hill and Glen stepped into one of those rows and went ass over teakettle all the way down? That's *still* one of the funniest things I ever saw!"

"That was *me*, idiot." And it *was* a funny memory but Spence did not feel like laughing. He did not like that group of people ahead of them. He liked even less the thought of Katie being in that house with so many residents of Denham. *Fucking devil worshippers, man*, Vic would say. That might have been nonsense but Spence drew no comfort from the knowledge. "Are you going or staying?"

As his friends voiced their opinions Spence started walking. Within a few seconds he could no longer hear their whispers. The complete silence around him magnified the sound of his sneakers on the dirt road. It was nearly lost to the sound of the blood pounding in his ears. *Just get to the main house. Take a look inside, make sure there isn't any (devil worshipping) trouble going on. Maybe you'll spot Katie in one of the rooms. She'll be serving food and drinks to the neighbors and laughing at rich people jokes. And you'll feel like an idiot for being nervous in the first place.*

He heard the footsteps coming up behind him. Spence suppressed a smile. Phil and Keith joined him. They were followed by Scott, Marcus, and Maria. No one spoke.

The woods on the left came to an abrupt end and the farmer's field appeared. It was larger than Spence remembered.

Cornstalks stretched nearly to the opposite end where the woods reclaimed their dominance. The slope of the hill grew steeper as it reached its apex. At the top of the hill, unseen from this angle, stood Greystone Manor. Spence never broke stride. He moved from the dirt road to the field and started up the hill.

The rows of corn began five feet from the edge of the road. Spence navigated the narrow strip of dirt and heard his friends keeping pace behind him. The hill had grown steeper in the years since he had last made this climb, or so he told himself. He was starting to labor by the time he reached the halfway point. His friends seemed in similar shape, judging by the sound of their breathing, Marcus and Maria loudest of all.

"I need a break," Maria whispered between deep breaths.

Spence didn't slow. "Go ahead. Catch your breath. We'll meet at the top." He meant the whole group. One glance at Scott and Phil told him they were not enjoying the steep incline any more than he was.

Only Keith seemed unaffected. "Out of shape bastards," he whispered.

The break was more of a pause; within a moment everyone had resumed the march up the hill.

The first thing they saw was the roof of the barn. They had just about crested the hill when the rest of the structure came into view. One of the large doors was open and light spilled from the inside. Spence could hear nothing but the breeze rustling the leaves of the large tree that stood watch between them and the barn.

Spence ran to the tree. He peeked around it at the open barn door. He saw no one, heard nothing. To his right was the driveway. He spotted Katie's Cruze right away, one among many cars parked there. Apart from the others, nestled against the side of Greystone, sat the ugly old muscle car. He still could not tell the model but it looked like a Chevy or perhaps an Olds. Its ancient paint was either white or yellow.

Spence checked the barn again. He waved his arm and the rest of the group joined him. He pointed to the open barn door and placed a finger to his lips. Five heads nodded their understanding. There was perhaps fifty feet of open ground between his current hiding spot and the barn. Spence crossed the distance in seconds. His back to the closed door, Spence leaned over as far as he dared and peeked inside.

The largest man Spence had ever seen sat at a worktable. He fiddled with something Spence could not make out. "Jesus," Spence whispered. *If this guy sees us and gets it into his head to chase after us…* The man seemed utterly absorbed tinkering with whatever was hidden in his giant bear paws.

Spence advanced to another large tree, this one close to the far side of Greystone. He turned his eyes toward the mansion. He found his sister and another girl standing outside a side door. Before Spence could do anything more than recognize her Katie and the other girl opened the door and went inside. His first instinct was to run to the door. Even if it was locked Katie was still close enough to it that she would see him.

And then what? What would he say? Why was he even here? She knew nothing of the urban legends of Denham. If he told her about the devil worshippers she would laugh at him. She would also be angry that he was checking up on her. As it was he had waited too long. She was likely deep inside the house by now, anyway.

Spence returned to the tree. "I saw Katie. For a second, anyway."

"Anything in the barn?" Marcus asked.

Spence nodded. "Yeah, the biggest son of a bitch I've ever seen. Remember when we saw the Big Show at WrestleMania? This guy is twice his size."

"Oh, get the fuck outta here," Marcus whispered.

"Hand to God," Spence replied. "So let's give the barn a wide berth and get around to the other side of the house. I'll go first."

"Wait." Maria placed her hand on Spence's arm. "Are you sure about this? I watch wrestling, too. If that guy is really as big as you say he is…"

"Just don't make any noise," Spence whispered back. He had no patience for anything more from Maria, not after he had finally seen Katie. "Follow me."

They skirted the barn in single file. Spence returned to the large tree that afforded a view of the side of Greystone. It was thick enough around for all of them to hide behind. There were many windows on this side of the house. Light spilled from most of them. The largest windows looked in on the mask room if he remembered correctly. Spence squinted at them.

There were some people inside the room, but Spence could not tell if Katie was one of them. He was simply too far away. He could see the masks still in their place upon the wall. The room was ablaze with light; numerous lamps, a chandelier, and at least one fireplace turned the room into a beacon bright enough to guide ships in the night.

More people began entering the room. They walked in slowly, single file. Each one lowered themselves either by leaning or kneeling in front of a high-backed chair. When they had finished greeting the chair's occupant they walked across the room and repeated the gesture to a second person seated in an identical chair. It took some time for the neighbors to file into the room and address the occupants of the chairs. When that part of the festivities concluded they took to standing in small groups talking amongst themselves.

Spence glanced over his shoulder. Five sets of eyes seemed fixed on the scene inside the mask room.

"Must be nice," Keith whispered. "Look at this place. I didn't see anything like this even in Europe." He whistled through his teeth.

"Same," Scott added. "I was in Spain once and I saw some serious places, old castles and shit. But even they don't stand up to Greystone."

"I'm gonna get in closer," Spence told them. "Stay or follow, it's up to you." He did not wait for anyone. Spence emerged from behind the tree and, ducking down, circled as fast as he could to the side of the house. He found himself beside one of the tall windows. He put his back to the wall and looked toward his friends. Phil, peeking around the tree, gave him a thumbs-up. Spence nodded.

He leaned an inch or two to his left and stole a quick glance inside the room. From this vantage point he could see the ancient man in the equally ancient tuxedo seated in the high-backed chair farthest from the door. He sat with his hands clasped in his lap, his eyes heavy and lidded. His guests continued to speak together in their small groups. Someone said something funny and others laughed. It might have been a scene from a movie that lit up the box office in 1920; even the clothing they sported appeared out of date.

A man stood stiffly by the door, dressed identically to the man in the chair. Spence couldn't begin to guess his age but it was still well south of the ancient man. One arm was bent and held in front of him. A white cloth was draped over the appendage. His other arm he held behind him. His eyes were attentive; they moved slowly about the room, missing nothing. His expression was utterly blank.

A woman in a maid's outfit stood at the opposite end of the room. Her posture was somewhat less statue-like than the man's but not by much. One of the guests—a man in a very expensive suit—talked to her and laughed at his own jokes. The woman's expression was pleasant enough, but Spence could just about read her mind. *Someone please come fetch your husband before he makes me do something we'll all regret.* Spence smiled at the thought.

Most of the guests turned in the direction of the door nearest the butler. Two young women entered the room, arms loaded with silver trays. They were dressed the same as the maid. Spence smiled at the sight of his sister. She smiled pleasantly and walked about the room. The guests helped themselves to whatever *hors d'ouevres* she and the other girl had brought. It occurred to Spence this would make a great picture with which to torture Katie. He could never risk it, of course. The flash would be a dead giveaway. Anyone glancing out the window would see him. But, damn, it would be funny to post it on social media and let the comments fly.

Marcus appeared next to him. Spence nearly jumped. He had the presence of mind not to make a sound, but it had been close.

"You jumpy fuck," Marcus whispered, and laughed.

"Fuck you," Spence replied.

"I'd rather fuck *her*," Marcus said, and pointed to Katie's partner. "Nice tits."

"Yeah, I'm sure Maria would be okay with that."

"She don't need to know nothing." Marcus leaned past Spence and looked through the window. "Fuck me. I never been this close before. Look at all that expensive shit they got in there. Makes you think."

"Yeah, makes you think what would happen if they caught you stealing any of it."

Marcus shrugged. "Ten years ago, I'd have gone for it."

Ten years ago you would have been stupid enough, yeah. "Back up, man. They're gonna see you."

Marcus lingered another moment. He glanced again at the other girl in the maid's outfit before he put his back to the house again. "Seen enough? Katie's fine. And look at all these rich assholes. She's probably gonna make a few grand in tips tonight. Let's get outta here."

Spence swallowed. He looked through the window again. Katie did seem fine. She was smiling pleasantly, making small talk with the guests. She held a tray in each hand and had tucked an empty beneath one arm. The other girl (*nice tits*) did much the same as she worked the other side of the room. Marcus was right. There wasn't much more to see here. And Spence remained aware that they were still in the most notorious place in all the Landing. Maybe it was time to go.

He nodded. Marcus made his way back to the tree. Once he reached it he motioned for Spence. Spence spared a final glance inside the mask room and then ran for the tree.

"Everything cool?" Phil asked.

Spence gave him the thumbs-up. "Yeah, she's okay." He glanced at Marcus. "Looks like she'll clean up in tips tonight."

"Lucky her," Phil replied. "We ready to go?"

"I guess so." Spence eyed the other tree, the one closest to the barn. The barn door remained open and light continued to spill onto the grounds. "Just be really quiet or Godzilla will hear us."

Spence led the way. He stopped at the first tree, careful to keep its bulk between him and the barn. He peeked around the tree for any sign of the big man's presence. If he were still inside that is where he remained. *Good. Stay there for another minute or two.* He motioned for the others to join him.

Spence looked again at the mass that was Greystone Manor. *This is the last time,* he thought. *I'll never come up here again. No reason to.* Now that he had seen his sister and knew she was okay he felt foolish for even coming up here in the first place. Yes, he had been concerned for Katie but at the end of the day he had to admit he had never genuinely believed her to be in danger from devil worshippers. So why had he dragged everyone back here?

To see the old crew, he thought. *Maybe to have one last night like the ones we had back in the day. Before various marriages, divorces, kids, moving out of state, and everything else had put an end to those endless nights.* And was there anything wrong with that? Spence did not believe there was. And his pretense for getting everyone together was not false; he really had been concerned for Katie.

It did not matter. His sister was safe and they could all go out for a drink when they got back to civilization. One last round…

"Where's Maria?"

Spence snapped back to reality. He looked at Marcus. His friend whipped his head around in every direction. The others mimicked him. Spence did, too. Maria Greer was not with them. Spence's eyes scanned the grounds around them. The barn, the tree nearest the house, the spot where he and Marcus had stood beside the window, no Maria.

"Maria!" Marcus hissed.

"Quiet," Phil whispered. "You're gonna get us caught."

"Maria!" Marcus called again, louder this time.

"Would you shut—"

"Fuck off," Marcus told him. "I need to find my wife right fucking now!"

Scott placed a hand on Marcus's shoulder. "Easy, man," he whispered. "We'll find her. Maybe she's squatting in the corn or something. God knows I need to piss, too. Or she's headed down the hill already. We'll catch up."

Spence didn't buy that for one second. Neither did anyone else, he was willing to bet. Maria was scared enough already. There was no way she would go anywhere alone. Spence's eyes turned toward the open barn door. She wouldn't…no. No way. But it was still more likely than Scott's suggestions. Spence took a step toward the barn.

That was when he heard the scream from inside Greystone Manor.

CHAPTER NINE

The Most Boring People on Earth

Katie stood in the doorway to the mask room. Mr. Exton stood beside the door. She watched the new arrivals as they finished greeting the Morley brothers. Each guest took their turn saying hello and making brief small talk with each man. Not for the first time Katie thought, *This is how it was in the Middle Ages. The peasants come to see their lord and pay homage to him.* Of course, these peasants were far from paupers, she knew. If Katie had one-tenth their money she would already have put Deacon's Landing in her rearview. *Next they'll doubtless ask for a favor, or for the Morleys to take their side in some dispute with a neighbor.* Katie found herself genuinely fascinated by the tableau. She flashed back to the portrait of Henry VII upstairs and wondered how many of these he had endured during his reign. They must have looked the same, at any rate.

The line finally came to the end and the guests began to congregate in smaller groups. Mr. Exton glanced at her and nodded his head ever so slightly. Katie took a deep breath and stepped across the threshold. Her feet throbbed and now her arms were starting to ache. The platters, three of them each for her and Amanda, were weighted down with enough finger foods to feed a few dozen people. There was not quite that number within the room but they weren't far off, either. Men and women dressed in very old and expensive clothes and sporting more jewelry than the British Royal Family turned in her direction. Katie smiled and made her way into the room.

She stopped before the nearest Morley brother. *Serve their Lordships first*, Ms. Palmer had instructed them. *Always. There are no exceptions to this rule. The guests will await their turn without complaint.* Katie still could not tell which brother was which. She bent her knees a bit and lowered the tray so this Morley could inspect what she had brought. Amanda crossed the room and did the same for his twin. The ancient man's hand shook a bit as it hovered over the cocktail shrimp. He selected one, then two, and waved her off without a word. Katie smiled and regained her full height. She stole a quick glance at Exton. He remained at his station near the door and did not return her look.

The first group of guests she came upon was a man and two women. The man's suit appeared as if it cost more than Katie's rent. He looked away from his two companions and regarded the trays in Katie's hands.

"Yes, thank you," he said as he helped himself to a cocktail shrimp. He took a small crystal bowl and placed the shrimp inside and then spooned some of the caviar on top of the shrimp. "Stanley. Robert Stanley III." He smiled the whitest smile Katie had ever seen.

Katie curtsied as much as her throbbing feet would allow. "Katherine Spencer."

"So nice to meet you, Ms. Spencer. This is my wife, Karen, and our neighbor, Eleanor Poole."

"Ladies," Katie acknowledged, and offered the platters.

The two women smiled and returned to their conversation. Robert Stanley III shrugged. He leaned in closer to Katie and whispered, "Women." Katie suppressed a smile before she moved on to the next group.

She met more of the residents of Aldebaran Road and emptied the first of her platters. The Buckinghams (owners of Buckingham Funeral Parlor on the corner of Palmer Street and Buscema Boulevard) were fans of the caviar. The Royces favored the smelliest cheese Katie had ever encountered in her life; they took chunks of it and ate it plain. Katie made a mental note not to get too close to them if they should want to speak with her during the evening. An elderly man named George Watts took every last bacon-wrapped Brussels sprout she had on the tray. Katie tucked the empty tray under her arm and continued to work the room.

Four men, identical in appearance and clothing, chatted amongst themselves. Katie approached them with her trays.

"Didn't you inform Charles of their Lordships' return?" one asked.

"I did," said another. "He couldn't find a flight in time. Gandhi International isn't known for their choice of carriers. I expect he will turn up later this week."

"Let's hope their Lordships don't note his absence," said another as he perused the offerings on Katie's trays.

Not only do they look and dress the same, they sound the same, too. Quadruplets? Katie pitied the poor woman who went through that.

Every so often she would cast a glance at Ms. Palmer, who stood on the far side of the room in Amanda's territory. The younger woman was stone-faced, but Katie could detect nothing in her body language that raised any red flags. Their service seemed to be meeting her standards. A quick glance at Mr. Exton reinforced her impression. *Maybe I get to keep my job for another day. Assuming my feet survive.*

Katie caught snippets of conversation. The neighbors, while clearly wealthy, also appeared to be the most boring people on earth. They spoke of their stock portfolios, the latest safety regulations being considered by the legislature in Hartford and how they would affect their factories and businesses, which countries were lifting or initiating embargos on which goods. It made her head spin. *If I ever hit it big, please don't let me turn into them.* She cast a quick glance at Amanda. Her fellow server was doing well on her side of the room. She had already emptied two trays and the guests were working on her third.

Katie finished her rounds and returned to Mr. Exton's side. "The guests seem to like the *hors d'ouevres*," she said in a lowered voice.

Exton nodded so slightly Katie could not be sure he had moved at all. He continued to stand impassively, expressionless.

"Should I go back to the kitchen to get more?"

"You and Ms. Regan shall remain on station." His tone was neutral, his voice low enough that no one else could hear.

"Yes, sir." Katie didn't know what she was meant to do. She had one tray left and no one showed interest in what was left of its contents. No one seemed to need her for anything. So she stood and tried not to make it obvious when she shifted her feet every few seconds. With nothing to do and no one to speak to she could no longer ignore the pain in her feet. *How many blisters do you think you have now? Ten? Fifteen?* Then, right on the heels of that, *Eyes on the prize, Spencer.* If Exton wanted her to stand next to him and do nothing, then she would smile while she did it.

The elderly George Watts knelt in front of the closest Morley brother. Katie could not hear the conversation. She imagined it was more rich person's talk. Watts was clearly asking for something. His eyes and body language suggested it was big, whatever it was. Katie disliked seeing the old man clearly begging for something. He all but prostrated himself before Lord Morley. Watts, his head bowed, took one of Morley's hands in his own. Morley pulled his hand free and glowered at Watts.

What kind of heartless asshole do you have to be to put an old man through that? Katie wanted to hug George Watts, take him by the hand and lead him out of the room. As it was more people were beginning to take note of what was happening. Katie scanned their faces, hoping someone would step forward and take hold of the old man. None did. The residents of Aldebaran Road seemed content to watch the spectacle unfold without taking any action at all. Katie's lips pressed into a thin line. If this continued she would get involved. It would be the end of her tenure at Greystone Manor, she was sure, but this was too much.

Lord Morley's hand curled into a fist and he brought it down hard on the arm rest. The elderly man started, his eyes wide. He snatched his hand back as if he had been bitten. The movement was too much. Watts lost his balance and stumbled backward into a seated position on the rug. He looked upon Lord Morley with wet, betrayed eyes.

Exton beat Katie to the punch. He moved instantly and quickly to Mr. Watts's side. He placed his hands beneath the elderly man's arms and lifted him from the floor. Watts could not take his eyes from Lord Morley. His expression remained as if his face were carved of stone.

Katie's eyes darted about the room. The guests of the Lords Morley regarded the scene with detachment. Not one of them seemed the least concerned for the elderly man. They stood with their drinks and their finger foods and simply watched. Across the room Ms. Palmer mirrored them. Only Amanda seemed to react. She wore the same expression of surprise as Katie.

Katie placed her platters on the nearest end table and moved to assist Mr. Exton. His head snapped in her direction. "Remain where you are, Ms. Spencer." His voice was calm, flat. She might have expected a shout, or at least an edge to his tone. It was most likely this that stopped Katie in her tracks. She stood next to the end table and did not know what to do.

Exton helped Watts to his feet. He brushed off the elderly man's trousers and jacket. "There you are, sir. Good as new."

Watts's eyes remained glued to Lord Morley. He did not acknowledge Exton in any way. He stood before Lord Morley. After a moment to collect himself he simply bowed his head and moved away. He walked slowly to the fireplace where someone handed him a drink; he downed it in one gulp.

Exton knelt before Lord Morley. He whispered something to him. It must have worked. The old lord patted Exton's arm and leaned back in his chair again. Exton looked at Katie. "Bring another bottle of the red for Lord Morley, Ms. Spencer. And an extra glass for Mr. Watts."

Katie's eyes moved from Exton to Morley to poor Mr. Watts. She knew without looking that both Ms. Palmer and Amanda were looking at her. So was everyone else in the room. Katie felt the blood rush to her cheeks. She turned on her heel and went to fetch the bottle.

When she returned to the mask room she found it in its pre-Watts state. She poured two glasses of red and brought one to Lord Morley. He smiled at her as he took the glass. "Thank you, my dear." His tone was pleasant if condescending.

"My Lord," she said in reply. It took effort but she managed to keep the contempt from her voice. Katie approached Mr. Watts. He sat in a chair next to the fireplace. His eyes were distant and it took him a moment to realize she was there. "Your wine, Mr. Watts," she said helpfully.

His eyes found hers. He took the glass from her and mumbled a thank you. It was all Katie could do not to place a hand on his shoulder and tell him it would be all right. *You would be perfectly justified if you hurled this glass right at the old bastard, Mr. Watts* She resisted the urge to turn and glare at Lord Morley. The spectacle was over; any reaction from her now would end her employment and land her back on square one. With this job she was closer to leaving Deacon's Landing now than she had ever been. *Eyes on the prize* would probably be enough to get her through the next six weeks. Unless this scene repeated itself. Then all bets were off.

Katie resumed her position next to Exton at the door. She saw that Amanda had not moved from her spot, either. She stood next to Ms. Palmer and tried to pretend nothing had happened. Katie wondered when their next break would present itself. She had a feeling she knew the topic of the conversation.

Slow, heavy footsteps drew Katie's attention toward the door nearest her and Exton. She expected to see Mr. Johnson enter the room; only he could produce footfalls that sounded like the t-rex from *Jurassic Park*. It was, however, not Mr. Johnson who entered the room. It was Martin Jacoby. And he was not alone.

Katie at first took the object slung over his shoulder to be a sack of some kind, perhaps containing more wood for the fireplaces. As the man walked past her Katie saw it was not a sack of wood at all. It was a woman.

The last tray slipped from Katie's hands. It produced no sound when it hit the rug. The contents of the tray pin-wheeled in every direction.

Jacoby strode to the center of the room. He leaned to one side and dumped his cargo onto the Oriental rug. The guests, the Morley brothers, even Exton and Palmer, displayed little reaction. Katie gasped.

The woman appeared semi-conscious; she mumbled and one arm waved weakly in the air as if she were trying to ward off a swarm of mosquitoes. She made no attempt to regain her feet or even to raise her head. Her long black hair obscured her features.

Katie did not think. She watched herself stride across the room to the woman's side and kneel beside her.

"Return to your station, Ms. Spencer," Exton told her.

Katie ignored him. She brushed some of the hair from the woman's face.

"What is this, Jacoby?" Exton asked.

"Found her nosing around outside. There are three more out there, three men. I figured I'd grab her because she was the easiest. The others probably won't leave without finding her."

"Why didn't you simply take them all?" The question came from the Morley seated closest to Katie.

"I'm a lover, uncle, not a fighter."

Katie barely heard any of it. Her attention was focused on the women in the center of the room. She looked familiar although Katie could not place where she had seen her before. "You're okay, you're gonna be okay," Katie assured her. The new arrival looked upon Katie with glazed eyes. A thin trickle of blood that originated somewhere within her black hair ran down her cheek to her jawline.

Katie's hand went to her pocket before she realized her phone was in her pocketbook in the third floor changing room. She whipped her head in Exton's direction. *Eyes on the prize* had gone out the window along with any chance of Katie continuing her employment with the Lords Morley. "Call an ambulance! *Now*, Exton! What the fuck are you standing there for?"

Exton remained where he was. So did everyone else in the room.

Amanda reached into her back pocket and pulled out her phone. She strode across the room in Katie's direction.

Ms. Palmer moved quickly to catch her. The younger woman produced something from her front pocket. It was thin and perhaps six inches in length. She jabbed it into Amanda's neck. Amanda spun. One hand went to the object stuck in her neck; the other slugged Palmer across her jaw. Palmer staggered back a step but appeared unharmed. Amanda's knees buckled and she went down on the edge of the Oriental rug.

Katie screamed. Then something slammed into the side of her neck. She spun, saw Exton standing over her. In one hand he held a syringe. Katie's hand had gone instinctively to her neck. Now her arm dropped, numb and useless. The sensation spread across her body and Katie fell backward onto the rug.

Her wide eyes darted about the room. No one, not the Morley brothers, not the guests, not even Mr. Watts, seemed the least concerned nor surprised by this turn of events. Their eyes regarded Katie with cold neutrality.

It was the last thing she saw before the darkness wrapped itself around her.

CHAPTER TEN

Still On The Clock

Spence ran back toward the house. His first few steps took him by the same path he used the first time, cautious, skirting around the light spilling from the windows. It was instinct, honed by many past expeditions to Greystone. He swore and consciously overrode the caution that had become part of the experience of being here. He bolted straight for the windows that looked in on the mask room. If anyone within saw him, so be it.

He did not have to concern himself with that. Marcus heard the scream, too. He shouted, "Maria!" and caught up to Spence in seconds.

Before they reached the window or their vantage spot beside it, the wealthy people within the mask room were looking out, looking at them. Spence did not care. He ran to the window and looked inside. A woman in a maid's outfit was dragging another (*nice tits*) toward the door on the far side of the room. The woman being dragged appeared unconscious or maybe even dead.

A portly man reached down and retrieved a cell phone from the floor. He said something to one of the seated men, nodded, and tossed the phone into the fireplace. Spence's eyes darted past the people standing about the room, past the two old fucks seated in their fancy chairs. He found Katie. She was lying on the floor next to Maria. Maria appeared conscious, if dazed; Katie's condition mirrored the other girl's.

"Katie!" Spence pounded on the window. Marcus was likewise shouting his wife's name.

One of the ancient men turned his head and glanced in their direction. His eyes met Spence's. The old man smiled.

Spence slammed his fist against the glass. The impact produced a dull *thud.* Spence pulled his hand back and shook it and swore. He shouted his sister's name again. Katie lay unresponsive on the floor. The man in the butler's outfit knelt beside her and lifted her from the floor as if she weighed nothing. He stood and carried her from the room.

"Don't you hurt her, you fucker!" Spence shouted. He pounded on the window with his other fist, with much less force than the first time. The men and women on the other side of the glass regarded him and Marcus for another moment before they returned their attention to each other.

Spence looked at the ground around him. He needed a rock, something big enough to break the glass. He found nothing; the grounds of Greystone had always been immaculate and that was something that had not changed over the years. "Fuck!" He started for the side of the house.

"Help!"

Spence stopped, turned.

The giant he had glimpsed inside the barn had emerged. He held Keith by his neck at least a foot above the ground. Keith's feet kicked at empty air, his body twisted in all directions as he tried to wriggle free. Phil was slamming his fists into the man's midsection, to no effect. He switched tactics and threw both his hands around the arm holding his brother. Scott sat on the ground and looked dazed. Even from this distance Spence could see the blood streaming from his nose and his mouth.

Spence did not hesitate. He started for his friends.

Phil made his intervention unnecessary. He grabbed at a hammer hanging from the giant's tool belt and swung for his head. Spence could hear the impact from fifty feet away. The giant released Keith and staggered backward. Keith dropped to the ground but sprang to his feet rather quickly. He rubbed his throat and coughed.

The big man was not down. He shook his head to clear it and his eyes found the Volokhov brothers again.

Phil ran to Scott and hauled him to his feet. The three of them staggered in the direction of the corn field. "Spence! Run!"

"They're taking her! They're taking her!" Marcus was shouting and slamming his open palms against the window. On the other side of the glass a disheveled man with greasy hair and filthy hands dragged Maria toward the nearest doorway. Katie and the other girl he had seen earlier on the side of the house were already gone from the room.

Spence turned back toward the giant. He was gone. *He's after Phil and the others.* Spence wanted to chase after them. The giant couldn't possibly move that quickly, but Phil and Keith were all but dragging Scott. Spence thought he could catch up to them easily enough. But Katie.

Marcus helped with his decision. He shouted, "You devil-worshipping pieces of shit! I'm gonna fucking kill every last fucking one of you if you hurt her!" The people inside the mask room appeared oblivious to the man and his threats. They carried on with their private conversations and sipped their wine as if three women had not just been dragged from their presence. Marcus bolted for the side of the house.

Spence stared at the empty doorway through which his sister had vanished. He punched the window a final time and failed to draw the attention of any of the room's occupants. He swore and ran after Marcus.

Spence found him at the side door where he had seen his sister and her friend taking their break. Marcus was struggling with the door handle and having no luck. The door remained sealed tight.

Marcus took note of Spence's presence. "Stand back, man." Marcus reared back and slammed his elbow into the door glass. The glass did not break. Marcus swore and backpedaled and tumbled off the steps. He rubbed his elbow and looked at the door with death in his eyes. "I think I just broke my elbow. Holy shit, this hurts!"

Spence knelt and examined the wounded appendage. Marcus squirmed and swore. "It's not broken. At least I don't think it is. What the fuck do I know?"

"We have to get in there, man. Maria's in there. They fucking took her!"

Hearing it spoken aloud raised the gooseflesh on Spence's arms. He had known on some level he would have to go inside Greystone, had known it since he saw Katie being carried from the room. But hearing it brought it to reality. Spence's seventeen year-old self whispered to him, *You're not serious, are you? You're not actually going to go* inside *Greystone Manor. Are you fucking crazy? Those devil-worshipping fuckers will eat your fucking heart.* Spence squashed the voice. His seventeen-year-old self could go fuck himself.

Spence eyed the door. "We're not getting in that way. Let's go around. Maybe we can find an open window or something."

"I can't lose her, Tom. No fucking way, man."

Spence helped Marcus to his feet. "You won't. And I'm not gonna lose Katie. C'mon. Let's find a way in."

They made their way around to the front of the house. Every window they tried was locked. Marcus had picked up a fist-sized smooth round rock he found bordering a group of hedges and he slammed it against the first window they came across. He succeeded in marring the glass. The window remained intact. "What the fuck," he whispered. "These fucking things are indestructible!" Spence shook his head. He had been thinking the same thing.

They rounded a corner and found themselves peeking at the front door. Spence realized he had never actually seen the front entrance to Greystone. It had always seemed too risky to approach whenever they ventured this close to the house. The front deck was spacious, the doors themselves tall and very solid-looking.

"I don't know if we should try a frontal assault," Marcus whispered.

Spence nodded. "Agreed. Too dangerous. Let's keep going."

They tried several more windows with no luck. They were now looking at the driveway. Katie's Cruze sat parked where Spence last saw it. *When she stepped out of that car she had no idea what was going to happen tonight.* Then, quickly, *She's okay. We'll find her and get her out of there and then we'll have a nice long talk with the Deacon's Landing PD.*

The corn field was to their left. They were close to completing a full circuit around the house and they still had not found a way inside. *It's taking too long. Your sister could be dead already. And even if she's still breathing, what do you think they're doing to her? Get in there, man. Or go home. Either or. Time to shit or get off the pot, as Keith would say.*

"I got one!" Marcus lifted the next window and it opened easily. He shook his arm and grimaced. His hand rubbed his elbow. "You sure it ain't broken?"

"No."

Marcus continued to rub his elbow. "Fuck it. Who cares? I knew there had to be a way in. Come on!"

Spence grabbed his friend's arm and pulled him back. "Hang on." He stepped closer and peered inside. The room beyond was black as pitch; Spence could not see a single detail. He waited for his eyes to adjust but they refused to penetrate the darkness. He turned back to Marcus. "We don't know what's in there. Or who."

"*Maria's* in there," Marcus hissed. "That's all that matters to me. You want to hang out here? Cool. Be my guest. I'll find Maria and your sister and get them both out."

Spence frowned. "That's not what I meant and you know it." He took a deep breath. "All I'm saying, man, is we have to be careful. Those assholes know we're out here and they probably know we're trying to get in. They'll be ready." Spence peered inside the room again. "Can't see a thing. Where's your lighter?"

"Maria has it."

"Great."

"Fuck it." Marcus placed his hands on either side of the window frame and pulled himself through with a grunt.

Spence heard something break, a dull thud, and Marcus swore under his breath. "Marcus!" Spence looked into the room. He could hear nothing, see nothing. He started when Marcus jumped to his feet and leaned along the window sill.

"I'm in."

"Could you make any more noise?"

"I'm a ninja, motherfucker."

"You couldn't sneak up on Helen Keller."

Marcus grinned and held out his hand. "Get in here, asshole. We're still on the clock."

Spence took the offered hand.

Two filthy hands appeared from the darkness behind Marcus. They wrapped themselves around Marcus's shoulders and wrenched him away from the window. Spence lost his grip on his friend's hand. He stumbled backward and nearly went down. Marcus yelped and disappeared into the darkness.

Spence ran back to the window. "Marcus!" He could still see nothing, hear nothing from within. No sound of a struggle, no shouts or curses. The room beyond the window was a void. "I'm coming, man! Hang on!" Spence grasped both sides of the window frame.

Something winged past his head and smashed against the house no more than an inch from the side of the window. Small pieces of the object pelted his arms, his face. Spence closed his eyes and turned his head away from the impact. When he opened his eyes again he saw a sizeable chip in the stone that made up the mansion's façade. Grey dust floated down from the impact spot. Spence turned.

The giant was striding across the driveway. He was dragging someone behind him, someone who was not struggling. From this distance and in the low light Spence could not tell who it was. The giant bent down and scooped another rock from the ground.

Spence sprinted for all he was worth toward the edge of the driveway and the cornfield beyond. The second rock missed as well, slicing through the air inches from Spence's head. The driveway ended thirty feet in front of him. He set a personal speed record in covering the distance. Spence leaped across the path that ran alongside the cornfield and threw himself into the sea of stalks.

He landed hard on the ground and the breath exploded from his lungs. He gave himself only a moment to catch his breath and then he was on his feet, running through the downward-sloping rows of corn stalks. He zig-zagged, stopped, knelt, ran again. It had probably been no more than thirty seconds since he entered the cornfield but to Spence it might have been a year. He stopped and listened. He heard no sound that would indicate the giant was chasing him. *Then again, you didn't hear anything just before someone grabbed Marcus, either,* seventeen year-old Spence reminded him. "Shut up," he whispered.

The giant did not seem to be in pursuit. Spence released a long, slow breath. It occurred to him he might try his cell again. It wouldn't work, or course, but it was worth a shot. *Sure, and let everyone for miles see the light from the screen. Christ, and I thought I was dumb.* "You were. Are. Whatever. Shut the fuck up."

He thought of making a run for it. He was far enough from the house and close enough to the road that he could probably make it back to the cars before anyone could catch him. And then what? His own car was back at the apartment. He didn't have keys to Marcus's car or Phil's. Was he to run along Route 26 until he made it all the way back to civilization? He seriously doubted he could manage that.

Not that any of it mattered because he could not leave. Katie was here and she was in trouble. His friends were here and they were in trouble as well. And they were here because *he* brought them here.

The giant had been dragging someone behind him. Spence couldn't see who it was but that hardly mattered. One of his friends was hurt, at the very least. It was all he allowed himself to think. And Katie and Maria and probably Marcus as well. There was only one direction for him.

"Fuck this."

Spence stood and tried to get his bearings. The stalks were too high for him to see anything. He started in the direction of the upward slope of the ground. After a few minutes he neared the top of the hill. Barely visible above the corn stalks was the highest point of Greystone's roof. He could see the weak light coming from the barn to his left.

Spence peeked through the stalks first at the barn and then at the house. He saw no one, heard nothing. In a burst of movement he sprinted from the edge of the cornfield to the barn. His eyes darted about the yard but he seemed to have this part of the grounds to himself.

He peeked around the door to the inside of the barn. The giant had not yet returned. *Probably dragging whoever that was into the house.* Spence needed him to take his time. He stepped into the barn. Despite the light from the fluorescent overheads and the lamp on the large work desk he did not trust that he had the run of the place. Quickly his eyes fell on a soil tiller. He scooped it up and held it like a samurai sword. It sucked but it might be enough to handle anyone who might be in here. *Except for that colossus*, he reminded himself. Yeah, except for him.

He scouted the entire barn in less than a minute. No one leaped at him from the shadowy corners. Spence turned his attention to the rows of farm implements and tools. He dropped the soil tiller and picked up a short-handled sledgehammer Yeah, this would do, and it would do quite nicely.

He was cautious as he approached the barn door. He raised the hammer, ready to bring it down on anyone who poked their head inside at the wrong time. No one did. Spence cleared the barn and made for the house.

CHAPTER ELEVEN

Ayudame

Katie had knee surgery when she was sixteen years old. A player from Naugatuck Regional had hit a line drive back to the pitcher's mound that ricocheted off her knee and Katie had gone down in agony. What she remembered most about the day of her surgery was the effect the anesthetic had on her. The anesthesiologist had hooked up the IV to her arm and a nurse wheeled her bed out of the prep room. "Count backwards from 100, please," the nurse told her. Katie made it as far as 97. She blinked and she found herself in the recovery room. That was what she found so disorienting about the anesthesia. Clearly she had been out for some time. Her knee was wrapped in a surgical bandage, she was in another room entirely. But she had not felt the passage of that time. Nor did she now.

She had been on the floor in the mask room. Exton, the Stanleys, both Lords Morley, even Mr. Watts, had been looking at her with no hint of emotion. She blinked, and now she was here.

The walls were made of stone. The air was cold and damp. The room reeked of mold. There was another scent, beneath the mold, faint but definitely there. It was unpleasant and caused Katie's nose to wrinkle. A single lightbulb dangled from a wire that disappeared into the ceiling. There was no finery in here. No portraits, no fireplaces, no bookshelves. The basement, perhaps. A part of the house no one was allowed to see.

Katie found herself lying on a table of some kind. She felt no restraints holding her down and yet she could not move anything aside from her head. There were other tables within the room.

Amanda lay on one, the woman brought in by Martin Jacoby on another. There were two other women there, as well. Katie could not see either face; the angle of her table prevented that. She could see both women wore outfits identical to hers. She caught sight of the rose tattoo poking out from the sleeve on one woman's arm. None of her roommates moved, nor gave any sign they were even conscious.

"Amanda?" Katie waited. Her friend remained still and she did not respond. Katie craned her neck as much as she was able and saw the other woman in a similar state. "Amanda? Amanda, wake up. Anyone? Is anyone alive in here?"

What if she's dead? What if they're all *dead?* The thought struck Katie like a fist. She could not tell if Amanda was breathing. *You might be the only one alive in here. These other four are dead and everyone upstairs thinks you are, too. So what do you think they'll do when they see you're still alive*? Katie squashed the thought.

She tried to lift her arms, failed. Her legs were likewise unresponsive. She settled for her fingers. It took effort but she managed to curl her hand into a fist. Katie could feel the sweat from the effort on her forehead. She tried to pound the table with her fist but that was apparently beyond her abilities. She concentrated on flexing her fingers. Maybe that would help snap the rest of her out of this paralysis.

That was one hell of a roofie Exton hit you with. It made Katie think of Bob Mason, the piece of shit she met the first (and last) time she let herself be dragged to Elements. It was a dive bar that masqueraded as a hip nightclub. Shannon and Dana had talked her into going for her twenty-first birthday. Mason seemed nice enough. He smiled a lot, dropped some obscure trivia that Katie verified with a quick Google search. And when she wasn't looking he slipped something into her Long Island iced tea. She could barely move after it hit. If it weren't for her friends coming to her rescue she would have been at the asshole's mercy. They all but carried her to the car, Katie's feet dragging uselessly along the ground. Dana had gone back inside and a minute later returned with a bruised hand and a look of satisfaction on her face. Katie could sure use her friends now. She felt just like she did that night.

It wasn't going to do her any good thinking of Shannon or Dana. They weren't here and they weren't on the way. "Okay, okay, okay," she whispered. "We need to get out of this." She was able to move her hand in a circular motion but no more. Everything north of her wrist was still down for the count. "Come on, come on, *move.*" The sweat on her forehead had spread to her face and neck and was migrating down to her chest. Still her arm would not budge.

"Can you help me?"

Katie would have jumped at the unexpected voice had she been capable of such movement. She turned her eyes to the mystery woman on the table across the room.

"Please. I need help. I can't move."

"Yes," Katie replied with too much desperation in her tone. She was relieved to find she wasn't the only one alive. "Yes, I'm here! Are you okay?"

"I can't move," the woman repeated. "I can't feel anything. Please help me." Her voice was soft, as if she did not want anyone but Katie to hear.

"I can't move, either," Katie informed her. "Exton injected me with something. Amanda, too. Is she breathing? Can you tell?"

The woman lowered her voice and switched to Spanish. Katie did not understand her but she recognized the tone of desperation and fear.

"I don't know Spanish, I'm sorry. I can't understand you. Can you tell if Amanda is alive?"

The woman either did not hear Katie or hadn't registered what she said. She continued in Spanish. Now her tone was full of fear bordering on hysteria.

"I can't…" Katie stopped. There seemed to be no point. She redirected her attention to her hands. Her fingers continued to flex but her arms remained dead at her side. Katie bore down and commanded her arms to move. She gritted her teeth and shut her eyes with the effort. Nothing. Katie exhaled loudly. Tears streamed weakly from her eyes. "God fucking *dammit!*"

Katie licked her lips. "Listen. My name is Katie Spencer. I live on Commercial Street in Deacon's Landing. What's your name?" Katie moved her head as much as she was able toward the other woman.

The woman's voice had become a whisper. She stared at the ceiling; tears streamed from her eyes.

"What's your name? Can you tell me that?"

"Maria," the woman replied after a few false starts. "Maria Greer." She sniffled and craned her neck to look at Katie. "You're Spence's sister?"

Katie's breath caught in her throat. "You know Tom?"

"His best friend is Marcus Greer. Marcus is my husband," she explained.

It hit Katie all at once. Maria had looked familiar when Jacoby first brought her to the mask room. Katie did not have the chance to place her then. "We met once, I think," Katie told her.

She hadn't seen Marcus in a long time but she remembered how she was always a bit creeped out whenever he would come over, some head-banging song blasting from that old car he drove. He had never actually hit on her but his eyes always seemed to imply that he wanted to. His behavior hadn't changed even when he brought his new girlfriend to a barbeque in Tom's backyard.

"At Tom's house. It was a cookout, I think. Do you remember?"

"I can't move," she stammered. The connection between them had put Maria's hysteria on pause for a moment. It was back on play now. Fresh tears streamed from her eyes. "*Ayudame*," she implored. "*Por favor, ayudame.*"

"Maria? Maria! Dammit!" Katie would have slammed her fist on the table if she could. Maria was gone again. She craned her neck in Amanda's direction. Her friend had not moved a muscle as far as Katie could tell. Nor had the other two women on the other side of the room. "Amanda! Amanda, can you hear me?" The only sound that reached her was the sobs coming from Maria.

Katie bore down again.

Not long after the twentieth time Katie tried to move she heard another groan from across the room. Katie's head snapped in that direction. It had come from Amanda, she was certain. Katie turned all her concentration toward her friend. Thankfully Maria had fallen silent a few minutes before. After several moments of silence, Katie said, "Amanda?"

She awaited a reply. The room remained silent. "Amanda, you with me? Come on, wake up! We're in trouble!"

The groan did not repeat itself. The room was so quiet Katie could hear the soft background buzz of the electric light dangling from the ceiling. She tried several more times to get Amanda's attention but her friend was out of it. *At least she's alive.* Katie felt some of the weight lift from her. She hadn't realized until that moment how much she liked Amanda Regan.

She called her name, willed the woman to regain consciousness. Amanda rewarded her with a second groan but remained otherwise unresponsive. Katie waited some more.

After a time she heard voices from outside the room. One she identified right away as Exton. His voice was faint but growing louder and more distinct by the moment. The other voice sounded as if its owner was a thousand years old. One of the Morley brothers. The voices grew in volume and clarity until their owners were right outside.

"Don't say anything," Katie whispered. She might have been speaking to Maria, or Amanda, or to herself. "No matter what they say, keep your mouth shut."

She received no acknowledgement from anyone. She was going to repeat her instructions but she was interrupted by the sound of a heavy door swinging open slowly.

Some light spilled into the room from the outside. Katie caught a glimpse of a simple lightbulb hanging from a wire from the ceiling. Two silhouettes stood framed by the light. One was thin and hunched over and leaned on the other. Both men entered the room.

William Morley—Katie thought it was William—perked up a bit when he surveyed the occupants of the room. His eyes settled on Maria, Amanda, and her in turn, the corners of his mouth turning up in an unpleasant smile. Katie could not help but notice the ancient man ignored the other two women in maid's outfits. "Well done, Exton," he told his companion. "Well done indeed."

Exton inclined his head slightly. "My Lord."

Morley walked slowly, assisted by Exton, to the table nearest him. Katie saw them stop and the ancient man's eyes moved slowly over Amanda's body. He leaned down and sniffed several times.

"Leave her alone!" Katie shouted and ignored her own advice.

Morley paid her no mind. Exton's head snapped up and he regarded Katie with cold, hard eyes. Katie stared venom at him.

"I said leave her alone, you fuckers!" She struggled against the poison in her system. Her hand twitched, and she could feel pins-and-needles in her wrist and forearm. That was all. "If you fucking hurt her…"

Morley straightened and looked at Exton. "No. Too much pollution in the blood. Give her to my brother. He doesn't mind that sort of thing."

Exton nodded. "Yes, my Lord." He guided Lord Morley to the next table, where Maria Greer quickly turned her head and averted her eyes. Her breathing had picked up the pace considerably. Tears streamed steadily down her cheeks.

"And this one?" Exton asked. "She's the one your nephew caught outside."

Morley leaned down and sniffed the woman on the table. He paused several times; at one point his expression became one of a man who had just smelled a particularly pleasant flower. Maria whimpered and Katie could see more tears leaving wet tracks across her cheeks. At last Morley stood straight and regarded the woman before him. "Her fear is certainly heady. But I'm afraid her blood is even more vile than the first one's. I'm not sure even Arthur would want her."

"Perhaps we can use her for the sacrament, my Lord," Exton offered helpfully.

Morley seemed to consider the suggestion. "Perhaps," he echoed. "His Majesty is not terribly selective. She would be of little use otherwise. I was going to suggest we give her to my dear nephew, but you may be on to something, Exton. We shall discuss it upstairs."

Exton guided the old man to Katie's side.

Katie's first instinct was to look away, to turn her head as far away from William Morley as was physically possible. She forced herself to look into his eyes, instead. She saw her image reflected in two pools of black that seemed to absorb all the warmth from her body. Katie shivered. She felt the tears well up in her eyes.

Morley leaned down and sniffed her as he had the other two women. After a moment he paused. Katie watched him look at Exton. Then he returned his attention to her. He sniffed again, descending from her head to her chest and proceeding downward. He paused when he reached the area between her legs. He sniffed in a lungful and this time his smile was unmistakable.

Katie wanted to scream. She pictured herself swinging her fist for all she was worth and connecting solidly with the old man's jaw. She could see the blood fly from his mouth, see the startled expression from Exton. The old man reeled and crashed to the floor, spitting blood and teeth. The expression in his black eyes was one of utter astonishment followed by a howl of pain.

None of that happened, of course. Katie's arm remained dead at her side.

After lingering in her sweet spot for several more moments Morley continued down her body and ended with her feet. At last he stood erect—or as close to erect as he could manage--and regarded Exton. "This one," he announced. "She is clean. Or, at least, clean enough by the standards of today's world. It's funny, my dear boy, but in my youth I would have spurned her as much as the other two. Now…"

"Shall I prepare her, my Lord?"

"Fuck you, Exton!" Katie shouted. She wanted to say more, to *do* more. In that moment her mind had gone blank except for an image of her pummeling Morley and Exton into the floor. Fresh tears spilled from her eyes. Her heart slammed against her ribs. "Fuck you!" she screamed. "Fuck you!"

Exton's eyes were wide. His lips moved but he produced no sound. He stared at Katie in utter shock. It took him several moments to recover. When he did he looked at William Morley. "My Lord," he stuttered, "forgive me. Had I known…"

Morley waved him off. He produced a sound that took Katie several moments to identify as laughter. The old man's shoulders shook, his whole body quivered with the display. A fit of coughing brought the laughter to an abrupt end. Morley's hands gripped the edge of the table; his arms shook with the effort to steady himself.

He's gonna die right here, Katie realized. *Listen to that cough. He's gonna spit blood in a second. Christ, if I could just move my arm this would be over right now.* But she could not move her arm. The pins-and-needles continued to go to work on her limbs but so far she was still glued to the table.

Exton placed his hands on Morley's shoulders until the tremors subsided and the coughing stopped. Morley steadied himself with a deep breath, then another. He took a kerchief from his breast pocket and dabbed at the corners of his mouth. He looked at the kerchief before shoving it back into the pocket from whence it came.

"That's quite enough, Exton," Morley said and shrugged off the other man's hands. He watched Exton retreat a step, then he turned his attention back to Katie. His smile returned. "You may look on me with disgust now," he told Katie conversationally, "but you should have seen me in my youth. I was far from this frail body before you today. Time has a way of humbling all. Don't you agree, Ms. Spencer?" He smiled again. "Now, where were we, my dear?"

"Let me out of here you old fucker!" Katie screamed.

"Por favor dios ayudanos," Maria mumbled from her table. Somehow, even above the pounding of the blood in her ears, Katie heard her. Whatever Maria said next was lost when Exton clamped his hand over her mouth. Maria's prayer became nothing but a muffled grunt.

Exton reached into the pocket of his coat and produced a syringe. He held it in front of her eyes. Maria fell quiet.

Morley's eyes had never left Katie's. "Such spirit!" His tone was one of approval, even excitement. "It has been some time since I encountered such tenacity in a woman. You, my dear, are a rare creature indeed."

Katie's fingers continued to clench and unclench. She could feel her wrist now, and part of her arm. She was close. *Keep talking, you old bastard. Just another couple minutes. Keep talking. Tell me how amazing I am. I'll show you something I'm willing to bet you've never seen before.*

Morley seemed to read her thoughts. "I am going to enjoy you, Ms. Spencer." He leaned down again.

Katie expected him to sniff her again, or maybe even to lift up her skirt and pull her panties down. She braced herself as best she could.

"No need to prepare this one, Exton. I prefer her just as she is." Morley's lips parted and Katie saw the long, sharp canine teeth. He leaned into her until his breath brushed her neck.

Her arm finally moved. Katie swung it with little strength and even less aim. The limb glanced off the side of Morley's head. Even that meager contact had a profound effect on the old man. He staggered back a step, his arm flailing to steady himself. He might have gone down had Exton not been there to catch him. William Morley sagged in the butler's arms for several seconds before Exton steadied him.

"My Lord! Are you unharmed?" Exton glared at Katie. "If you have injured His Lordship..."

"I'm quite all right, Exton," Morley told him. He straitened as best he could and adjusted his tuxedo. He regarded Katie with both surprise and admiration. "Yes, quite spirited." His smile was wide enough to swallow her car. He resumed his place next to the table. He leaned down.

Someone on the other side of the room screamed.

When those sharp teeth penetrated her neck, Katie did, as well.

CHAPTER TWELVE

A Wolf Confronted by Three Very Small Mice

Spence put his back to the house. He craned his neck and looked through the large window at the people assembled inside the mask room. The denizens of Denham had returned to their drinks and their conversation as if nothing out of the ordinary had occurred. One of the old men was gone from the room, but the other sat in his high-backed chair and drank what looked like dark, expensive wine. *I'll drown you in that shit, you old bastard.* In truth Spence could have taken his sledgehammer and bludgeoned every last person inside Greystone for what had been done to Katie. And he would have done it with a smile on his face. But first he had to find her.

He left the mask room behind. He returned to the corner of the house and peeked at the spot where he had seen his sister and the other maid just before they had gone back inside. The steps were clear of people. A single light above the door was bright enough to clear the area of shadows almost to where Spence stood. Anyone who looked out that door, or even the windows between here and there, would spot him easily. *So what? It's not like they don't know we're here. They have at least three of us in the house already.* And that wasn't counting Katie. Spence thought of his sister lying on the Oriental rug like a discarded doll. His hands squeezed the handle of the sledgehammer.

Before he could step around the corner someone hissed his name from the darkness. Spence whirled and raised the hammer. He saw no one. He narrowed his eyes and took in his surroundings. Between the light from the house and the barn in the distance was a zone of darkness into which he could see little in the way of detail. He heard his name again. It was coming from the other side of the tree. Spence saw someone poke their head out, followed by a hand waving him over.

"Spence," the voice hissed. "Over here." The hand gestured again.

Spence looked back in the direction of the mask room. He could see little from this angle but from what he could tell no one had heard the voice except him. He pressed his finger to his lips, the universal gesture to *shut the hell up.*

Two forms emerged from behind the tree. He recognized Keith right away. No one else in the group was close to his size. The other, smaller form limped to catch up. They took care to stay out of the light coming from the mask room and joined him. The second form belonged to Scott. Even in the semi-darkness Spence could see the blood that had caked and dried beneath Scott's nose and on his chin.

"You okay?" Spence whispered.

"No," Scott whispered back. "I can't even see okay from where I am. That fucker broke my nose and I have one hell of a headache. But I think I'll live."

Spence looked at Keith and mouthed, *What happened?*

Keith bulked up his arms and puffed out his chest and nodded in the direction of the barn.

Spence nodded back. Right. Of course. The giant from the barn.

"He grabbed Phil," Keith whispered, his voice full of guilt. "We got separated. Last I saw he was dragging him here."

"I saw him," Spence whispered back. He paused. "Right after someone grabbed Marcus."

"Wait, he's in there, too?" Scott asked. His voice rose in pitch and volume.

"Shh. They know we're out here, but they might not know where exactly," Spence told them. "They looked right at us. They did something to Katie. I don't know what. She was out cold on the floor. And they grabbed Maria, too."

Scott held up both hands. "Okay, we need to go get the cops."

"How?" Keith asked. "Phones don't work up here. I know, I tried. And Phil and Marcus had the keys. You know how to hotwire a car?"

"Maybe we just need to get clear of this place," Scott suggested, "until we get a signal. Then we can call 'em."

"You go," Spence whispered. "They have my sister in there. I'm gonna get her."

"I'm with you," Keith answered immediately.

They looked at Scott. Spence wouldn't blame him one bit if he decided to go for help. It might even be the smart thing to do. But Scott did not look like a man who could make it all the way back to town on foot. He swayed slightly from side to side and every few seconds his eyes lost focus. Spence said nothing and waited for his old friend to make up his mind.

"Okay, okay, I'm with you," Scott said at last. "But someone better grab that big bastard if we see him again. I'm not going another round with him."

"What's the plan?" Keith asked.

Spence shrugged. "Find a way in. Find Katie and everyone else and get out of Dodge." He hefted the sledgehammer. "If anyone gets in our way…" He allowed his voice to trail off.

Scott swallowed. Keith's lips disappeared but he nodded.

"I'm thinking that door right there." Spence peeked around the corner again.

Another woman in a maid's outfit emerged from within Greystone Manor. She closed the door behind her and walked down the few steps. She looked younger than Katie but her body language suggested someone older. Spence watched her fish a cigarette out of her pocket and light it. She angled her head up and exhaled a cloud of smoke into the night sky.

There was a good seventy feet between him and the maid.

Spence turned back to his friends. "She's our ticket inside. Stay here until I signal you. If this goes south run like hell. Got it?"

Scott nodded. Keith looked less than thrilled with the idea. "Don't let it go south," he whispered.

Spence hefted the hammer. It was heavy and reassuring in his hand. He took a deep breath.

Spence ran for all he was worth. He covered the distance in seconds. The maid looked up, startled, but she had become aware of his presence too late. She scrambled up the steps and had her hand on the doorknob when Spence grabbed for her.

She started to scream but Spence wedged his forearm against her throat. Her scream died instantly. His momentum carried them both into the door. It rattled in its frame but remained closed. One of the glass panels cracked a bit when the woman's head slammed against it. She struggled, and she was stronger than she appeared, but Spence had had enough of this place and the people who called it home. He shifted his stance and shoved his forearm against her throat with even more force.

"Stop," he hissed. "Stop right now or I'll cave in your skull." He showed her the hammer. Her eyes fell on it and she ceased her struggle. She shifted her gaze from the hammer to the man holding it.

"Now I'm gonna ease off here. If you try to scream or run or do anything I don't like..." He showed her the hammer again. "Got it?" The woman nodded. He pulled his forearm back a few inches. "Where's my sister?"

"Who is your sister?" she asked. Her tone was neutral. No fear, not even a hint of worry. She may as well have asked him for the time.

"Katie Spencer. You assholes attacked her. I want her back right fucking now. And if she's hurt, well, you definitely won't like what happens next. Understand?"

"I was unaware Ms. Spencer had any siblings."

Spence reapplied his forearm. She gasped but her eyes remained fixed on him. She had returned to being the age-indiscriminate woman whom Spence had seen on her smoke break. The surprise and fear she had displayed at his initial appearance were gone. "I won't ask again."

The woman's impassive eyes had locked themselves onto Spence's angry and fearful ones. She seemed to study him, a scientist trying to decide if this species of bacteria was new or already catalogued. She came to a decision after a long pause. "I believe she is in the cellar. I can bring you to her."

Spence backed off a few inches. "Good decision." He waved over his friends without taking his eyes from the maid.

She did not react to the two new arrivals. She did not monitor their approach nor did she seem surprised at their appearance. Her eyes never left Spence.

This chick ain't right, seventeen-year-old Spence told him. *Yeah, she looked surprised when we rolled up on her, but she got over it pretty quick. Right now it's three against one and she looks about as worried as a wolf confronted by three very small mice.* His younger voice wasn't wrong; the maid seemed completely nonchalant about her current situation.

She also displayed no discomfort. Her head hit the glass hard enough to crack it, the same glass Marcus had tried to break with his elbow. Spence glanced at the cracked glass. There might have been a couple strands of blonde hair embedded there—it was difficult to tell in this light—but there was no blood. *Hard-headed*, Spence thought.

"We really doing this?" Scott whispered. "Going inside Greystone?" His voice dripped both fear and surprise, as if Spence's plan had been an abstract until this very moment.

"Hey, my brother's in there," Keith reminded him. "And Spence's sister. You wanna leave them here? Don't pull a fucking Greer on us."

Scott swallowed and said no more.

Spence looked back at his friends. Keith nodded. Scott's expression said he wanted to be anywhere but here. "Inside," Spence said to the maid. He removed his forearm from her neck and took a step back to allow her to turn around.

She placed her hand on the doorknob and turned it. The door opened silently. She started across the threshold.

Spence wrapped his free hand around her arm. "Nothing stupid," he whispered in her ear. He held the sledgehammer in front of her eyes. "Or else."

The maid stepped into the house. Spence followed her.

They were inside a small alcove. Cabinets lined the walls, making it cramped for four people. The floor was off-white linoleum and polished to a sheen. Spence could just about see his reflection in the floor.

We're inside, his younger self exclaimed. *We're actually inside* Greystone fucking Manor! *Maybe this wasn't such a great idea. We should get outta here right now!*

Spence's mind flashed back to all the nights they had come to Denham. All the close calls, the clone car, the drums in the woods, running through the cornfield, all of it. In all those nights spent here it had never occurred to him, to any of them, to try to go *inside* any of the houses, let alone the main house. Even getting close enough to look inside had been pretty goddamned daring of them. *If you had told me back then one day I'd be sneaking into this house I'd have said you were insane.* And yet here they were. Spence needed a moment and he took it. It wouldn't do Katie a bit of good if he was too freaked out to help her.

"Where's the cellar?" he asked when at last he gathered himself.

"This way, please, Mr. Spencer," the maid replied.

They exited the alcove and emerged into a long hallway. Spence looked both ways, saw no one. Voices reached him but they were far away. He could make out nothing of the conversations.

"Keep your eyes open for a phone. A landline. Two old fucks here, they're bound to have one."

"Good idea," Keith replied.

"Hey, I don't like this, man," Scott whispered. "She sounds like she's giving us a goddamned tour. She's gonna fuck us the first chance she gets. We can still get outta here, Spence."

Spence ignored him. Once he had Katie he would be very willing to get away from this house and this street and never see either again for the rest of his life. But first he needed to find Katie.

They moved silently along the hallway. Doors lined the walls, each one closed. Spence tensed a bit as they passed each one. He didn't think anyone would come charging out at them but there was always that chance. Then what would they do? Would he really swing the sledgehammer to keep them quiet? Was he prepared to bludgeon someone to death simply to keep their presence a secret? Could he kill?

Well, yes, he believed he could. If he got his hands on whichever asshole attacked his sister he believed he might very well end the man, or woman. If it cost him prison time, so be it. At least Katie would be safe. Part of him hoped it didn't come to that. He wanted his sister back, safe and sound. And his friends. He would settle for that.

The hallway ended and split into two directions. The maid took a right and Spence followed her. The voices he heard earlier had faded to nothing. In fact Spence didn't hear a sound except for their soft footfalls on the strip of carpet that ran down the center of the hallway.

"Where's the cellar?" Spence leaned in close and whispered into the maid's ear. "If you're leading us into a trap—"

"It is this way, Mr. Spencer," she interrupted. "I assure you, I am taking you to your sister."

"She better be okay." He prodded her forward with the sledgehammer. "I swear to Christ, she better be okay. Get me?"

"I do." Her voice carried no hint of emotion.

Spence began to sweat. *Scott was right. She's way too calm for this. Maybe she* is *leading us into a trap.* On the heels of that, *Then what? Am I supposed to threaten her again? Let's just hope she's really taking us to Katie. We'll deal with anything else after that.*

As they passed a door Spence heard a toilet flush from the other side. He froze. *This is it. This is it. Now we're fucked.* The paralysis lasted only a split-second. He shoved the maid forward. The hallway ended fifteen feet ahead at yet another T-junction. They had only to reach it before the occupant of the bathroom emerged into the hallway and they would be okay. They nearly made it.

The door swung open and a middle-aged man stagger-stepped out of the room. He was dressed in a very expensive looking three-piece suit. In one hand he held a short glass of what looked like bourbon; his free hand he placed against the wall in an obvious attempt to steady himself. He had emerged from the bathroom directly next to Keith and Scott. He looked at them, blinked several times. Saliva dripped from the corner of his mouth. "Who're you?" he drooled.

Keith did not hesitate. His fist shot forward and caught the man square on the nose. Blood spurted. The glass fell from his hand. Expensive bourbon splashed onto the floor, the walls, the man himself. He staggered back against the wall. His knees buckled and he slid down until he assumed a seated position on the floor. He looked at Keith through half-lidded eyes before his head lolled to the side.

"Jesus." It was Scott who said it. "One and done. God *damn*, Keith!"

Spence was going to tell them to drag the man back into the bathroom from whence he came. He got as far as opening his mouth. The maid brought her fist down in a sweeping arc. She caught him squarely in the groin. Spence *huffed* and he dropped to his knees. The hammer landed on the floor with a dull *thud*. His hands moved to protect the injured area. The maid took off. Spence grabbed for her, missed. She rounded the corner in the hallway and vanished from his sight.

Keith was right after her. He made the turn and stopped. "What the fuck?" He looked back at his brother's friends. "She's gone."

Spence couldn't get his legs under him. His groin throbbed and he felt the bile rising in his throat. It took all he had to prevent himself from vomiting all over the floor. Scott reached down and got a hand under Spence's arm. He braced himself against the wall and lifted as well as he could. Spence staggered to his feet, his hands still covering his groin.

"What? Where?"

Keith held his position at the end of the hallway. "There are no doors here, man. There are windows but they're closed. She's *gone.*"

Spence leaned a bit on Scott and the two of them joined Keith. Spence's eyes took in the new hallway. As Keith had said there were no doors here. One wall was made up mostly of windows. They appeared locked to Spence. He could see nothing outside the windows but pitch darkness. Other than a few paintings on the opposite wall the hallway was featureless.

"Where the hell'd she go?" Scott asked.

"Oh, man, this is bad," Keith said by way of answer. "She's gonna bring the goddamned cavalry down on us."

"We're not leaving," Spence told him.

Keith regarded him with a half-smile. "Of course not. But we'd better get a move on. Can you walk?"

Spence nodded. He stood up straight and took his weight off Scott. "Grab the hammer. And find a fucking phone while you're at it."

Keith went back into the previous hallway and returned with the makeshift weapon. He looked down both hallways before his eyes settled on Spence. "Now what? Which way is the cellar?"

Spence shrugged. "Pick one."

Keith did as he was asked.

CHAPTER THIRTEEN

All The Indica in The World

Amanda felt as if she had just awoken the morning after the world's greatest party. Her head swam rather pleasantly. There was a slight buzzing behind her eyes. She was no stranger to mornings like this, although it had been some time since the last one. She allowed her head to swim in the invisible ocean. How long she indulged herself she could not say. She might have remained that way even longer but for the voices nearby. At first she couldn't make out a single word, only that the voices sounded angry. Were the neighbors at it again? That was a recurring problem in West Philly. No one seemed to respect a hangover anymore. She was going to tell them to shut up but there was something wrong with her mouth. Her lips moved but she couldn't speak. Amanda tried again. She heard a rattle in her throat, nothing more. *Progress*, she thought. *Soon you'll be speaking in full sentences like a normal person.*

The voices continued and now Amanda was able to catch a few words. "Fuck you, Exton!" someone shouted. The voice sounded familiar. And she knew someone named Exton, she was sure of it. Wasn't he one of the endless goons who worked security at O'Toole's? The dive bar's owner was known to be a prick to his customers—the ones uninterested in purchasing anything illegal, anyway—but he was downright savage to his employees. There was always a new bartender, always a new guy at the door, always some new hulking thug following the owner around in case anyone tried to get rough with him. Amanda had always wondered why the cops simply didn't shut down the place. There was certainly enough trouble there to do so. But that couldn't be it. Amanda hadn't been there in months. Had, in fact, left the bar and the city behind when she applied...

Everything came back to her at once. Her eyes snapped open. She was lying on something cold and unyielding. And for some reason she could not move.

Someone nearby, a woman, was saying something in Spanish. Amanda had no idea what the words meant but it sounded like a prayer. It ended abruptly.

Amanda was able to move her head but only a few inches. She turned in the direction of the voices. The woman who had been dumped on the floor in the mask room lay on a nearby table. Exton stood over her. On the other side of the room she found Katie. The girl was laid out on an identical table and one of the Morley brothers stood beside her.

"No need to prepare this one, Exton. I prefer her just as she is," the old man announced.

Katie looked terrified, although Amanda couldn't see much from this angle. She tried to speak again and managed a muffled grunt. *What the hell did they hit me with? Did they break my neck? Why can't I move?*

She tried again to speak. This time she produced what sounded like a moan. She was getting closer, she knew it.

Katie swung her arm clumsily through the air. She connected weakly with the side of Morley's head. The ancient man staggered a step before Exton caught him and steadied him. The old bastard said something and then he resumed his place next to Katie's table. He leaned down.

Amanda found her voice at last. She screamed. It echoed off the damp stone walls of the room.

Morley had his face pressed against the side of the girl's neck. Katie's head thrashed against the table, but weakly. A scream erupted from somewhere deep within her soul. Amanda's eyes opened wide when she heard the gurgling sound coming from her new friend.

"Leave her alone!" she finally cried. She was aware of the return of her ability to speak only on a subconscious level. All her focus was on what was occurring on the other side of the room.

Katie's legs managed to lift off the table a few inches. Her arm dropped and dangled off the side. The gurgling sound continued for another few moments. Then she lay still.

Amanda realized she had been holding her breath. She gulped air. Her eyes moved to her arms. She willed them to move. Her brow creased with the effort and sweat beaded on her cheeks. She managed to move a few of her fingers but nothing more. She gave up with a loud expulsion of breath. Her eyes returned to her new friend.

Morley stood erect once again. He blocked any view Amanda had of Katie's face. "Mmm." Morley inclined his head as if he were studying the girl on the table. "Quite magnificent." He turned.

His chin was covered with blood. It dripped from the corners of his mouth and onto the floor. His eyes were black and devoid of pupils. His teeth…

"Jesus Christ," Amanda whispered.

Morley's black eyes turned in her direction.

Amanda swallowed. "What…What did you do?" Then, with much more anger, *"What did you do to her?"*

Morley's lips turned up at the corners. The long, sharp teeth were stained crimson. He flicked his tongue across them and smiled again.

"Come, Exton." He strode across the room. It would not occur to Amanda until later that his stride was strong and confident, not that of the ancient man she had met upstairs. Exton turned on his heel and followed Morley through the door. It closed behind them. Amanda heard a lock engage from the other side.

Her eyes went immediately to Katie. She lay on the table, unmoving. The side of her neck was covered with blood. It was difficult to see from this angle whether or not she was breathing.

"Katie? Katie, can you hear me?" When the girl did not stir Amanda raised her voice. "Katie, answer me! Wake up! *Katie!*" Amanda waited. Katie did not move.

Amanda banged her head against the table. She could move that much, at least. The pain blasted away the last of the clouds in her head. She took several deep breaths, willed her heart to slow down. At last she opened her eyes and turned her head.

She craned her neck to the see the woman on the table closest to her. "Can you tell if she's breathing?"

"*Por favor dios ayudanos,*" the woman replied.

Amanda tried again to move. "God*damnit!*" She swallowed again. "Okay, I can't move. Can you?"

Tears spilled down the woman's cheeks. She shook her head with what seemed like much effort. "I can't," came the reply. "They injected us with something. We're gonna die down here, just like them." More tears. The breath hitched in her throat and cut off anything else she planned to say.

Amanda's eyes darted about the room. She spotted two more tables. Atop each one lay the body of a woman dressed identically to Amanda and Katie. She could see both women clearly. Their necks were brown with dried blood.

"Holy Mother of God," Amanda whispered. Her eyes whipped back in Katie's direction. "Katie, wake up! Come on, honey, open your eyes. Talk to me. *Katie!*"

Her friend neither moved nor replied.

Amanda licked her lips. She eyed the crying woman. "Listen, we have to get to Katie. We have to see if she's alive. Get her to a hospital, I don't know. She can bleed out if we don't. Try to move again."

The woman appeared to make no effort to follow Amanda's advice. Or maybe she was trying. It was difficult to tell from this angle. And Amanda was trying with everything she had. Aside from her hands and her head she could not move at all.

Whatever they hit me with is doing its job. I feel like I smoked all the indica in the world. And what's the cure for that? Time. But Katie might not have time.

Amanda rested her head against the table. She thought of Katie. She pictured the two of them in the kitchen, in the secret passage, outside on the steps. Amanda thought of her smile and the dimples that sprung into existence when it appeared. She couldn't bring herself to look at Katie now. She did not want to see the blood, and she didn't want to know if the girl had stopped breathing.

"Just hang on, Katie," Amanda whispered. "Just hang on. I'll get you out of here, I promise."

She went to work getting the rest of her hand to move.

*****

Spence was the first to hear the voices. Two of them, a man and a woman. The slight echo told him they were in a rather large room ahead. He looked back at Keith and Scott and repeated the *Shh* gesture. They nodded their understanding. Spence put his back to the wall as he approached the open doorway. He grimaced as he walked. His groin still hurt like hell but it seemed his testicles had recovered a bit. Best not to think about that for now.. He could see black-and-red linoleum and what looked to be a stainless steel table. The wall he could see from this angle appeared made of white tile.

Spence stopped short of the doorway. He leaned forward to get a better look at the room. It was the largest kitchen he had ever seen. Ovens, sinks, enough counter space to prepare food for a hundred people.

A portly woman in a black chef's outfit busied herself at one of the sinks. "All I'm saying is Mr. Exton could have waited until after the gusts were finished with their drinks," she said to someone out of Spence's line-of-sight. "I wash and clean enough glasses whenever their Lordships aren't here. It isn't fair to make me do them when I'm supposed to have a staff working for me."

The unmistakable sound of an empty beer can being crushed in someone's hand. A pause. The sound of a refrigerator door being opened then closed, followed by the sound of a new beer can being opened. "Blame Exton, not me," a man replied. "He's the one who knocked out that Katie chick. She was the one, too." The sound of guzzling followed by a loud belch.

The chef winced and snapped a dishtowel in the unseen man's direction. "You are disgusting, Mr. Jacoby."

The man leaned in and planted a quick kiss on the chef's cheek. She recoiled as if she had been bitten by a snake. "Get away, get away!"

Spence saw the man for only a second. It was long enough to see the grime on his hands. The man who grabbed Marcus. Spence's hands balled into fists. He retreated from the doorway.

Keith and Scott looked expectantly at him.

"Two," Spence whispered. "A man and a woman. I'm pretty sure the guy is the one who grabbed Marcus." He paused. "And his name is Jacoby."

"*Martin* Jacoby?" Scott's voice rose an octave.

"I assume," Spence replied.

"Who the fuck is Martin Jacoby?" Keith asked.

"I don't know the dude personally," Scott told him, "but his name's always in the police blotter. Motherfucker gets arrested every other day. Drugs, mugging, B&E, you name it."

"He's kind of a celebrity in the Landing," Spence said.

"So he's an asshole," Keith replied. "So what?"

"So nothing," Spence told him. "We're still going in. We just make sure we grab him first."

Scott swallowed. "Are we sure about this?"

"*Very*," Keith hissed. He displayed the hammer. "We find out where my brother is, and Katie, and we fucking clean house. Why are we even talking about this?"

"There's a good forty feet between the door and them. Scott's in no condition to run that distance. I can probably do it but I can't promise anything. That leaves you."

The corner of Keith's mouth ticked upward. "Spence, it'll be my goddamned pleasure."

Spence regarded him. The annoying little shit from back in the day was gone. The man in front of him was ripped like an action movie hero and he sounded like one. Keith looked ready and more than willing. "Just don't fuck anyone up," Spence whispered. "We need to find out where everyone is. We need them to talk."

"Yeah, yeah, yeah," Keith replied. "We gonna do this?"

"Lemme check if they're still where I saw them. I'll wave you through if they are."

Keith gripped the hammer so tightly his knuckles turned white. "Make it fast."

Spence left them behind and returned to his spot near the kitchen doorway. The chef still stood at the sink with her back to the door. The man was gone from his sight although Spence could hear the refrigerator door open again. He took a deep breath.

This is really it. You're about to get into a fight with two people inside Greystone Manor. Hell of a night, isn't it?

Without taking his eyes from the chef Spence waved his hand in Keith's direction.

Keith plowed past him. Spence followed him inside.

Jacoby looked up, the latest beer can halfway to his lips. His eyes widened.

Keith stopped and hurled the hammer like the God of Thunder himself.

The distance was too great. Jacoby had plenty of time to duck out of its way. He swore and scrambled backward. The hammer struck the wall and sent chips of tile in all directions. The chef turned at the sound of the impact.

Keith covered the distance at a speed that surprised Spence. Three, maybe four seconds after he threw the hammer he had reached the two occupants of the kitchen. He threw a haymaker at Jacoby.

Spence concentrated on the chef. At first she was too surprised to do anything. She gaped at the new arrival, one hand still drying the glass held in the other. Then she threw the glass into the sink and lunged to her left. Her hand came up with a rolling pin that looked heavy and solid.

Spence's groin throbbed and promised to up the wattage but it was too late to stop. He grabbed for the arm holding the rolling pin. The woman was far stronger than she appeared. She tried to bring it down on his head and nearly succeeded. Spence was able to deflect the path of her arm and the rolling pin passed within an inch of his shoulder. She shifted her feet and threw her weight behind the move.

Spence lost all semblance of balance. He crashed to the floor but managed to keep his hand on the chef's arm. *Christ, if she decides to just fall on me...*

Scott threw himself at her. The sudden unexpected weight caused the chef to backpedal. Her feet flew out from under her and she landed on the floor with a loud grunt.

Spence scrambled to his feet, gasped at the pulsing throb that originated deep inside his testicles. He groaned and sank back to one knee.

Scott threw himself atop the chef. She was still trying to scramble to her feet. Spence could see Scott holding on for dear life. The woman was winning the battle.

"Could use a hand here," Scott grunted through gritted teeth.

The chef's arms flailed and beat against the man on top of her. Had she still possessed the rolling pin it would have been over already. As it was Scott looked like he would have the upper hand for perhaps another few seconds before she freed herself from him.

Spence's eyes darted every which way until they fell upon the rolling pin. It had rolled across the floor, perhaps fifteen feet away, when the chef dropped it. Spence scrambled after it. Looks had not been deceiving. It felt as if it weighed fifty pounds. Spence's groin shrieked when he lifted it. *How the hell is she strong enough to use this?* "I'll ask her," he told himself.

Spence staggered back to the spot where the chef had just managed to throw Scott from her. Scott skidded across the linoleum and crashed into one of the legs supporting a prep table. Spence swung the rolling pin in his best Aaron Judge imitation. It connected solidly with the woman's meaty left arm and bounced off. She howled. Spence raised the rolling pin again.

The chef's eyes narrowed with laser focus on Spence. Her lips pulled back from her teeth. She screeched something incoherent and charged her target.

Spence half-stepped aside and swung the rolling pin again. This time it struck the woman on the back of her neck. Her momentum carried both of them to the floor. She landed atop Spence. He might have screamed, or, at least, grunted, but the air had been driven from his lungs quite thoroughly. He lay on the cold linoleum beneath the chef and gasped for air.

"I gotcha, bro." Scott appeared next to him on hands and knees. Fresh beads of blood dotted the left side of his face but he seemed none the worse for his experience. "Hang on." He shoved the unmoving woman. She rolled a few inches and Spence imagined his ribs snapping like twigs beneath her weight. He grunted. Scott took a deep breath and tried again. This time the chef rolled off Spence and came to rest on her back next to him.

Air flooded Spence's lungs and he gulped it greedily. He allowed himself several breaths while he felt his chest and sides with his hands. There was no pain, only relief at having the weight lifted from him.

"Jesus, she was fucking tough," Scott commented.

"You ain't lying," Spence replied. Thank God they'd only had to deal with her and not the other guy, too...

"Keith!" Spence pushed himself into a seated position on the floor. Until that moment he'd forgotten about Jacoby and Keith.

He saw Keith sitting on the kitchen floor, blood dripping from the corner of his mouth. He wiped at it and grimaced. Beside him, Jacoby was sprawled as if he were making snow angels.

"You okay?" Spence asked.

Keith sniffled and spat blood onto the linoleum. "Fucker was tougher than he looked. But he was nice enough to show me something. Take a look at this."

Spence first looked at the chef. She was in much the same state as Jacoby. Her chest rose and fell in long, deep breaths. *At least you're not a murderer.* Yet, *anyway.* Scott offered a hand and Spence allowed his friend to pull him to his feet. His legs wobbled and the dull pain in his groin was back but he still felt better than he had with the chef's weight on top of him.

Keith pushed himself to his feet when they joined him. In addition to the blood dribbling from his mouth there was a fresh, dark bruise on his right arm. He rubbed it absently. Jacoby was still among the living as well. His nose was clearly broken and blood seeped from both nostrils and formed thin streams down the side of his face. Keith indicated the wall to his left. "Check this shit out."

A wall panel had been moved aside. Beyond it, between the kitchen and the outside wall was a passage. It was dark but Spence could see a lightbulb hanging from the ceiling ten feet inside.

"A fucking secret passage? Now I've seen it all," Scott remarked.

"He tried to get in there," Keith explained.

Spence found a light switch on the wall just inside the passage. He flicked it and the dangling lightbulb came to life. Perhaps fifteen feet beyond it was another. "This could lead to the basement. But since both these assholes are out cold we can't ask them."

Keith held up both hands. "Hey, don't look at me. There were two of you and you still barely beat her ass. I was one-on-one, here. It was him or me."

"What do we do with them?" Scott asked. "We can't just leave them here. We made enough of a racket. Someone's bound to come looking."

Spence looked back at the chef. "You think you can drag her somewhere? She weighs more than the three of us combined."

Scott smirked. "Okay, I didn't think that through."

"Let's just go. We find my brother and Katie and we get outta here."

Spence could not agree more. "I'll go first," he announced. He didn't wait for the others. He stepped inside the secret passage.

CHAPTER FOURTEEN

A Proper Scrap

Amanda felt the sweat on her forehead. Her breaths came in short, quick gasps. Her stomach muscles screamed at her and promised much pain if she did not stop at once. Amanda didn't stop. She had managed to move both her arms, although she found she had little control of them. They flailed and thumped against the edges of the table upon which she lay. Still, she had made quite a bit of progress.

She had no idea how long it had been since Exton and Morley left the room. What she was keenly aware of, however, was Katie had not moved an inch or made a sound. Every few moments Amanda would pause her efforts and crane her neck to get a better look at the other girl. She couldn't see much from this angle, could not even tell if Katie was breathing. "Just hang on, Katie," she would whisper. "I'm coming to get you. I'll get you out of here."

Amanda didn't hear much from the other woman, either. Some whispered prayers in Spanish but nothing more. She could barely see the other woman from her current position. Either she was unable to move as of yet, or she wasn't trying. Neither was good news.

"Okay, okay, okay. Move, bitch," Amanda told herself. "Move your feet." She could feel her toes wiggling inside her shoes. She was even able to turn her feet from side to side. Her knees tensed but they as yet refused to do more. "Come on, come on, come *on*," Amanda said through gritted teeth. "Move!"

Her right knee bent. Not much. A few inches, perhaps. Amanda bore down. Her stomach muscles screeched their protest. She could almost feel the muscles in her leg trying to obey her commands. Nothing more happened.

Amanda released her breath and lay back on the table. Her chest heaved and her stomach felt as if it had taken several blows from a professional boxer. The sweat dripped down the side of her head. "Okay," she whispered. "Ten second break. Then you're gonna move those fucking legs and you're gonna get to Katie. That's the deal." Amanda closed her eyes and counted slowly to ten.

****

Spence paused the first time they came across a window inside the passage. It looked in on a richly-appointed room. Paintings hung on the walls, the furniture was old but in original condition. A fire crackled along merrily in the fireplace.

Scott whistled through his teeth. "God *damn*, he whispered. "Look at that shit."

Spence ignored him. Katie was not in there. No one was. And they had yet to find the cellar or a phone. He moved on.

Ahead of them was another window. More light spilled into the passage from the other side. Spence approached it and looked through.

Unlike the previous room this one was most certainly not devoid of people. The inhabitants of Aldebaran Road were gathered here just as they had been when Spence saw the room from outside the house. The two old fuckers sat in their high-backed chairs, each sipping a glass of wine. Spence could not tell which one had smiled at him earlier. The butler in the tuxedo stood by a doorway, hands behind his back. The woman who had escaped him stood on the other side of the room, her pose identical to the tuxedoed man's. Spence's groin voiced its displeasure at the sight of her.

He spotted four men standing together near the fireplace. They were dressed identically down to their eyeglasses. "The clones," Spence whispered.

Scott jockeyed for a spot from which to see. "Holy shit!" he whispered. "It's really them! Goddamn, I wish Johnny B was here to see this. He'd freak the fuck out!"

An elderly man knelt in front of one of the old men. His head was bowed, his arms at his sides. The men and women who called this street their home stood in silence and watched. No one sipped their drink, no one moved. Their eyes were fixed on the elderly man and the ancient one who sat in front of him.

Spence leaned in a bit closer. He could hear nothing from the other side of this strange, colored window. The old man in the chair moved his lips but no sound reached Spence.

The elderly man on his knees seemed to respond positively to whatever the old fuck in the chair told him. He smiled. Then he lifted his head and tilted it back. His lips parted and he opened his mouth.

"The fuck is this?" Keith whispered.

Spence shushed him. It seemed unnecessary. Spence himself had barely heard Keith. Certainly no one in the room could have. He shook his head in answer to the question.

The seated old man extended his left arm and held it above the elderly man's mouth. His right hand moved to his wrist and the fingers uncurled. The old man's fingernails looked as if they hadn't been trimmed in years; they were long and yellow. The old man ran one of his fingers along his wrist. Something spurted from the skin but it did not look like blood. It was milky white in color and thick enough to ooze. The old man turned his arm so the viscous substance dripped down. The elderly man opened his mouth wider and let whatever it was fall upon his tongue.

"Jesus, fuck," Scott whispered. His hand covered his mouth.

The elderly man convulsed. He tumbled from his kneeling position and doubled over on the floor. His body thrashed and he let loose a scream that Spence had no trouble hearing. The others in the room stood their ground. They were all smiling now.

"They fucking poisoned him!" Keith exclaimed. His voice was still a whisper but Spence cringed nonetheless. His eyes darted about the room but it seemed no one had heard a strange noise from the other side of the wall, not with the elderly man screaming.

Spence glared at Keith. *Quiet*, he mouthed.

The elderly man's spasms continued another few moments. Then his muscles released all at once and he lay still.

Jesus, Keith was right. They did *poison the old dude.*

The elderly man stirred. His fingers dug small trenches into the Oriental rug. His hands flattened against it and he pushed himself to his knees. He appeared unsteady; he teetered so much Spence thought he would collapse again. Instead he leaned forward. The old man's hand still dangled in the air. The elderly man took it in his and planted a kiss on it.

Although Spence could still hear nothing, he saw the elderly man's lips say, *Thank you, my Lord.* He regained his feet and something about the movement raised the gooseflesh on Spence's arms. It took him a moment to figure it out. *He's moving like he's twenty years old. Look at him. No shaking, no weakness whatsoever. What the hell did I just see?* The elderly man strode across the room and accepted a drink from someone. He raised the glass in the direction of the two old men in their chairs. The gesture was repeated by the others.

"To Lord William Morley!" the elderly man shouted in a robust, younger man's voice. "A truer friend to us has never existed!"

"To Lord William Morley!" the others echoed.

Spence could barely hear them. Were the walls really that thick?

Several people were clapping the elderly man on the back. Some shook his hand. One man even feinted a right cross at the elderly man's jaw. The elderly man faked the impact and returned the gesture. All laughed.

"What the hell are we seeing?" Keith whispered.

"Hey, Spence, that's the chick who smashed you in the balls," Scott said and pointed at the maid.

Spence grimaced. "I noticed," he whispered. "Why hasn't she told anyone about us?"

"Who fucking cares?" Keith asked. "Let's leave these assholes to their party and find my brother and Katie."

Keith was right. Spence took a last look inside the mask room.

The butler strode from one end of the room to the other. Several people stepped aside. As they did Spence caught his first look at two men kneeling on the Oriental rug in the middle of the room. Their hands were bound behind their backs and their heads were down.

Spence's breath caught in his throat.

Keith saw them at the same moment. Before Spence could wrap his mind around what he was seeing Keith charged the window and pounded on it. "Phil!" he shouted.

Every head inside the room turned in the direction of the window.

Keith slammed his fists against the colored glass. It quivered in its frame. Spence's feet were glued to the ground. His lips parted but he had lost the ability to speak. He stared at Phil and Marcus. They had turned toward the window like everyone else. Phil appeared dazed; Marcus's eyes were wide with terror.

A spider-web crack appeared in the window. Keith struck it again and shouted his brother's name.

The people within the room gasped and pointed at the window. A woman held her hand to her mouth. A fat man in an expensive suit balled his hands into fists. Many faces twisted into anger. The elderly man seemed to look through the window and he smiled at Spence.

Keith's next blow punched a hole in the window. Colored glass rained onto the hardwood and skittered in every direction. Keith struck it again and the hole widened a bit.

"Phil! Phil! Hang on! I'm coming!" He struck the window again.

"There are your miscreants, Ms. Palmer," the old man who had bled the white pus said to the maid. His voice was calm. He may as well have been discussing the weather.

"I knew they would present themselves sooner or later," the other old man added. "Exton, summon Johnson. Dealing with their kind is just his speed."

The butler bowed his head. "At once, my Lord." He walked back across the room. He grasped a rope hanging from the ceiling to the side of the doorway and pulled it once.

Keith had widened the hole nearly enough for him to climb through. Another blow would do the job. And still Spence could not move.

"Keith!" Marcus shouted. "Keith, man, get us outta here! Hurry!"

His eyes were wide but they were fixed on Keith. Phil had neither spoken nor moved since he saw his brother on the other side of the window. He swayed slightly, his half-lidded eyes would focus on him for a moment before they glazed over again. His face was a mass of bruises; his lips were swollen and bloody.

Keith succeeded in creating an opening for himself. He placed his hands on either side of the hole.

Spence at last regained the ability to move. He tackled Keith. The two of them went down in a heap. The old floorboards beneath them creaked their protest. Keith's hands struggled to find purchase on Spence and he finally succeeded in shoving him aside. Keith scrambled to his feet.

"No!" Spence shouted. He stood and grabbed Keith. "There's too many! Keith, there's too many! We have to move, man!"

Keith continued to struggle. His eyes remained fixed on Phil.

"Help us!" Marcus shouted.

The women in the room had congregated on the far side, as far from the hole in the wall and the intruders as possible. They spoke amongst themselves and seemed more than a little amused by the scene. Some of them pointed and whispered something to another and they laughed. Their men were angry. They grimaced and made threatening gestures at these unwanted invaders on the other side of the wall. Some had taken protective positions between Spence's group and the women. The maid stood beside the women and simply watched. The two old men had not moved from their chairs. They wore an identical expression of nonchalance.

The elderly man crossed the room and stood before them. "May I, my Lords?" He nodded in the direction of the hole in the wall.

The old men looked at one another. "Why would you want to dirty yourself dealing with their kind?" one of them asked.

"It is beneath you, Mr. Watts," said the other.

"As a token of my appreciation, my Lords," the elderly man replied. "I am most grateful to you." He smiled.

The lords exchanged another glance. One shrugged. "Very well," he said. "But leave at least one alive. The more for the sacrament, the better."

Watts bowed from the waist. "Their Lordships are too kind." He turned in the direction of the hole in the wall.

Spence had seen enough. He shoved Keith away from the window. Keith started to resist but Spence was having none of it. "We have to go, man. Right now." He shoved again. Keith stumbled but kept his feet under him. He started to move down the passage. Spence did not have to look over his shoulder to know if Scott was with them. He heard his old friend's footfalls behind him.

It was only after they had traveled perhaps fifty feet that Spence realized they had gone the wrong way. It had been his intention to return to the kitchen. He had gotten turned around and shoved Keith in the wrong direction. Spence stopped, turned. "Wait, this is the wrong way," he told his friends. He took a single step the way they had come. He froze.

The elderly man, Watts, stood twenty feet in front of him. His wrinkled hands were balled into fists. His head was tilted down slightly but his eyes were glued to the three men before him.

"I have not had a proper scrap in many a year," Watts told them. "This should be great fun!"

"Spence?" Scott asked. His tone was equal measure scared and incredulous.

Spence held up both hands. "Come on, man. You don't want to fight us. It's three against one. Turn around and go back to your martini."

Watts tilted his head to one side and then the other. Spence could hear the cracks twenty feet away.

"Fuck you!" Keith shouted. He flew past Spence and charged Watts.

Watts planted his feet. His fist shot forward at the last moment. Keith's head snapped back and his knees buckled. He staggered against the wall. Watts grabbed him with both hands and hurled him straight up. Keith crashed into the ceiling and fell straight down. Dust plumed beneath him and floated down from above. Keith tried to rise. He got one knee and one arm under him. Watts reached down and wrapped his fingers around Keith's throat. Keith hands clamped onto the elderly man's wrist.

Spence snapped out of his momentary paralysis and sprinted forward as fast as his throbbing groin would allow. "Let him go! Let him go!"

Watts threw a backhand and Spence's world went dark. He felt hands place themselves under his arms followed by the sensation of being dragged backward. His mouth was full of something hot and coppery. He opened his eyes.

Watts's hand remained around Keith's throat. He held the younger man at least two feet above the floor. The elderly man's arm did not shake with the effort. It seemed, in fact, holding Keith aloft required no effort at all. Keith's legs kicked the air weakly. Spence heard the younger man wheezing for breath. Watts turned his eyes from Keith to Spence and Scott. He smiled.

Watts turned his wrist. Spence heard the *snap*. Keith's legs kicked more violently and his arms flailed and then he was still. Watts regarded him for a moment. He opened his hand and Keith dropped to the floor. He landed awkwardly and did not move.

"Jesus H. Christ!" Scott shouted.

Watts brushed off some of the dust that had settled on his sleeves. "So, who's next? You, perhaps?" He indicated Spence with a nod of his head.

Spence rose to his feet. He spat blood and a molar onto the floor. Then he shoved Scott down the passage and followed after him.

"Spence, did you see that? We have to help Keith!"

"We can't," Spence replied. He looked over his shoulder. Watts was walking at a leisurely pace behind them. Keith lay in a heap where he fell. "Keep going!"

The passageway made a sharp turn to the right. Spence kept one hand on Scott's shoulder and tried to increase their pace. Another check over their shoulder showed Watts was still there. He maintained his slow pace but somehow the distance between them remained unchanged.

They passed several more windows. Spence looked through each one without breaking stride. Every room he saw was deserted. The floorboards creaked loudly with each step and dust plumed into the air. They ran through several cobwebs before Spence realized the lights hanging from the ceiling were becoming fewer and farther between.

"I don't think anyone's been here in a long time," Scott said between deep breaths.

"Yeah." Spence was winded himself. Maybe they should have stood their ground against Watts. Now neither of them had the strength to deal with him. If (*when*) he caught up to them it was going to be ugly.

"We have to get out of this fucking fun house, man," Scott remarked. "There has to be a secret door or something. Don't all these secret passages have secret doors?"

"How the hell do I know? Look ahead. There's another turn. Let's see if we can find a way out that way."

Scott no longer needed prodding. If anything he was pulling ahead of Spence a bit. His groin was still sore, yes, but it was more than that. The initial adrenaline surge brought on when the elderly man dropped Keith was gone. Spence was not only winded, he felt cold, as well. His legs shook and he needed to keep one hand on the stone wall to his left. He glanced over his shoulder before they reached the turn in the passage. Watts was still there, still walking, still no more than twenty feet behind them.

Spence rounded the turn. The passageway ended ten feet in front of them.

CHAPTER FIFTEEN

Hard Part's Done

Philip Volokhov's world was a haze of half-remembered agony. He could recall bits and pieces of his former life when his mind snapped back into focus, but it never lasted long. Each time he came to he had to start all over again. He remembered running from the mansion. Two were with him and he was pretty sure one of them was his brother; the identity of the other was just beyond his grasp. Someone was hurt so they could not move fast enough. One of them—Keith, he thought—was assisting the injured member of their group. Someone else was chasing them but here his memory clouded over. It was someone *big*, he remembered that much, but nothing more than that. They had to hide for some reason. Phil found himself alone, kneeling in the woods on the side of the road. Then pain. Then he was here.

The Oriental rug was thick and cushioned his knees as he knelt in the center of the mask room. Many people were in the room and something unexpected had happened. The sound of glass breaking. Someone was shouting his name. Then the haze rolled in again and Phil thought of nothing at all.

When his mind awoke, he was still kneeling on the rug. His hands were restrained behind his back. Whatever it was it was soft and stretchable. A fabric of some kind. He became aware that someone was kneeling beside him. Phil turned in that direction. Marcus looked far beyond scared. His eyes were wide and darted left then right in quick succession. He looked at the faces of the people within the room. He babbled something about letting him go. The audience seemed amused by his frantic pleas. Some laughed, more than one toasted him with their drink before taking a sip.

Someone new entered the room. More accurately, he burst through the doorway out of breath and bleeding from his nose. He so obviously did not belong to this group of well-dressed high society people. His clothes were dirty, his hair looked as if it hadn't seen shampoo in months. His hands were covered with grime. He started to address one of the old men in the fancy chairs before he stuttered when he saw the broken window behind Phil and Marcus.

"Yes, yes, out with it," one of the old men chastised him. "We are old, not immortal!"

The new arrival looked sheepishly at the old man who spoke. He walked around the side of the chairs to stand before them. "There were six of them," he began. "They attacked us in the kitchen. Poor Ms. Arnold caught a beating!"

One of the old men looked at the other. "Six? I saw only three."

"As did I," the other concurred.

"I do believe our dearest nephew is inflating their numbers so his defeat seems more reasonable."

Both old men returned their attention to their nephew.

"Does it matter? There are assholes loose inside the house! Counting the ones I grabbed already, that makes at least six of them, maybe more. Do you plan to do anything about it?" He placed his hands on his hips and awaited an answer.

"He's so excitable," remarked one.

"Mmm, yes. His side of the family always was." He drummed his old fingers on the arm of his old chair. "Be at ease, dear boy. Mr. Watts is seeing to the intruders. You may return to the kitchen. Ms. Palmer will accompany you and see to your injuries and those of Ms. Arnold."

The woman in the maid's outfit crossed the room. She walked past the nephew and stood by the doorway. "Mr. Jacoby?"

"I want them myself," Jacoby announced, stabbing his chest with his finger. "Especially the big one with the ink. I owe him."

One of the old men waved him off. "Ms. Palmer will tend to you. We shall discuss this later."

Jacoby was clearly of a mind to continue the conversation. He looked at his uncles and changed his mind. "Fucking bullshit," he mumbled as he headed back the way he came. Palmer followed him out.

One of the old men turned to his twin. "I do believe it is my turn now, dear brother." His tone was conversational.

The other nodded his agreement. "It is indeed. And you have your choice. There are still two of them down there."

"Then I shall take my time deciding." He pushed himself from the chair.

"And do remember to drain her completely. It caused such a bother last time."

"That happened only once. I know what I'm doing, dear brother." The butler was at his side instantly. "Lead the way, dear Exton, lead the way. I have not feasted since early this morning. I am becoming famished."

"As you say, my Lord," Exton replied. He led the way from the room.

The men and women returned to their conversations. Phil felt something brush his hand. He turned in Marcus's direction.

"That window right there," he whispered and inclined his head toward the broken opening in the wall behind them. "Your brother and Spence were in there. I'm gonna go for it. Follow me."

Phil tried to speak but his mouth didn't work. His tongue felt as if it had tripled in size. He managed a mumble but even he didn't understand what he said. The sound bore no resemblance to any human language.

All at once Marcus sprang to his feet. A few heads turned in his direction. "Fuck you devil-worshipping motherfuckers!" he shouted. He raced across the floor and hurled himself through the broken window. Phil heard him grunt as he landed on the other side. Silence for a few seconds. Then, "Holy shit! Keith!"

Phil tried to pronounce his brother's name. He had no better luck than when he tried to reply to Marcus a moment before.

Marcus reappeared in the window. "Phil, I'm real sorry, man. Fuck all of you!" He bolted from sight.

One of the men in the expensive suits turned to another. "Devil worshippers? Is that still a thing?"

"Apparently so," his companion replied. "Some rumors just refuse to die."

"Indeed."

Although Phil could not comprehend everything he had just witnessed—the haze was coming back once again—he was left with a single thought that followed him into the vast expanse of nothingness.

He left me again.

****

Amanda's legs dangled off the side of the table. She could feel them, actually *feel* them, and she even had some measure of control. Her right arm obeyed her commands, albeit sluggishly. Her left arm remained dead down to her wrist. She had tried twice already to roll herself to the edge but both attempts had left her gasping for air and feeling the burn in the pit of her stomach. Her face, neck, and arms were coated with sweat. But she was almost there. She knew it.

The other woman had fallen quiet some time ago. Amanda still could not get a good look at her but she thought her reluctant roommate was still alive. Amanda could just about make out the rise and fall of her chest. At first Amanda narrated what she was up to. She gave the woman constant updates about every muscle she was able to move and how much. But her neighbor had stopped responding. She prayed in Spanish and English and back to Spanish again. Amanda had stopped the progress reports. She needed every ounce of strength she had left.

She took several deep breaths, felt the damp air saturate her lungs. *This is it. Gonna work this time. It has to. Get to Katie and find our way out of here. We'll walk if we have to but we're putting this place in the rearview forever. Let the cops deal with these assholes.* More deep breaths. The air felt cool on her skin. Her arms glistened with sweat. Amanda took a final breath and held it.

She flung herself onto her side. Her success surprised her, so much so that she couldn't stop herself from falling off the edge of the table. The ground was hard unyielding stone and Amanda grunted when she landed. The breath exploded from her on impact. She moaned and blinked back tears. Her eyes remained closed until her heart slowed its rhythm and the stars stopped winking at her. She took a long breath, held it, released it, and opened her eyes.

"I made it," she announced, although she didn't know if she was updating the other woman or Katie or just confirming for herself. "Hard part's done. We're getting out of this." She got her knees under her and placed her right hand on the tabletop. Using every obedient muscle in her body Amanda hauled herself to her feet. A ball of lead had formed in her stomach and threatened to drag her down to the floor again. Amanda waited for the span of several breaths before she tried to move again.

Her eyes fell on Katie. Her friend had not moved since Morley assaulted her. The blood on the side of her neck was darkening. She did not appear to be breathing. "No," Amanda whispered. She took her first step toward Katie.

The sound of a hinge creaking somewhere behind froze her in place. If Morley had chosen that moment to return and finish the job he had started there was nothing she could do to stop him. She had barely enough control of her limbs to walk.

Voices. Far away but getting closer quickly. No words that Amanda could identify, more like a scream or shout. Amanda braced herself against the table and turned. At first she saw no one. Nothing seemed out of the ordinary as far as she could tell. Her eyes fell upon the corner of the room. It was cloaked mostly in shadow but there was just enough light to see a panel in the ceiling had opened. Amanda started.

A number of bodies fell from the open panel.

Amanda screamed.

****

Spence placed himself in front of Scott. It was the last thing he could do for his friend. If Watts was strong enough to do what he did to Keith then Spence had little chance of doing anything beyond dying. He could hear the old man's footsteps. They were getting closer. Any second he would appear from around the corner and that would be that.

"I'll take him," Spence whispered to Scott. "When I do, get past him. Go back out through the kitchen and get outside. Then don't stop until you hit civilization. Understand?"

"I ain't leaving, man," Scott replied. "Fuck that. We can take this asshole."

No, we can't. Spence didn't say that but he knew it was true. He suspected Scott knew it, too. Spence backed up one more step. A quick look over his shoulder told him they were out of room. They had maybe ten feet between them and the corner and the man who would soon round that corner. It would have to do. The footsteps were louder but slowing down. He was here. Spence braced himself.

Watts turned the corner. He stopped, regarded the two men, smiled. "Now, where were we?"

"You killed Keith, you fucker!" Scott jabbed a finger at him.

His smile widened.

"Come get some," Spence told him.

"With pleasure." Watts strode toward them.

Someone rounded the corner at a high rate of speed and crashed into him. Watts stumbled forward. His hands went to the wall and his feet skidded along the floorboards. Spence drew back his fist and let it fly with everything he had. The impact snapped Watts's head back and his knees buckled.

Scott shouted something unintelligible and moved around Spence. He rained punches on the elderly man's unprotected head. Watts sank to one knee.

Spence looked past him to the body that had propelled him forward. Marcus had sunk against the wall after the collision. His hands were still bound behind his back but his eyes were clear. "Marcus!"

"Spence!"

Watts sprang to his feet. The sudden violent move sent Scott backpedaling. His arm caught Spence's shoulder for balance. Spence almost went down; the wall was close enough for him to brace himself against it or he would have collapsed in a tangle of arms and legs. It took him a moment to realize he had grasped something embedded in the wall. The light was poor but he could feel a metallic handle. *Jesus Christ, there* is *a secret door.*

Watts spun on his heels. Marcus had regained his feet. He threw himself at the elderly man, a wide receiver shouldering his way through the defense toward the end zone. Watts caught him and used Marcus's momentum to throw him against the wall. Marcus wailed at the impact. He crumpled to the floor.

Spence charged him. Watts's hand made for this throat. Spence twisted out of the way and the elderly man's hand glanced off his shoulder. Spence leaped onto Watts's back.

Marcus recovered enough to push himself to his feet. He used the wall to keep his balance. Watts lashed out with his foot. It caught Marcus in the bread basket and pinned him to the wall. Blood spurted from Marcus's lips.

Spence screamed, "*No!*" and hauled back with everything he had. He succeeded in pulling Watts a few steps away from Marcus.

The elderly man spun again. In the cramped passageway Spence was able to hang on. He pulled back again, in the direction of the end of the corridor, away from Marcus.

Marcus slid down the wall. He sat on the floor and looked at Spence. "Fucking devil worshippers." Blood bubbled on his lips and dribbled down his chin.

Spence was losing his grip. Watts turned in every direction. His hands flailed and tried to grab at Spence but so far he failed to find purchase. That wasn't going to matter if Spence lost hold of the elderly man. His sense of balance was gone, he could no longer even tell which direction they were facing at any given moment. The elderly man's movements were violent and fast. The passageway became a blur.

The jerking stopped when Scott wrapped his arms around Watts's waist. The elderly man stopped and concentrated on this new threat.

Spence saw his last chance. He pulled back with everything he had. "Scott, go back!" he shouted. Somehow Scott heard him and understood what he meant. The three of them staggered in the direction of the end of the passageway.

Spence's fingers brushed the metal handle but Watts was still thrashing violently. It flashed past him again and he failed to grasp it. *One more time. That's all I have left.* All he had to do was grab that handle. That would put an end to the old bastard's thrashing about. All they had to do was open the secret door and shove the old fuck through it. Then they could at the very least grab Marcus and get away.

The handle flashed past him again. Spence touched it but failed to grasp it. Watts twisted again and Spence lost his grip. He crashed into the wall and his hand fell upon the handle. It swung down easily under his weight.

The floor opened beneath them. One moment Spence was wondering how long he would have before Watts turned on him. The next he was in freefall.

CHAPTER SIXTEEN

Waste of White

She couldn't tell how many bodies fell through the open panel in the ceiling. Three, maybe four. They landed roughly and atop each other. Amanda's first thought was, *They're killing everybody. This whole thing was a just a way for them to gather victims. And you're gonna be next if you don't find a way out of here.* But she realized she had been incorrect. At least one of the unfortunates was still alive. She heard a grunt and an exclamation from the small pile of bodies. Her first instinct was to run to them, see who it was and if they needed help or could provide it for her. She stopped herself. She was in no condition to run anywhere, nor could she hope to fight off anyone if they proved to be hostile. Amanda shrank back against the table and prayed.

"Son of a bitch, that hurt," one of them, a man, said. He rolled off the pile and lay on the floor, flat on his back. He sucked in air in great gulps.

Another survivor followed the first. He extricated himself from a third who did not move. The second man pulled himself away and very quickly regarded the one who had yet to move. He was tense, this second man; his body language indicated he expected trouble from the third. The third man did not move at all. The first man threw a hand onto the other woman's table and used it to haul himself to his feet.

They haven't noticed you yet but they're about to. Amanda braced herself. It was all she could do. If any or all of them came at her it was over. She did not have nearly enough control of her limbs to put up a fight.

The first man helped the second to his feet. Both regarded the third. He was dressed in an expensive suit and he was very old. He had been upstairs before Palmer made her move, Amanda knew that much. She thought she might have brought the man a drink but she could not be certain. She had served many people and their faces were a blur.

The second man delivered a vicious kick to the third. The third man lay where he fell. "Yeah, think he's dead," the second man remarked matter-of-factly. "Secret door my ass. That was a fucking *trap* door!"

"It got us outta there, didn't it?" the first asked.

"Can't argue with that." The second man nudged the third again before he finally looked up.

"Maria!" He moved around the table and lifted the other woman's head in his hands. "Maria, are you okay?"

Maria opened her eyes. Even from her vantage point several feet away Amanda saw recognition there. "Spence!"

"Jesus! We're gonna get you outta here." He lifted her into a seated position on the table. "What happened? Are you okay?"

"I can't move much," Maria told him. "Those assholes injected me with something. Spence…" Her voice trailed off. She inclined her head toward the other table.

Spence's eyes followed hers. They went wide when he saw the woman on the table. "Katie!" He ran for her. If he saw Amanda, he gave no indication. He bolted past her without even a glance in her direction. He reached the table and checked the body atop it. "Wake up, Katie," he told her. His voice was gentle, but it rose in volume and desperation as the woman on the table failed to respond to him. He tapped her cheeks, nudged her, even opened her eyes with his thumbs. Katie did not move. He placed his ear against her chest and listened. "Jesus, no!" He clambered onto the table and straddled her. He placed both hands on her chest and began CPR. "Come on, Katie, come on. Wake up!"

Amanda's eyes moved to the first man. He had taken up position beside Maria. He had one hand on her back to steady her. Maria swayed slightly, her legs dangled off the edge of the table. They wore identical expressions of misery.

Spence continued his attempts to revive Katie. The pressure of his hands had caused one of her arms to hang off the edge of the table. It was the only movement she made. "Come on, Katie. Come on, Katie! *Come on, Katie!*" Katie remained motionless.

Spence leaped from the table. He raised his fist and brought it down hard on Katie's chest. "*Breathe!*" He slammed her chest several more times. Her body shook with each impact. Nothing happened.

Amanda cringed each time his fist slammed down. After several more impacts she covered her ears and closed her eyes. "Stop it! Stop it! She's gone," she screamed.

Spence froze, his arm raised high. He turned in her direction and blinked. His lips trembled but he produced no sound. After several more moments his eyes focused on her. His arm dropped to his side. "What…What happened?"

Amanda wiped tears from her eyes. Her voice hitched in her throat. "Morley," she said after several attempts. "Morley bit her on the neck. Like some kind of fucking vampire or something."

"Bit her on the neck." His voice held no hint of emotion.

Amanda walked slowly around the table and approached her friend. The blood on the side of Katie's neck was mostly dry now. It had turned a dark crimson, almost brown. "He just leaned over her. We couldn't move. She couldn't stop him." Tears welled in her eyes. Amanda did not attempt to wipe them away.

Spence brushed a stray lock of hair from Katie's eyes. His own were wet. When the tears came they fell in fat, salty drops onto Katie's cheeks and neck. He cradled her head in his hands.

"I'm so sorry." It was the only thing Amanda could think to say.

"What about Marcus?" Maria asked the first man. "Where is he?"

The first man swallowed. "He went down. That old fuck over there kicked him in the gut." He strode across the room and kicked the third man in the side. "Fucking kicked him in the gut!" His foot flew again. "How's it feel, asshole? How's it fucking feel? Don't like it when it happens to you, *do you?*" He was shouting now. With each blow the aged body quivered. "Fucking piece of shit!" He spat on the corpse and kicked it again.

"Is he alive?" Maria had to shout to be heard.

After a few more kicks the first man stopped. "I think so. I don't know. This prick was a lot stronger than he looked." He spat on the corpse again.

"Spence, I'm sorry," Maria told him. "I'm so, so sorry. But we have to find my husband. Please!"

Spence had not moved from Katie's side. He cradled her head and cried and sniffled.

Amanda remained silent. What could she say? This was obviously Katie's brother. The other two were his friends. Had she been able to she might have walked out of the room. It seemed the decent thing to do at the moment. But she was not at all certain how far she would make it. The door seemed very far away. Amanda remained where she stood and willed her body to shake off whatever Palmer had injected into her.

"Fucking hell," the first man exclaimed. He had moved to the other side of the room where the two other maids lay on their tables. "Jesus, look at this. Two more over here." He placed a finger beneath one's jaw and turned her head to the side. Dried blood coated the dead woman's neck. "Same as..." He didn't finish his sentence.

"Spence, *please.*" Fresh tears traced tracks of clean flesh down Maria's cheeks.

Spence looked up. He appeared dazed, as if he noticed the room and its occupants for the first time. His eyes were wet. His nose was runny. He sniffled and wiped his nose with his arm. He swallowed several times before he laid his sister's head back upon the table.

The first man crossed the distance between them and placed his arm on Spence's shoulders. "I'm so sorry, bro. Everyone liked Katie, you know that. Let's get her out of here, okay?"

Spence grasped his friend's arm and squeezed. He sniffled again and nodded. "Scott, help Maria. You. Can you walk?"

Amanda eyed the closed door. "I think so. Maybe. I guess we'll find out."

Spence hefted his sister's body from the table. He cringed but seemed capable of supporting the weight. Scott took Maria's arm and draped it across his shoulders. When he took her off the table Maria's legs sagged and the two teetered. Scott grunted and shifted his feet. He looked expectantly at Spence.

"Get the door," Spence told Amanda.

Her legs were still unsteady, but her strength seemed to be returning to her, although much slower than she would have preferred. She used the tables for support until she left them behind. Her steps were slow, as if the floor was made of thin ice and she was afraid of falling through. At last she reached the door.

The knob failed to turn in her hand. "It's locked," she announced.

The first man, Scott, propped Maria against a table and approached the door. "Get out of the way," he told her. When Amanda did as she was told he kicked the doorknob from the side. It took two more such blows before the knob cracked and sailed into the corner of the room. "Ain't locked no more." He returned to Maria.

Amanda opened the door. She half-expected to find one of the Morleys waiting on the other side, or maybe it would be Exton or that creep Jacoby. No one was there. She leaned through the opening and looked about.

The basement was large and draped in shadow. A lightbulb dangled on a wire from the ceiling above the door. Another was positioned perhaps forty feet away at the base of a staircase.

"It's clear," she announced. "And I see some stairs."

"Lead the way," Spence told her.

Amanda leaned against the wall outside the room to stop herself from collapsing to the floor. Her first steps out of the room were hesitant. Each moment her feet remained under her gave her a bit more confidence. She pushed herself from the wall. She teetered momentarily but her legs cooperated. Amanda headed for the stairs.

She was nearly there when she heard the voices. One old and somewhat frail but with a tone used to command, the other younger and stronger and supplicating. Amanda's heart leaped into her throat. She turned back toward the others. They must have read her expression because they all started looking for a place to hide. Beyond the light above the door from which they emerged the basement was a sea of shadow. Spence decided for all of them. He disappeared into the darkness with his sister. Scott swung Maria around and followed his friend. Amanda moved as quickly as she was able, thin ice be damned.

Beyond the last light she could see nothing. She held her arms out in front of her. "Spence? Maria?" Her voice was a whisper; she could barely hear it herself.

"Here," came the whispered reply somewhere to her left.

Amanda moved in that direction. She could see nothing, could hear nothing but the sound of footsteps on the stairs somewhere behind her. She increased her pace as much as she dared. A hand brushed hers and Amanda gasped.

"Shh," someone said.

Amanda advanced a few feet farther before she felt the others in the darkness. They seemed to be crouched low. Amanda willed her feet to stay where they were and lowered herself to their level.

The two voices were getting louder and closer. Amanda recognized Exton's, and the other was obviously one of the Morleys. "Did you leave the door open, Exton?"

"No, my Lord. I am sure of it."

They entered the light above the doorway. Exton peered inside. "Mr. Watts." His voice held a trace of surprise. He disappeared into the room. After a moment, "I fear he is dead, my Lord."

Morley waved his hand in a dismissive gesture. "Waste of white. I knew we should have let him die. The man hasn't been useful since the Somme. But that's my brother for you. He always becomes magnanimous after he's fed."

"The others are gone, sir," Exton told him from inside the room. "You don't think Ms. Spencer…"

Morley harrumphed. "My brother swore he drained her completely. This is the work of those hooligans we saw in the servants' passage, I am sure of it. They can't have gone far. Tell the neighbors to find them. It's about time they did something to earn their keep."

Exton reappeared in the doorway. "At once, my Lord." He led the way back to the stairs. Morley followed him out of the light.

Amanda expected them to turn, to come roaring out of the darkness directly at her and the others. She may have regained the ability to walk but she was in no condition to fight if their hiding place was discovered. She held her breath and braced herself. Both men emerged into the light at the bottom of the stairs and proceeded up. Amanda did not move a muscle until she heard the door at the top of the stairs close. She expelled the breath and took another.

"What the fuck is the Somme?" Scott whispered.

"It's in France, I think," Amanda whispered back without much thought.

"That's helpful," Scott replied.

"Who cares?" Maria asked somewhat rhetorically. "Can we go find my husband now?"

"We have to get outside," Spence announced.

Maria started to protest.

"We're in no condition to look for anyone right now. I have to get Katie out of here. I'm not leaving her in this fucking place. And you still can't walk. We make it back to the cars. You guys can stay there. I'll come back for Phil and Marcus."

"What about Keith? Is he at the cars already?"

Spence did not reply. Nor did Scott.

"How do you plan to accomplish that?" Scott asked. "Those assholes are gonna be looking for us. It was bad enough when it was just that big bastard outside. Now it's the whole street. And it's not like we can move fast. I gotta tell ya, Spence, I ain't liking our chances."

"You want to stay down here?"

"Fuck that. Wait. New girl. Do you have a car?"

Amanda shrugged although no one could see the gesture. "Yeah. It's a Corolla and it's parked in the driveway. But the keys are in my pocketbook and that's in a bathroom on the third floor."

"For Christ's sake." Scott clearly did not like her answer.

"We'll make it," was Spence's reply. "You. Maid. Lead the way."

"Amanda. My name is Amanda."

"Amanda. Lead the way."

She rose to her full height. There was nothing within arm's reach to use for balance so Amanda simply walked in the direction of the stairs. Her legs felt stronger, surer. She stayed close to the wall just in case. She heard the others behind her, mostly Maria's feet dragging along the floor. No one spoke. Amanda approached the stairs.

She expected to see Exton at the top waiting for them. He would smile and descend slowly, a hypodermic in each hand.

She craned her neck to peek at the top of the stairs. There was no one there. She waved the others forward.

She used the handrail when she climbed the stairs. There was no reason to push her luck.

CHAPTER SEVENTEEN

The Other Side of Aldebaran

Scott was right about their chances. They were next to nil. As he mounted each step, the weight of his sister heavy in his arms, Spence knew it was a hell of a long shot. But he also meant what he'd said; there was no way he would leave Katie inside this house. If that meant fighting his way through every asshole in here, then that's what he would do. *And if they're all as strong as that Watts dickhead you won't make it ten feet.* It didn't matter. He was going to get Katie out of Greystone.

Amanda stopped at the top of the stairs. She placed her hand on the doorknob and it turned easily. "Not locked," she whispered over her shoulder.

"Open it very slowly," Spence instructed her. "Take a peek."

A sliver of light appeared as the door opened a crack. Amanda leaned into it. After a moment she said, "I don't see anyone."

"Do you know the fastest way out of here?" Spence asked.

"I think so," she replied. "There's a servants' entrance on the side of the house. I think that's pretty close."

"Lead the way."

She started to open the door, stopped. "What if someone sees us?"

Yeah, what if someone sees us? seventeen-year-old Spence asked. *You're carrying Katie and Scott has his hands full with Maria. That leaves Miss Amanda here as your sole means of protection. You're so fucked.* Spence shrugged. "Hope they don't."

"That's fucking reassuring," she replied. She opened the door and took a better look at whatever was on the other side. "Coast is clear. Follow me."

Spence followed her. He had to exit the stairs sideways to allow Katie to fit through. On the other side he found a narrow hallway. Small paintings hung on the walls every few feet. Most were portraits of what looked to be old English lords and ladies. A strip of faded carpet ran down the center of the hardwood in either direction. Ornate wall sconces kept the area well-lit. As Amanda had said there was no one within sight.

"This way." She turned right, one hand on the wall to steady herself.

Spence looked back. Scott was still supporting most of Maria's weight. Sweat dripped from his hair and his breathing was labored. Maria's feet struggled for purchase on the carpet. She would take two or three steps and then her feet would drag again. *Yeah, this ain't looking too good. One can barely walk, one can't, Scott's winded—not that he was ever much good in a fight to begin with—and you're carrying Katie. Right now you couldn't take a piss, let alone someone in a fight.* Spence willed his younger self to shut up.

The hallway ended ahead of them and branched to the left and right. Amanda paused. She looked both ways, looked back at Spence. He saw the question in her eyes.

"You're lost."

Amanda shook her head. "No, not exactly. I'm just not sure which direction it is. I've been getting turned around in this place since I first got here."

"Figure it out," Scott hissed. "This ain't getting any easier." He repositioned his hands and hefted Maria.

Amanda licked her lips. "This way I think." She turned left.

They moved slowly into the new hallway. It looked much like the one they had just left behind. More paintings, more worn carpet in the center. Spence couldn't blame Amanda for being unsure of their path. If he were out front he would be guessing at every turn.

Amanda froze.

Spence's heart stopped beating. Was someone headed their way? The hallway looked like it turned fifteen feet ahead. If someone came around that corner…

He heard the voices. Three, maybe four, all male. Spence couldn't make out much of the conversation, but he caught the words "portfolio" and "Dow." The voices grew louder. Every muscle in Spence's body corded. He would have to put Katie on the floor. He started to kneel.

"It's okay," Amanda whispered. "They're turning off."

Spence exhaled and rose to his full height again. His arms were starting to ache, and his legs weren't far behind.

"We really need to get out of here," Scott whispered. His breathing was even more labored than it had been just a few moments before.

"Keep going," Spence told Amanda.

At the end of the hallway Amanda stopped and peeked around the corner. "Yeah, this is the way," she announced.

When Spence took the corner he knew she was right. He had been here before, when he grabbed the maid outside. She had brought them into the house somewhere very close by. He shifted his grip on Katie's body and followed Amanda.

The door was ahead of them. Amanda reached it first and waited for the others. She looked outside and then at Spence. She nodded.

The door opened easily and Spence felt the cool night air invade their small alcove. The gooseflesh rose on his arms and neck and he realized for the first time he was sweating quite profusely.

Amanda was through the door instantly. Her head whipped in all directions before she said, "Clear."

Spence crossed the threshold followed by Scott and Maria. The temperature had dropped since he had entered Greystone. His breath frosted the air. He looked down at his sister. She produced no such mist. Spence swallowed.

"Where's your car?" Amanda asked.

"The other side of Aldebaran," Spence replied.

Amanda's face fell. "Are you kidding me? How the hell are we supposed to get all the way down this street without being seen?"

"We'll make it," he told her. "Just keep your eyes open."

"Tom, we can't leave Marcus," Maria said. "He's still in that house."

"We're not leaving him," Spence told her. "But first we get back to the cars."

Amanda did not wait for an invite. She took off toward the corner of the house. Before Spence and the others joined her she had already scanned the area ahead of them. "I don't see anyone." She did not wait for confirmation. She scurried, half-bent, across the front lawn. She made it to the tree line next to the driveway entrance and waited.

Spence was feeling the weight now. He was moving much slower than he would have thought. His arms felt as if they were made of lead. His legs were starting to quiver. Reluctantly he knelt and placed Katie on the cold, damp grass. He brushed a lock of hair from her face.

Scott followed his lead. He lowered Maria onto her knees. Then he collapsed onto the ground next to her. His chest heaved and he sucked in great gulps of cold air.

You're in bad shape already and you haven't even made it off the property yet, his younger self informed him. *How do you expect to make it all the way to the other side of Route 26? Magic?* Spence did not believe he had been this obnoxious back then although his teachers might disagree. In any event the voice was correct. He felt at the moment he couldn't even make it to the paved half of Aldebaran Road let alone all the way to where they had parked. And Scott was in even worse shape.

"We go in stages," he announced through gasps of air. "Go, rest, go, rest, until we're there." It was all he could think to do.

"Flashlights!" Amanda hissed.

Spence crouched down instinctively. He followed Amanda's eyes.

They were cell phones, not flashlights. Four of them perhaps one hundred feet away. The beams of light swept the darkness ahead of the men holding them. The men appeared to be in no rush; their pace was casual. Their lights probed the darkness in every direction, but slowly, as if these men expected to find nothing and were doing their best to achieve that goal.

"We can't stay here," Amanda said quite unnecessarily.

Spence slid his arm beneath his sister's body. He looked at Scott. The poor bastard was still sucking in lungfuls of air. One hand massaged his injured leg although he had not complained about it. At the same time his eyes were wide and filled with fear. Spence lifted with his legs. He teetered for a moment before he shifted his grip on Katie's body. It took effort but he managed to sling her over his left shoulder. It was somewhat easier to bear the weight and he cursed himself for not thinking of this sooner. It would still be slow going to the cars but he thought perhaps he would have a slightly easier time of it now. He checked to make sure Scott had Maria and then he nodded to Amanda.

She stepped around the closed gate to the property and onto the unpaved section of Aldebaran Road.

****

The argument had been going on for some time. The old man who had left with the butler returned to his fancy chair and had some harsh words for his brother. Phil could not remember much of what had been said:

(*Wasted your white*)

(*Only one for the sacrament, and a* male *at that*)

(*Who will feed me?*)

(*Let them get away*)

(*Looking for them*)

Phil couldn't believe the two old men had the physical fortitude to keep up an argument too long so his periods of unconsciousness must be getting shorter. That was probably a good sign. He was still on his knees so the simple fact that he hadn't fallen onto his face was another factor in his favor. And aside from the two old men and the butler everyone else had cleared out of the room. Phil did not remember them leaving. One moment they were there the next they were not. He wished he could remember.

The one thing he did remember, quite vividly, was Marcus throwing himself through the window in the wall. He had disappeared after that. *Son of a bitch left me again.* It was his first thought every time the world swam back into focus. In any other place he would be angry, even furious. He found he could not waste the energy thinking about Marcus. Not now. When he got out of here, though...

The three men in the room paid him no mind. Phil may as well have been the family dog. They argued without regard for their words. Phil wished he had been more lucid. It's possible he might have picked up something useful. As it was he had to assume Keith and the others got away. That was something else in his favor. Marcus wouldn't hesitate to leave him behind but Keith was another matter entirely. *He* would come back for him. Phil hoped it was sooner rather than later.

The argument continued until the clock on the wall tolled. Both men ceased speaking immediately and regarded the ancient timepiece. Phil turned his head as much as he was able. Midnight. Was that supposed to mean something?

"And we're nearly out of time," one of the men said to the other.

"If we must use a male in the sacrament then so be it. His Majesty will have to understand. The services we have provided over the years should be more than enough to compensate for this poor offering."

The other nodded. "Indeed."

They pushed themselves to their feet.

The butler approached them. "Shall I send for Master Edgar, my Lords?"

Both men scoffed. Their facial expressions turned quite sour.

"That bore?" one of them said. "I do not believe his presence is required. Perhaps the next time."

"Yes," the other concurred. "Leave our dear baby brother where he is for now. This night has been most trying, Exton. I fear I do not have the strength of stomach to tolerate his presence."

The butler bowed from the waist. "Very good, my Lords."

One of the brothers looked askance at Phil. "Prepare him. He will have to do."

"At once, my Lords."

The butler approached him. Phil started to squirm but rough hands hauled him to his feet. The butler slung Phil over his shoulder as if he weighed nothing. The world started to swim out of focus again.

****

Somehow they had managed to make it to the halfway point of Aldebaran Road. The dirt ended abruptly and the asphalt took over. Spence was more winded than he had ever been. His arms and legs were long past pain; he felt almost nothing at all.

"I need to stop for a minute," Scott announced through great gulps of air. Then, to Maria, "Can you stand?"

"I think so." Maria took a hesitant step away from him. She teetered a bit but her legs held her upright. "Yeah, I think I'm okay."

Scott dropped to his knees, gasping. "Thank God! No offense, Maria." Another deep breath. "Jesus, I need to quit smoking!"

"Amen," Maria replied.

Spence lowered himself as carefully as he was able and placed Katie on the road. He knelt beside her and stroked her hair. "Katie, I'm so sorry," he whispered. "I'm so sorry, honey. I should have told you. I should have gotten here sooner." Tears dropped upon her cheeks. Spence wiped them away.

Now that they were away from the house his mind flooded with images of his sister throughout her short life. Opening presents on Christmas morning, dressed for church on Easter Sunday, playing in the backyard at their house on Everett Street, riding her bike around the neighborhood. He had been less than an ideal brother. He remembered teasing her relentlessly, pulling the heads off her Barbie dolls, banging away on his drum kit in his room while she was trying to study in the next. He had once dropped a water balloon on her head when she was standing on the front deck with her date to the prom. His timing had been perfect; the balloon exploded just as their mother snapped a photo to commemorate the occasion. Spence made copies of the picture and would tape them to the walls of her bedroom whenever the opportunity presented itself. "I'm so goddamned sorry, Katie. I never meant any of it. I was just being an asshole. Forgive me, please." He wiped more of his tears from her cheeks.

Spence came to realize someone had placed their hand on his shoulder. He pulled his eyes from his sister and saw it was Maria. Her eyes were wet with tears. She shifted her weight from foot to foot. "Tom, I'm so sorry about Katie. I didn't know her well but I wish I did. But we have to go."

Spence looked about. Scott was still on his knees, head down, breathing heavily. *He won't make it.* The thought was sudden and cold-blooded and absolutely correct. They had made it halfway from Greystone to Route 26 and his friend was nearing the end of the line. *No way he makes it all the way to the cars dragging Maria along. And for that matter, there's no way you're getting there, either. Neither one of you is in any condition to continue this way.* Scott would never admit it, Spence knew. If he called for them to get moving again Scott would without complaint. But they would not make it to 26, not like this.

Spence swallowed. "That's it," he said. "We can't do this."

Three sets of eyes turned in his direction. Scott was the first to speak. "Come on, man, we got this." He spoke between deep breaths.

What he said next was out of his mouth before he knew he would speak. "We have to leave Katie here. We won't make it unless we do." He closed his eyes. Hearing it aloud made him want to vomit. The thought of leaving his sister here…

"God, Spence, I'm so sorry," Maria told him. "I think you're right."

"That's fucking bullshit!" Scott exclaimed. He wiped sweat from his forehead and face. "And that's a pretty fucked up thing to say, Maria. Maybe we should leave you here, too."

Maria started to protest.

Amanda, who had walked about thirty feet farther up the road and was looking in both directions, turned back toward them. "I can stay with her."

Spence turned to her. Her eyes darted from Katie's body to Spence to the road ahead of them. She fidgeted with her outfit, her feet shifted. *I don't want to,* her body language practically screamed. *I can't even begin to tell you how much I don't want to stay here. But if I don't maybe no one gets to leave.* "You sure? You wanted to get out of here as much as us."

Amanda started back toward them. She still moved slowly, as if unsure of her balance. "I don't *want* to, if that's what you're asking. But I have eyes. You and your friend here can't go much farther. I'll stay with Katie. We can hide in the woods. Once you get to your car come back and get us."

Spence got one knee under him. He placed his hand on his sister's cheek. "Are you sure, Amanda?"

"Hell no," she replied. She had reached them. She knelt down beside Spence and looked at Katie. "I didn't know her for long. But she was nice. We got along really well. And she didn't deserve this." She paused, swallowed. "So if staying here with her while you get the car means we can get her away from this fucking place, I'm in."

"Those assholes are actively looking for us," Scott said with a wave toward Greystone. "What happens if they come this way?"

"We'll be in the woods," Amanda answered. "We'll stay down, go quiet. They won't even know we're there."

"I hate this idea," Scott told her.

Amanda shrugged.

Spence lifted his sister's body from the cold pavement. His legs protested and promised him a world of pain tomorrow. He carried her into the woods on the side of the road. He made it perhaps fifteen feet before he knelt and placed Katie on a bed of old, dry leaves. He brushed a stray lock of hair from her eyes. "I'm so, so sorry, Katie. I swear to God I am. Please believe me."

Amanda joined him. "I couldn't see this far into the woods from the road. We'll be okay here. I'll watch her. I promise." She placed her hand on his shoulder.

"Just…Just…"

"I know."

Spence squeezed her hand. Then he knelt and kissed Katie's forehead. "I'll be back for you. I promise on Mom's grave. I'll be back for you." His tears fell on her cheeks, her neck. He wiped them away.

"We'll be okay," Amanda told him.

Spence spared one more look at his sister. He used a tree to help him regain his feet. "I promise."

Scott and Maria stood by the boundary between the blacktop and the woods. Neither spoke.

Spence swallowed and left his sister behind. He emerged onto the road and started toward 26 without looking at them.

They had made it perhaps one hundred yards from the start of the blacktop when Scott stopped before the entrance to a driveway. "You think all the assholes who live here are at Greystone?" he asked everyone.

Maria shrugged. "What does that have to do with anything?"

"There's no signal out here, and we can't use our phones anyway because they'll see the light." He grinned. "I'm gonna break into this motherfucker and use their phone to call the cops."

Spence's first thought was, *Jesus, tonight* is *the night for firsts. Going inside Greystone was bad enough. Now we're breaking into a house at Denham.* He gave voice to his second thought. "That's not a bad idea. Assuming they have a landline. Hit 911 and call in the cavalry. Good thinking."

Scott eyed them both. "You guys should stay here. It'll be faster if I go alone."

"We should hide," Maria offered. "In case someone comes by."

Spence could not argue her logic. "Be fast, man. Get in, make the call, get out. No bonus points for being a hero."

Scott grinned. "You know me."

Spence did. He made for the woods and found a spot big enough for him and Maria. They waited in silence. Maria placed her hand on his shoulder. Spence placed his on hers.

Spence glanced at the sky, hidden by the canopy of leaves far above his head. "Gonna get you out of here. I swear to God

I'm gonna get you as far from this fucking place as I can. I promise, Katie."

"What if that house has an alarm?" Maria whispered. "If he sets it off…"

"Let's hope they have one of those window stickers saying the house is wired," Spence whispered back. *Because if he does set off an alarm we're well and truly fucked.* The good news was he had yet to hear anything from the house. He hoped that meant Scott was already inside and calling the DLPD. Spence allowed himself to hope.

He heard the footsteps before he saw Scott emerge from the darkness of the driveway. His breathing was fast and shallow. He stopped in the middle of the road and placed his hands on his knees. "Jesus Christ," he muttered just loud enough for Spence to hear.

Spence stood and walked to the edge of the woods. "What happened? Did you get in?"

Scott shook his head. "Nope. They have a giant fucking dog, or maybe it's a wolf, I don't know. As soon as I touched the doorknob the fucker jumped for me. Slammed against the door so hard it cracked one of the glass panels. I thought it was gonna come right through the door. I just about pissed myself. Ain't calling for help from there, I can tell you that."

"Maybe the next one." Spence motioned for Maria to rejoin them.

Scott was staring back along the road in the direction of Greystone Manor. His lips moved but he produced no sound. He raised his arm and pointed.

Someone was walking in their direction. It was one person as far as Spence could tell. The absence of streetlights threw the road into near-total darkness. It was possible there were others. Spence's muscles tensed. They were caught. This person—or *persons*—were already too close not to have seen them.

If there's just one beat him into the ground and run. If there are others… Spence's hands balled into fists.

"Marcus!" Maria broke from Scott and wobbled past Spence before he could grab for her. She moved as fast as she was able and threw herself at the shadow she took to be her husband. The shadow staggered back and both went down on the blacktop.

Scott ran for them. He was swallowed by the shadows. After several moments Spence heard Scott say, "Thought we lost you, man!"

Spence 's eyes cut through the darkness the closer he got until he could at last see the shadow man was indeed Marcus. Scott helped him to his feet. Marcus leaned to his right and held his hand over his gut.

"You okay?" Spence asked.

Scott lifted Maria from the road as Marcus said, "Been better. That old fuck busted me up pretty good. Been coughing up blood since I woke up. I can feel my ribs grinding together." He smiled. "Good to see you fuckers, though."

Maria wrapped her arms around his neck and kissed him. Marcus grunted. "Easy, babe, easy. I ain't one-hundred-percent here."

She kissed him several more times before she backed up a step. "Come on, honey, let's get out of here."

Scott took one of Marcus's arms and draped it across his shoulders. "C'mon, bro."

"Thanks, man." They made it two steps before Marcus asked, "You guys didn't find Katie, did you?" Maria whispered something to him. Marcus's face fell. "Oh, Jesus. Spence, I'm real sorry, man."

Spence found he could not reply.

Marcus cleared his throat and said, "Got some revenge, though," and smiled. He coughed suddenly and violently. He dropped to one knee and spat blood upon the ground.

Maria placed both hands on her husband's shoulders. "Breathe, Marcus, just breathe. You'll be okay. Just hang on."

The coughing persisted for another moment before Marcus got it under control. He wiped at his chin and then wiped his hand across his jeans. "I'm all right, babe." He looked up at Spence. "I followed that secret passage to the kitchen. Some fat broad was in there. Looked like someone worked her over pretty good. She was just getting on her knees so I kicked her square in the mouth. Down she went." He smiled a bloody smile. "Hurt like a motherfucker but felt good at the same time. I heard someone else coming so I got the hell out of there." He rose to his feet with another grunt.

Maria kissed his cheek and ran her hands through his thinning hair. "I love you, baby. Don't ever leave me. Promise!"

"I promise," Marcus told her.

Maria turned to Scott. "I got him, Scott. I got him."

Scott backed up a step. "We're gonna break into a house and use their phone to call the cops," he informed Marcus.

Marcus shook his head. "Fuck that." He patted his front left pocket. "I'm for getting the fuck out of here right now. We'll all fit in the Torino, no problem."

"What about Phil?" Spence asked.

Marcus tilted his head in the direction of Greystone. "We can't help him. There's too many of those fuckers. We need the cops. And, um, I saw Keith…"

"We know," Spence cut him off.

"Guys, seriously, we need to go," Maria prodded.

"Katie's back there in the woods," Scott said. "With another girl who worked there. We had to leave them behind. When we get to the car we have to come back for them."

"I didn't see anyone." Marcus spat more blood onto the blacktop.

"That's a good thing," Scott replied.

"Okay, so we get to the car, come back and get Katie and the other broad, and then we go to the cops. Do I have all that right?"

"As rain," Scott told him.

"Then let's go."

They went. Marcus leaned on Maria. She visibly struggled beneath his weight but she managed. He stopped at random intervals and coughed and spat blood onto the ground. Spence led the way. He moved steadily now, and looked back constantly as if to speed up his companions. He hated the idea of Katie lying on the cold ground and he wanted to get her away from here as fast as they were able. Since they found Marcus and now had a realistic goal ahead of them Spence found he was able to move with a bit more speed.

Ahead of them a light appeared in the darkness. Maria stopped and gasped.

"It's cool," Scott told her. "It's not a car, it's the streetlight at the start of the road." He turned toward Spence. "We're almost there."

Spence kept his eyes on the light. It grew in size and intensity and welcomed them out of the darkness of Aldebaran Road. Ahead of them perhaps fifty yards was Marcus's Gran Torino. Spence first heard and then saw a car drive past on Route 26. Maria shrieked and waved her free arm but she was too late. The driver had not seen them, had no reason to even look down the side street. The sound of the car's engine was already gone.

"Doesn't matter," Marcus told her. "We're here."

They reached the cross street. Spence eyed the lone house that stood sentinel at the top of Aldebaran Road. Its appearance had not changed since they arrived. A couple lights on, the Beamer in the driveway. No sign of people. They continued ahead.

The dark silhouettes of Phil's Equinox and Marcus's Gran Torino sat on the left side of the road. Scott ran to them and waited. Maria helped Marcus to the driver's door of the old Ford.

Spence eyed both vehicles. *When we were last here Katie was still alive. So was Keith. Phil was here and Marcus didn't sound like he was dying.* On the heels of that, *Jesus. I am so sorry. This is all on me.*

Marcus unlocked the driver's door and opened it. He stepped back and Maria reached across the front seat and unlocked the other door. Then she moved the seat forward and stepped back.

"Spence, I'm real sorry," Marcus said again. "Katie was a sweet girl. Don't worry. The cops will get those fuckers." He took a cigarette from the pack on the dash and lit it. "Fuck me, I needed this." He offered the pack to Scott.

"Fuck that. I'm quitting," Scott told him.

"This isn't a good time for a smoke break, babe," Maria informed him.

Marcus handed her the pack and the lighter. She shook one from the pack and lit it.

Spence scowled. "Can we go—"

"Car!" Scott shouted.

Spence at first thought his friend meant another car was cutting by on Route 26. He looked and saw the headlights racing up Aldebaran. A heartbeat later he heard the big block V8 of the yellow-white muscle car. "Oh, shit."

"Fuck that!" Marcus shouted. He threw himself into the driver's seat and fired up the Gran Torino. Maria dove into the passenger seat. Marcus jammed the car into gear and slammed his foot onto the gas pedal. The Gran Torino's tires smoked and the car flew forward. It fishtailed onto Route 26 and disappeared from view.

The car they had seen parked at Greystone Manor, the one that had stopped next to their hiding spot in the woods, mimicked the Gran Torino. It took the corner at a high rate of speed and nearly wound up in the woods before it straightened out. The driver gunned the engine and this car, too, was gone.

Spence and Scott remained frozen in place next to where the Gran Torino had been parked. They could still hear the two cars in the distance but the sound faded after another moment and the world went silent.

Spence had lost the power of speech.

Scott had not. "He fucking did it again."

CHAPTER EIGHTEEN

Another For the Fire

Spence stood and tried to wrap his head around what had just happened. In the back of his mind a single phrase, spoken by Phil Volokhov eleven years earlier, played on a constant loop: *He fucking left me there, Spence.* The phrase repeated until it made its way past his subconscious. Then the next sentence in Phil's rant came back to him: *Next time you see him, tell him I'm gonna fucking kill him.*

Spence hadn't been there himself. *The Night of the Carnival*, as it came to be known in Deacon's Landing, was something he heard from the inside of a cell at the old Deacon's Landing Police Department. He was lying on a cot bored to tears. Daniels had caught him holding a baggie of crystal and couldn't haul him into jail fast enough. The hell of it was the baggie wasn't even his. He had been holding it for his girlfriend, Simona. Of course there was no point arguing that with Officer Daniels. Every meth head and crackhead on the planet protested the drugs weren't theirs. And it wasn't like Spence didn't have a record. So he kept his mouth shut and stayed in his cell while Simona Carter tweaked with someone else at the carnival.

He could hear the explosions from his cell. Misset Park was only a few blocks from the station house. Had his cell boasted a window he would have run to it and peeked through. As it was he had to rely on half-heard shouts from the cops in the station.

He was released on a PTA the next day; the cops had far bigger concerns than a simple holding charge, even if it was for a felony. Spence walked out of jail and could see the white smoke rising slowly from the direction of the park. He tried to walk past and see for himself what had occurred but the entire area was cordoned off. He walked home instead.

He got the gist of it from the morning news. Even CNN was carrying the story. Apparently some asshat had set off a bunch of explosions at the carnival. The authorities were still counting the dead. A few days after that Spence would learn Simona was among them.

The day after the destruction Phil called him. He and Marcus and a few others had been smoking weed in the woods that bordered the park. One of Deacon's Landing's finest, someone who clearly knew about that particular spot, had gone fishing. He reeled in Phil. The worst part was, Phil told Spence, he had been the one to see the cop coming. He hissed a warning to his companions and he started to run. Marcus collided with him and knocked him down. Phil's knee struck a rock so hard Phil thought he had broken his kneecap. Marcus looked at him and bolted. The officer had just put the handcuffs on Phil when the first explosion went off. That was the last Phil saw of Marcus Greer.

Standing opposite Aldebaran Road, Spence knew beyond a doubt he too had seen Marcus for the last time. There was no way his friend—and the term no longer applied—could dare show himself after this. If he was smart he'd keep driving until he got to the opposite coast. Even that might not do it.

"I can't believe that asshole did that," Scott remarked. His tone was incredulous.

Spence had lost both the power of speech and the ability to move. He had yet to budge since Marcus high-tailed it onto Route 26.

Scott swallowed. "Motherfucker just left us here. Can you believe that?" When Spence offered no reply Scott shrugged and said, "Maybe I can hotwire Phil's car." He walked to the side of the narrow road and began scanning the ground with his eyes. He stopped, knelt, and came up with a rock the size of his fist. "This should do it."

"Stop," Spence told him. He surprised himself by being able to speak. He had, until that moment, thought Marcus's departure had muted him for life.

Scott hefted the rock. "Why? This'll get through the window no problem."

Spence still hadn't pulled his eyes from the end of the road where he had last seen the Gran Torino. "Do you know how to hotwire a car?"

"Well, no, but I'm sure I can figure it out."

"And can you figure out how to cut the alarm when you smash the window?" At last he turned from the road and regarded his friend. "You may as well set up trumpets and a spotlight to broadcast our location. You'll bring them right to us."

"So? The alarm can wail all the way to the police station for all I care! This is our only option."

Spence shook his head. "No, it isn't." He took a deep breath, felt the cold air saturate his lungs. It rid him of the last of the cobwebs that had covered his brain when he saw Marcus leave them behind. He exhaled slowly. "We're going back to get Amanda and Katie and Phil."

"Are you kidding me?" Scott asked. "Spence, we barely got out of there. You want to go back? Are you crazy?"

Spence placed his hands in his pockets and faced his friend. "It was always my plan. I figured I'd get you guys away from there and go back for Phil. They *killed* her, Scott. And Keith. What do you think they're gonna do to Phil? I'm not leaving him back there. You don't want to come? Don't. Smash the window, set off the car alarm, and good luck hotwiring this thing before all those assholes show up. Maybe you *will* make it back to the Landing. But I'm staying."

"This is insane," Scott announced.

Hell yeah it is, Spence's younger self chimed in. *You fought one guy in there and he was old as fuck and you* still *barely beat him. What are you gonna do when that big bastard from the barn shows up? You're fresh out of trapdoors.*

For once, Spence told his younger self, *you proved yourself useful.*

"There's plenty of shit in the barn I can use as weapons," Spence told him. "I'm gonna get something, maybe a lot of somethings, whatever I can carry. Then I'm gonna go in that house again and I'm gonna beat all the ass until I find Phil. Then we grab Amanda's car keys and we drive out of here together."

"Spence, this is *so* not a good plan," Scott told him. "Look, I'm not for leaving your sister and Phil behind. And that Amanda chick seems cool. But that's not the point. They're looking for us. They're probably all over the road and the woods. You won't get anywhere near the house."

"I'm not leaving them," he replied.

"Did I say insane? You're way past that," Scott told him. "You won't make it. My plan at least has a chance of success."

"Then go for it. I'm not forcing you to come with me. It's probably better if you don't. Drive out of here or walk. I'll go back for Katie and the others." He started for 26. When he reached it he stopped, turned. "Good luck."

Scott tossed the rock into the woods. "Son of a bitch." He started after Spence. "Now I wish I said yes to that cigarette."

Spence crossed the street and stepped onto Aldebaran Road. He walked in silence; Scott kept pace beside him. His mind was once again filled with images of Katie. This time he saw her jabbed in the neck by the butler. He saw her lying on the floor of the mask room. Then inside the room in the cellar. In the woods with Amanda kneeling beside her. Brushing her hair from her closed eyes. His hands had curled into fists at some point. He squeezed so hard he could feel trickles of blood welling up between his fingers.

The first time they scattered into the woods was a false alarm. Scott thought he heard voices ahead of them but after a few moments crouched down behind a thick maple tree no one presented themselves. They resumed their trek to Greystone Manor. They had made it nearly to the edge of the dirt road when they heard voices ahead of them.

There were two, male and female. The male voice was filled with anger; its female counterpart was screaming and clearly terrified.

Spence broke into a full sprint.

A portly man in an expensive suit had one hand clamped onto Amanda's arm. He yanked and pulled her along the dirt. Her feet skidded and kicked up small clouds of dust. She beat at his arm with her free hand and screamed.

"Gonna get you back to their Lordships," the man grunted. "You should never have run away, Miss Missy. They're gonna take care of you real good."

Amanda screamed, "Let go of me!" She continued to flail against his hold.

Spence reached them and leaped.

The man never saw him coming.

Spence's elbow smashed into the man's face. His nose gave way with a spray of blood. The man staggered back. He released his hold on Amanda's arm. She backpedaled and lost her balance. Her captor's face was hidden by his large hands. Blood streamed between his fingers and pattered onto his coat, his shirt.

Spence slammed his fist into the man's hands. His head jerked back and he dropped to his knees. He looked up dumbly at Spence. Then he teetered and fell onto his back. His breath plumed into the air in thick white streams. He neither moved nor made a sound.

Amanda was already back on her feet. She rushed the prone man and slammed her foot into his side. "Fucker!" She kicked him again then hopped back and limped away. "Son of a bitch!"

Scott reached her. "You okay?"

"No," she spat. "Asshole saw me. I got too close to the road. My own fault." She examined her arm and her fingers traced the path of the welts caused by the large man's grip.

"I don't think he'll be doing that again anytime soon."

"Good!" She approached him as if she were going to kick him again. But she apparently thought better of it. She instead spat on him. "Fuck you, you piece of shit!"

Spence emerged from the woods with Katie's body.

"What happened?" Amanda asked. "I thought you were going for the cars. And where's Maria? Jesus, did that guy get her?"

"What guy?" Scott asked.

"We were in the woods for only a couple minutes when I saw someone walk by, headed in your direction. Did that guy grab Maria?"

Scott swallowed. "That was Marcus. He's gone. So is Maria. They left us there when that car came up after us."

"Martin Jacoby."

"I guess."

"So your friend left us here? Nice fucking friend."

"We'll deal with that later." Spence, Katie's body in his arms, started in the direction of Greystone. "We're gonna find your car keys and our friend Phil and we're getting out of here."

"You're going back?" She could not or would not keep the surprise from her tone. "You can't be serious."

"I'm afraid he is," Scott told her when Spence made no reply. He followed after Spence. "You coming?"

Amanda stood her ground and shook her head and swore. Then she ran after them.

They had reached the edge of the cornfield. Spence stopped and nodded. "Through here. We get to the barn and find whatever we can use. Then we find Phil and Amanda's keys."

He took a step in that direction when Scott hissed, "Car!"

Spence's head whipped around. The headlights were still a ways off but they were getting closer. He could hear the throaty roar of the old muscle car as its driver navigated the road at far too great a speed.

His first thought, foolish as it was, was, *Marcus came back! He lost that asshole Jacoby and he came back for us! There's no way he would leave his friends behind, not again.* But no. This car was louder than the Gran Torino, and Marcus, crazy as he is, would never drive that fast on this road.

Spence didn't have to say anything. Scott and Amanda crashed into the woods and disappeared from his view. Spence followed them as quickly as he was able.

The old yellow-white monstrosity drew nearer. The driver must have slammed on the brakes because a great cloud of dust rose from the dirt road around the tires and the back end swerved a bit. The car stopped directly across from them.

Spence got his first close-up look at the car. It was an Olds; the *442* signage on the front fender said as much.

The driver's door opened. The man from the kitchen planted one foot on the dirt. "I have your friend here," he announced to the woods. He glanced back inside the car. "She don't look too good. I think she needs a doctor."

Spence ground his teeth with so much force he was surprised the man couldn't hear him.

"Your other friend is back in his car," Jacoby continued. "I don't think you'll be talking to him anytime soon. Or, you know, ever. I wish I could say I'm sorry about that but he was a bit of an asshole, wasn't he? I think he thought that beat up piece of shit could outrun me. He was most definitely wrong about that." The man paused as if he expected them to charge out of the woods. He did not hide his disappointment when no one presented themselves. "Anyway, I'm bringing this one back to Greystone and my uncles. Enjoy the rest of your evening, losers."

He waited another few moments. With a frown of disappointment he slid back behind the wheel and closed the door. "Fucking pussies." He spat on the road and threw the car into gear. The 442 shot forward in a cloud of dust and was gone from their sight.

"Maria. He was talking about Maria," Scott said when he crept onto the road. He checked both ways before he waved to the others.

The dust was still thick in the air when Spence and Amanda joined him. Spence regarded the road ahead of them before he set off for the cornfield.

"Spence, did you hear me? Did you hear *him*? He has Maria. And he said Marcus is dead!"

"I heard him," Spence answered. He could not allow himself to think of Marcus right now.

He crossed the threshold into the cornfield. The narrow dirt path that ran alongside the rows of corn stretched out and up before him. He knelt and placed his sister's body onto the ground. "I won't be long, Katie, I promise." He kissed her forehead.

He stood and looked up the hill. He could see neither Greystone nor the barn, not from here. But he would very soon. Phil was still inside Greystone, and possibly Maria now, as well. He thought of the barn and nothing more.

****

The woman in the maid's uniform, the one he had heard addressed as Ms. Palmer, flailed her arms and her legs kicked weakly in the air. The old man's mouth was fixed on her neck as if it were welded there. Several thin streams of pink fluid trickled down her neck and stained the white collar of her uniform. Her mouth was open wide but the only sound that escaped her was a low register gurgle. Her eyes were clenched shut but every few seconds they would snap open before closing again.

Phil felt that was the image he would take to his grave. Her eyes. They did not move when she opened them. It looked as if she were staring at something on the other side of the room that only she could see. They never found him, never pleaded with him. Yet they told him everything he would ever want to know about the horror that had suddenly thrust itself upon her.

She had squealed when the old man grabbed her from behind. At first she resisted, throwing her arms back and trying to free herself. The old man's grip was firm, far too strong for someone of his apparent age. Her struggles were meaningless. The old man drew his head back and revealed long teeth that ended in sharp points. Those points penetrated the woman's neck. Her expression of surprise and terror was replaced momentarily by one of, not just pain, but *agony*. Her efforts to free herself diminished greatly after a moment or two.

At last the old man pulled his mouth away from the maid's neck. He threw his head back and roared at the ceiling. Droplets of the pink stuff flew from his mouth and dribbled down his chin. The sound set up shop at the base of Phil's spine and froze him in place far more effectively than the restraints holding his arms behind his back. The old man lowered his head, eyes closed. His body quivered for a few moments, a drug addict reacting to a long-awaited fix. His eyes snapped open again.

He did not look at the dead woman in his arms. Instead he threw the body to the floor with enough force to make it bounce before it settled. Phil could not take his eyes from her. The woman's eyes were closed—a fact for which he was grateful—but her mouth still hung agape. The wound in her neck, two small punctures in a sea of stained and ruined skin, did not produce any blood.

"Gods, that is so much better!" the old man proclaimed. He thumped his chest with one fist. "I should have done that hours ago."

"Yes," his twin agreed from his high-backed chair. He had not moved at all during the past few minutes other than to sip from the wine glass in his hand. "And now we are deprived of all our maids. Well done, Arthur."

Arthur turned toward his brother. "We have Exton here! Isn't that right, Exton?"

The butler in the tuxedo, hands clasped behind his back, nodded his head stiffly. "As always, my Lord, I am at your service." His voice was flat, professional. He did not spare a glance at the dead woman lying five feet from his expensive shoes.

"You see?" Arthur said to his brother in that tone all siblings use to one-up each other. "Exton will see to everything. Where would we be without you, dear Exton?"

"I am sure your Lordships would be fine without my humble services, sir," came the reply.

Arthur scoffed and resumed his place in his chair. He leaned back, closed his eyes, and breathed deeply.

"This still leaves us short-staffed, dear brother," his twin said. "And I'm sure the white you just consumed will wreak havoc with your ulcers."

Arthur waved him off. "I just gave it to her yesterday. It's still fresh enough. Do not fret over my health, dear William. I feel like a young man again!"

"If I may be so bold," Exton started, "there are three more interviews scheduled for tomorrow, my Lords. The staff shortage shall be remedied by dinner."

"There, you see? All is taken care of." Arthur looked for the first time at the corpse at his feet. "Exton, be a good man and add this to the fire. It should be quite impressive this time."

Exton nodded. "As your Lordships wish." He started for the corpse.

Someone entered the room before Exton could reach the dead woman. Phil could not remember the man's name but he knew he was the nephew of the two old men. He dragged a body behind him.

"A gift for my dear uncles," he announced. He tossed the body onto the floor at their feet.

"Maria!" Phil instinctively tried to reach for her before he remembered his arms were bound behind him. He fell forward and wound up on his stomach. "Jesus, Maria!" Phil worked against whatever restrained his arms but it was unyielding and tore the flesh from his wrists. Exton closed his hand around the back of Phil's neck and pulled him back onto his knees. Phil tried to head-butt him but the butler had already moved out of range. "Maria, wake up! Maria!"

"I ran them down," the nephew announced. "Drove them right off the road. We'll need a tow truck to get the car out of there before someone sees it. She was the only one who made it." He noticed for the first time the dead woman on the floor. "Unless my uncles don't need her, in which case I'd be happy—"

"She is dead, my Lords," announced Exton. He knelt by Maria, his hand on her neck. "Most likely internal injuries, if I had to guess."

William Morley regarded his nephew.

"Hey, don't look at me." The nephew held up both hands. "She was alive when I got here."

"Don't touch her!" Phil screamed. "Don't you fucking touch her!"

"Someone's got balls," the nephew remarked. He smiled and sauntered across the room until he stood in front of Phil. He glanced back over his shoulder at his uncles. Then he slammed his fist against the side of Phil's head.

Stars exploded across his vision and Phil went down on his side. He had the presence of mind to sweep his legs across the floor. He felt them connect with the nephew's boots. The nephew yelped and crashed onto the floor.

"Son of a bitch!" The nephew scrambled to his feet. "Got some fight in ya. I like that." He reached down and wrapped his hands around Phil's arm.

"Leave him," one of the old men ordered.

"Yes, we need him for the Sacrament," the other agreed.

Phil regarded the nephew. He still held Phil's arm. His other hand was balled into a fist and his knuckles were white. He glared at his uncles for a long moment. Phil was certain he would ignore them and clobber him anyway. He braced himself for the blow.

It never came. The nephew released his hold on Phil's arm and stepped away. He looked at Phil. "Don't get too excited. What they're gonna do to you is way worse than what I was gonna do."

Phil managed to right himself. There was much he wanted to say to the nephew, to the other men in the room. Instead he looked at Maria.

"And this one, my Lords?" Exton asked with a nod at Maria's corpse.

"Another for the fire," Arthur told him. "It should be quite impressive, indeed."

"I shall see to it personally, my Lords." Exton knelt and scooped up Maria's body as if it weighted next to nothing.

"Leave her alone!" Phil shouted.

Exton ignored him. With Maria over his shoulder he knelt next to the maid's corpse. He grasped her ankle and returned to his full height. He exited the room, one corpse slung over his shoulder and the other bumping along the floor.

Phil watched him go. After the butler and his cargo were out of his sight he turned to the two old men. Arthur dabbed a kerchief along his jaw. William sipped his wine.

CHAPTER NINETEEN

The Procession of Masks

Spence crouched behind the tree. The barn stood before him. Its doors were wide open. Light spilled from inside. He could hear nothing from within although he might not be close enough. His eyes moved across the grounds. No one was in evidence. Against his will he looked toward Greystone Manor. His eyes fixed on the windows of the mask room. Looking through those windows was the last time he saw his sister alive. Before his thoughts could turn fully to Katie he squashed them. He could not help her. Phil, on the other hand, might still be alive. He needed to keep his focus on his friend.

They had hidden inside the cornfield once on their way up the hill. They spotted another group of Denham men on their way down the hill toward the road. There were three in total. They swept the area with the light from their phones and talked of Miami's come from behind win against the Dbacks in the NLDS. Spence's blood boiled at the insignificance of their topic of conversation. Katie was dead. So was Keith and probably Marcus. And they were going on about a baseball game. Spence had resisted the urge to jump out of the field and beat them into the ground. Once they were gone he returned to the path up the hill, Scott and Amanda in tow.

"What do you think?" Scott asked. He stood behind Spence and peeked at the barn.

"Could be empty," Spence offered.

"Could be full of assholes who want to kill us, too," Scott replied.

"You didn't have to come," Spence reminded him.

"Yeah, yeah, yeah."

Spence glanced back at the two people behind him. "Stay here. I'll check the barn." He did not wait for their consent or protest. He left the tree behind and ran to the side of the barn. Now that he was close enough he could hear music coming from within the structure. Static accompanied the song and drowned out most of the music. Spence glanced back at Scott. Scott gave him a thumbs-up. Spence nodded.

He made his way to the front of the barn. He peeked inside. No one was present. His eyes whipped over the walls, the workbench. He wouldn't have minded finding another hammer like the one they had left inside the kitchen. Spence stepped inside the barn.

The lamp on the workbench was bright and illuminated much of the area around it. Spence saw screwdrivers, pliers, a rubber mallet. He hefted the mallet for a moment before he tossed it aside. He looked about the walls. Shovels, tillers, tampers, rakes, hedge trimmers, a pole saw...

Spence pulled the pole saw from its niche on the wall. It was perhaps five feet in length. He found the wheel to adjust the length and extended it to eight feet. He swung it slowly several times. *Too long now.* He shortened it back to its five foot length. It was gas-powered so Spence checked the small fuel tank. It was full. He took several more practice swings until he felt comfortable with its weight and length. *You know what you have to do now, right? Test the thing.*

Spence took his hand away from the start button. Starting the pole saw would bring everybody running. *We'll test it on the first son of a bitch who comes between us and Phil.* He regarded the business end and was satisfied by the teeth. They were sharp and glinted in the light from the workbench.

Spence cast his eyes about for anything else that would make a suitable weapon. His shadow on the wall vanished suddenly, enveloped by a much larger shadow. Spence spun.

The giant stood perhaps ten feet behind him. His arms were at his side, his hands flexed and looked to be about the size of two baked hams. He smiled.

The image of Katie lying on the table in the basement flashed in front of his eyes. "You're fucking dead." The giant gave no indication he heard Spence's whispered threat. Spence pressed the starter button on the pole saw. The motor squealed. Nothing happened. He pressed it again and several more times after that. The giant remained where he stood. His hands continued to open and close.

Spence took a single stride and swung the pole saw for all he was worth. He struck the giant man across his chest. The metal pole bent. The target it had struck did not move. Spence pulled it back, examined it. The pole had nearly snapped with the impact; the upper part of it hung at an odd angle from the handle.

Spence swung it again. The pole snapped quite obediently. Spence spun and buried the broken end of the pole in the giant's chest. The man staggered back, one hand wrapped around the pole. Spence drove forward with all his weight. The pole penetrated another two inches, perhaps three. The giant swung one arm at him. Spence ducked under it but lost his grip on the pole. The giant wrapped both hands around it and pulled it free. Blood and puss spurted form the wound and stained his shirt a light pink. He tossed the pole aside.

Spence grabbed a shovel off the wall, a large, heavy spade. When the giant turned to face him, Spence swung for his head. The sound reminded Spence of church bells on a Sunday morning. The man's head tilted to one side. More blood/puss spurted, this time from his ear. Spence pulled back on the shovel and swung it a second time.

The giant caught it mid-arc. His fingers squeezed the handle. Spence heard the sound of splintering wood. He yanked back on it but the giant's grip was firm. Spence tried again. The giant swung and this time Spence could not get out of the way. The backhand caught him on the side of his head.

The world went dark. The lights returned long enough for Spence to realize he was flat on his back on the other side of the barn. The giant strode toward him. His hands flexed again. Then the darkness returned.

When the world swam back into focus Spence realized the giant was holding him off the ground. One meaty hand had hold of Spence's shirt. Spence's feet kicked weakly at the air. His hands clawed at the bear paw that held him.

The giant drew him closer until their noses were inches apart. He looked at Spence as an entomologist might a new species of insect. "You got fight in you." His voice was stone being fed through a grinder. "The Lords will be pleased."

Spence struck his arms, his face. The giant's grip did not falter, his expression remained unchanged. Spence saw the wound produced by the broken pole. He jammed his thumb into it.

The giant managed to hold his expression for a moment. Then his lips pulled back from his teeth. His eyes narrowed. Fresh sweat bloomed on his forehead and cheeks. With a grunt he released his grip. Spence landed awkwardly and stumbled. The giant took a single step back. He regarded the wound on his chest. He dabbed it with his finger and then wiped it on his shirt.

Spence regained his feet. His eyes whipped about but there was nothing on this side of the barn he could see that would be useful. Spence stood his ground and waited for the giant to grab for him again.

He looked like he wanted to. His eyes were focused on Spence. His hands no longer flexed; they were balled into fists that looked strong enough to punch through steel. He took a single step forward. His legs shook with the effort.

Spence braced himself.

The giant fell forward. He landed face down on the dirt floor. So surprised by this was Spence it took him a moment to notice the garden shears protruding from the back of the man's neck. Spence stared dumbly at them.

Amanda stood behind the fallen giant. Her hands covered her mouth and tears spilled from her eyes. "Oh, Jesus, Oh, Jesus," she mumbled.

Scott joined her. He placed his arms on her shoulders and looked at the giant. "Holy shit!"

"I killed Mr. Johnson," Amanda said through more tears. Her voice was muffled by her hands. "I killed Mr. Johnson."

"I won't complain," Spence told her. He suddenly felt both sore and cold. He rubbed the side of his head. There was already a rather large bump there. He winced and regarded the giant again. "Is that blood? It doesn't look right."

Scott stepped around Amanda as if he wanted to get a closer look at the pinkish fluid seeping from the wound in the back of the giant's neck. He stopped a few feet short of his goal. "I don't know, man. And I ain't getting any closer to look."

"Jesus, I killed him," Amanda mumbled.

Spence walked around the body. He found he did not want to inspect the wound any more than did Scott. He placed his hands on Amanda's arms. When she made no move to acknowledge him he shook her. Her eyes snapped back into focus. Her hands remained over her mouth.

"If you didn't I'd be dead right now. And the two of you would have been next. You did what you had to do. Are you listening? You did what you had to do."

Amanda's hands moved away from her mouth. She wiped the tears from her eyes and sniffled. Then she ran for the nearest corner of the barn, knelt, and vomited onto the ground.

"Crazy son of a bitch," Scott said. "You actually ran *toward* this guy. What were you thinking?"

"I was pissed," Spence admitted.

He walked to Amanda and knelt beside her. He patted her back. "Scott, watch the door."

"On it."

Spence continued to pat Amanda's back. "It's okay. You're okay."

Amanda spat onto the floor and wiped her lips and chin. "I just killed Mr. Johnson. Jesus, I fucking *killed* him."

Spence brushed the hair from her eyes and placed his other arm around her. "It's okay, Amanda. You did what you had to do."

She coughed and spat again. Her arms shook with the effort of keeping her from collapsing to the ground. She tried to speak, failed. It came out as a gurgle. She spat again.

Spence remained at her side. He alternated between patting her back and hugging her. The trembling continued for some time. He whispered encouragements to her, told her it would be all right. Eventually she got hold of herself. Spence helped her to her feet.

"I can't do that again," she told him. Her eyes were wide and wet. Tears continued to spill down her cheeks. "I can't." She shook her head and sniffled.

Spence pulled her close and wrapped his arms around her. "You won't have to." He hoped that was the truth. "We're gonna get out of here as soon as we find Phil and Maria. Then you'll never have to see this place again. I promise."

Amanda held onto him for several more moments. Then she pushed away from him. Her eyes went to the body on the ground. Fresh tears welled up.

"Don't look at him. Come on, let's go." He kept his hand on her back. He guided her past the corpse and toward the door where Scott was keeping an eye on their immediate surroundings. "You two stay here for a minute. We still need to find something we can use in case we run into any more assholes."

Grab the garden shears, his younger self instructed. *They clearly work*. Spence didn't think he'd be able to pull them from the dead man's neck. The thought of even touching them caused the bile in his stomach to rise. He stepped around the body and retrieved the shovel from where it had landed. He grabbed another off the wall. Spence found a claw hammer and stuffed it into his belt. There might be something more formidable he hadn't found yet but they had stayed here too long already. He was surprised no one seemed to have heard the fight and come running. There was no reason to push their luck.

He tossed the second shovel to Scott when he joined them.

"Haven't seen a soul," Scott told him. "Maybe they all went home for the night. It's pretty late."

Spence shrugged. "We find Phil and Maria and we go. Let's hope Phil still has his keys with him."

"I know where mine are." Amanda's voice was flat, timid. She did not look at them when she spoke. "In my pocketbook. Third floor servants' bathroom. I'm pretty sure I can find my way there."

Spence looked at Scott. "I'd rather have two chances than one," Scott told him with a shrug.

Spence most certainly did not want to wander around the inside of Greystone. But since they had to go back inside the house anyway… "If we don't find Phil and Maria right away we'll try the third floor for Amanda's keys. But *only* if we don't find them first."

Amanda neither agreed nor disagreed. She simply stood between them, eyes on the ground.

Scott placed his hands on her shoulders. "Are you sure you're up to this?"

Amanda's eyes went back to the corpse on the ground behind them. She sniffled and wiped her eyes and nose. "Let's just go," she choked.

Spence made sure Scott was ready before he made his way to the tree between the barn and the house. He could see one side of the mask room from here but there was no sign of Phil or Maria. He waited for the others to join him before he raced across the grass. He placed his back against the house to the right of the mask room windows. Spence swallowed and peeked inside.

The room was deserted. The fire in the fireplace was down to glowing embers. Several glasses stood on tables and the fireplace mantle. Some still contained the dregs of wine or champagne. Most were empty. His eyes lingered on the broken two-way mirror through which he had seen Phil and Marcus kneeling on the Oriental rug. Spence motioned for Scott and Amanda to join him.

"Room's empty. The party either broke up or moved. I don't see Phil or Maria in there."

"They could be anywhere," Scott said.

"Yeah. They might have been taken into that basement room."

Amanda shook her head emphatically. "I'm not going back in there. No way. I can't. Please don't make me."

"Let's see about getting inside first. Marcus and I found an open window around the front. And there's that side door we came out of before."

"It'll be locked," Amanda told him. "Unless we get lucky and Palmer is on a smoke break, that won't be an option."

"One thing at a time." Spence looked again inside the mask room. No one had presented themselves. He made for the side of the house. The side door was closed and Palmer was not present. Spence swore. He motioned the others to join him.

When they did Amanda asked, "Did you notice anything about the mask room?"

Spence looked at Scott before he answered. "Lots of empty glasses, the hole in that two-way mirror. Why?"

Amanda swallowed. "It was the first thing I noticed when I looked." She paused, took a deep breath. "The masks are gone."

****

There were at least thirty people in the procession. Phil was right in the middle of the line. A man he had heard referred to as Mr. Stanley had his fingers wrapped around Phil's upper arm. When Phil slowed his pace Stanley would yank hard enough to cause Phil to stumble. He even tried to drop to his knees once, but the man was stronger than he looked. Not only did he prevent Phil from falling, he did not even break his stride. Phil could feel the bruise beginning to rise from beneath the man's grip. He would have cursed him if he thought it would do any good. If Stanley could be provoked into letting go of his arm for even a moment Phil would run as fast as his legs would take him. But Stanley did not release him, didn't even shift his grip. Phil continued to drag his feet but his new captor would have none of it.

The worst part was Phil did not even know what the man looked like. He had been dragged from the room by the nephew, the one who had carried Maria's body back inside Greystone. The nephew tossed Phil into a dark room where both time and sound did not exist. Phil had found a wall and used it to leverage himself to his feet. In the darkness he bumped into several pieces of furniture and eventually wound up flat on his back. The next time the door opened there was a man at the threshold wearing one of the masks from the mask room wall. The thing was hideous. Its cheeks were full, its lips pulled back in a grotesque smile, its nose elongated. The masked man who would eventually be named as Stanley by another man in an equally hideous mask grabbed Phil and hauled him to his feet.

They had filed out the front door of Greystone Manor. The people who drank and gossiped and watched him and Marcus with impassive eyes were waiting. All were masked except the two Morley brothers. Phil had scanned their outfits looking for the butler and the nephew. He spotted neither but in the darkness it was likely he had simply missed them. He had scores to settle with both of them. If the opportunity presented itself—and if Stanley would just relax his grip a little—Phil might be able to give them a parting gift before he ran for his car.

The procession of masks made its way down the driveway and onto Aldebaran Road. On the opposite side stood the open field where, once upon a time, he, Marcus, and Vic had gotten lost. The inhabitants of Denham crossed the street and walked into the field. The wild grass, tall in his memory, had been trimmed recently, judging by the smell that reached his nostrils. It was still knee-high. The fallen blades provided a soft cushion beneath his sneakers.

The field was complete darkness. No one carried a flashlight, no one used their phone as a light source. The moon was gone from the sky. Yet no one broke stride. Whatever their destination they seemed to know the route by memory.

The hill sloped down gently ahead of them. Phil's sneakers slipped a bit on the damp grass. Stanley was there to make sure he did not fall. His fingers dug into the flesh of Phil's arm. Phil squealed and pulled back. Stanley pulled, too. Phil's feet left the ground but only momentarily. He skidded on the grass but Stanley held him upright.

"When I get out of this I'm gonna break your fucking neck."

Stanley did not reply. The mask hid any hint of reaction to Phil's threat. The man simply continued to walk and drag Phil alongside him.

At the bottom of the hill the ground levelled and remained that way as far as Phil could see in any direction. He might have come this way that night they got lost. He might even be standing on the spot where Vic sat on the ground and drew his map to try to figure out where they were. Then again that spot could be a mile away. There was no way to know.

The masked people continued to walk for several more minutes. At last they stopped. Phil could see they were breaking into two groups, each one walking in the opposite direction from the other and forming something of a circle. When Stanley forced him forward Phil caught sight of what stood in the center.

A thick pole had been driven into the ground. Seated around it, with their backs to it, were four bodies. The nearest one looked like the elderly man who had chased after his brother and Spence. The old bastard's head hung to the side at an impossible angle. Phil could not see the other three from his current position. All four sat on a bed of what looked like hay.

Standing on either side of the pole were the Morley brothers. Neither wore a mask although their expressions were as blank. One of them—Phil could not tell them apart—motioned for Stanley to bring him forward. *Another one for the fire.* Phil tore his arm loose from Stanley's grip. The man's fingernails raked across the skin of his arm. Phil barely noticed. He ran as fast as he was able with his arms bound behind him.

"Mr. Stanley, restrain him!" one of the Morleys shouted.

Something very large and very heavy struck Phil behind his knees. He sprawled onto the ground and skidded several feet. When he finally came to a stop he turned over and tried to get back on his feet. Stanley rose from the ground where he had landed after he tackled Phil. His mask was gone. His face was twisted with rage. He advanced on Phil.

Phil tried to kick him. His foot skipped off the side of Stanley's thigh and Stanley had him. His hand closed around Phil's arm and he lifted him clear off the ground.

"Try that again, you little bastard," he hissed through clenched teeth. His breath stunk of bourbon and cigars.

"Leave him unharmed, Mr. Stanley," one of the Morleys commanded.

Stanley lowered Phil to the ground. His expression was a mix of anger, embarrassment, and disappointment. "Of course, my Lords." His hand squeezed Phil's arm with enough force Phil imagined he could hear the bones splintering. He grunted his pain. Stanley dragged him back the way they had come. The man bent and retrieved his mask from the ground and returned it to his face.

Phil caught sight of the body seated next to the elderly man's. The pain in his arm was driven instantly from his mind. "Keith!" He shrieked his brother's name several times. Keith neither moved nor looked his way. His eyes stared blankly at the ground.

Phil had no memory of what happened next. He saw his brother, tried to move in his direction; when his mind returned to reality he was lying on his stomach. Someone had hold of his ankle and was dragging him across the wet grass, away from the bodies propped against the pole. His face was wet, whether from tears or the grass or a combination of both.

"Keith, no." His voice was barely a whisper. He caught a glimpse of the two other bodies and recognized them as Maria and Palmer. His eyes returned to his brother. "Jesus, no, please."

Stanley continued to drag Phil across the wet grass. He stopped in front of the Morleys and released his grip. "Apologies, my Lords," Phil heard him say. There seemed no reply. Stanley's hands clamped down on Phil's shoulders and he hauled him to his knees.

From this angle the thick pole obscured Keith's body, rendering it nothing more than a dark lump of shadow.

"Where is Exton?" one of the Morleys asked.

"He should be here momentarily, William. Patience, dear brother," the other answered.

"We can start without him," William remarked. "Ms. Arnold, if you would?"

A rather large woman, her face hidden by another grotesque mask, separated herself from the group. She walked slowly, her stride betraying a slight limp, toward the pole and the bodies. From within her coat she produced a slender kitchen lighter. She knelt between the elderly corpse and Maria's. She looked back over her shoulder. She must have received the signal she wanted because her next move was to click the lighter to life and hold it to the straw at the base of the pole.

Phil did not move at all.

CHAPTER TWENTY

A Temporary Reprieve

The side door was indeed locked. Spence considered breaking one of the panes and reaching in to unlock it. He remembered Marcus's attempt and its result and just as quickly he discarded the idea. No one inside Greystone knew they were here. They might soon enough but there was no reason to give them a warning. He checked the front of the house and was careful to avoid looking at the parking area. He had no wish to see Katie's Cruze sitting in its spot. No one was in evidence. He advanced slowly and stayed low. The front deck was deserted, the front doors closed. Spence made his way to the window through which Marcus had disappeared. The window was still open.

His two companions were crouched behind him. He knelt down and leaned into them. "This is the way in. We go in quiet, find Phil and Maria, and get back out. If we come across anybody…" He let his voice trail off. He hefted the shovel and pulled up his shirt to show them the hammer stuffed into his belt. It was nonsense, of course. There were a couple dozen people in there, at least. If they were as strong as that old asshole from the secret passage two shovels and a claw hammer weren't going to do jack shit. "We work with what we've got," he said to them as much as to himself. "Ready?"

"Not remotely," Scott whispered.

Amanda said nothing.

Spence stood and looked through the open window. As before he could see nothing of the room on the other side. Jacoby had grabbed Marcus as soon as he made it through. If that asshole was still there, waiting for him... It was awkward climbing through the window while maintaining his hold on the shovel. He did it but also managed to bang his elbow on the window frame. He suppressed a yelp. He felt carpet beneath his feet, smelled the dust in the air. Spence braced himself. He held the shovel at the ready. No one grabbed for him. The room was as silent as a crypt. "Clear."

Scott handed him the shovel before he climbed through. Then he reached back and helped Amanda.

"Any idea where we are?" Spence asked as he handed the shovel back to Scott. He could not see much of Amanda, but he got the impression she was shaking her head.

"Not really, no," she replied. "I don't think I've been in this section of the house.

"Door's over there, I think," Scott offered. "The wall opposite the window."

Spence crossed the room slowly. He held the shovel out in front of him at knee-height. He found a few pieces of furniture to either side of him but the path forward seemed free of obstacles. It took him only a moment to find the door.

"Got it. Walk straight ahead. Don't trip over anything." He did not wait. He turned the doorknob. A sliver of light illuminated his face. On the other side of the door was a hallway. He spotted more portraits along the walls; they appeared to be the wives of Henry VIII. When Scott and Amanda reached him, he opened the door a further few inches. "Hallway's clear. I think we go right, in the direction of the front doors."

"There are stairs in the foyer that go to the upper floors. My keys are up there"

"How do we get to the cellar?"

"Yeah, we didn't take the conventional route last time," Scott added.

"I'm not exactly sure," she told them, "and I'm not going back down there so you can bag that idea right now."

Spence did not reply. He still felt the cellar was the most likely place to find Phil and Maria. If Amanda wanted to stay up here, or even go after her keys on her own, he wouldn't stop her. He exited the room. Both ends of the hallway were free of people. Spence turned right. He could see the foyer ahead. More paintings on the walls, even a few tapestries. He heard no one, saw no one. It occurred to him he hadn't heard a sound since he came inside.

That's because it's a fucking trap, you idiot, seventeen-year-old Spence said helpfully. *They're all in one of the rooms, maybe even the basement. When you go down there they'll jump out and yell* "Surprise!" *like a bunch of assholes and then you're fucked. Amanda's the smart one. She'll find her keys and drive out of here while you and Scotty-boy get carved up by the natives.*

The idea seemed both plausible and preposterous at the same time. *They don't need to take us by surprise*, Spence told his younger self. *They've been doing just fine all night without it.* Seventeen-year-old Spence had no reply to that.

The foyer was large, cavernous. The staircase that led to the second level was wide and made of hand-carved wood. Two hallways led deeper inside the house on either side of the stairs. Another hallway continued straight ahead of them. No one leaped at them from any direction.

"Is this where we part company?" Spence asked.

Amanda's eyes were glued to the staircase. "I have to go up there."

"Hey, Spence, man, we can't let her go alone." Scott hefted the shovel and his eyes moved from hallway to hallway. "And who's to say Phil and Maria aren't up there? Upstairs is just as easy as downstairs. And this way she can get her keys and then we'll have a way out of here."

If that asshole in the 442 doesn't run us off the road, too. Yet he could not fault Scott's logic, even if his motive was transparent. "I guess. Okay, we'll try for your keys first. But if we don't find our friends up there I'm heading downstairs. That's the deal."

"Cool," Scott replied.

Amanda said nothing. She reached the base of the stairs and looked up. She placed her hand on the wood rail but just as quickly pulled it back. Her first step was tentative. Her eyes remained glued to the second floor landing. It took several steps before she picked up the pace.

Spence walked around her and took the lead. He held the shovel at the ready. No one presented themselves. At the top he scanned the hallways in either direction and came up empty. "It's clear," he whispered.

When Amanda reached the landing she turned purposefully to her left. "This way. The stairs to the third floor are over here."

They were. The staircase to the third floor was not as wide or as elaborate as the one they had just ascended. The banister was still hand-carved wood, though, and the carpet was soft and thick.

They moved slowly, too slowly for Spence's taste. By the time he reached the third-floor landing Amanda and Scott were only halfway up the steps. He took the opportunity to scan his surroundings. More hallways leading in different directions, more portraits displayed on the walls, more doors than he could count. No one was in sight nor could he hear anything.

"Good so far," he whispered to them when they joined him. "Where to?"

Amanda nodded her head toward the hallway on the left and whispered, "Third door down, I think."

The third door turned out to be a guest bedroom. It was larger than Spence's apartment. The bed looked big enough to sleep five people. Ornate end tables and dressers filled out the room. There were more paintings on the walls. They looked like landscapes but the artist had been overly fond of the color yellow.

Fields of grass that should have been green were instead ochre. Even the skies were sickly yellow orange. For reasons Spence could not begin to identify the color scheme of the paintings made the gooseflesh rise on his arms.

'This doesn't look like a staff bathroom," Scott whispered.

"It's one of these doors," Amanda told him.

Scott looked down the hallway. "There are seven more. Remember the right one before someone decides to come up here and call it a night."

Amanda stepped out of the room. Spence lingered long enough to examine the paintings one last time before he followed her.

"This one looks familiar," she announced. She pointed to a portrait on the wall. "I remember this painting." She opened the door and peeked inside. "Bingo."

Spence glanced inside the room. It was large although not as large as the bedroom. He could just about squeeze his apartment in there. Amanda was on the far side of the room where she opened a floor-to-ceiling cabinet. She emerged a moment later with her pocketbook. She reached inside, pulled her keys triumphantly from its innards. "Got 'em."

"Let's get outta here," Scott suggested. His voice was still a whisper but he had increased the volume a few decibels. The appearance of Amanda's car keys seemed to have emboldened him.

"We still have to find Phil and Maria," Spence reminded him.

Scott's face fell. "We can come back with the cops. Turn this whole fucking house upside down until we find them. That's the smart move."

What if they're dead by the time we get back? he wanted to ask. Instead, he said, "You go. I'm gonna check out the rest of the rooms up here." He started for the next door.

"Son of a bitch," he heard Scott mutter.

Spence reached the next door. He had his hand on the handle when Scott and Amanda joined him. "Thought you were going," he whispered.

"I'm not going alone," Amanda whispered back. She had both hands on Scott's shoulders. Her keyring dangled from one finger.

"Just hurry," Scott added.

Spence nodded. There was no point in waiting. He turned the handle.

The door opposite theirs opened. Martin Jacoby had been wiping his arm across his chin. He froze. So did Spence and Scott. Amanda gasped and threw herself against the wall to put as much distance between them as possible.

Jacoby had emerged from yet another bedroom. Exton stood at the foot of the bed. He had been buttoning his shirt but he likewise froze when he saw them.

"Holy shit," Jacoby remarked. His tone was conversational. He smiled. "And here I thought you got away. It really *is* my lucky night, Exton."

Scott swung the shovel. Jacoby ducked under it and grabbed for Amanda. She screamed. Her arms flailed against him, striking several times but without much strength. She screamed, "*No!*" every time her fists struck him.

Spence shoved him with the handle of his shovel. Jacoby backed up a few steps but he had a solid grip on Amanda's arm. He swung her around until she stood between them.

Exton emerged from the room so quickly he crashed into Scott. The shovel flew from Scott's hands and skittered across the floor. Exton grabbed Scott's arms and hurled him the length of the hallway. Scott landed with a grunt and rolled along the floor until he hit the wall.

Spence swung his shovel and felt the satisfying shudder in his arms when it connected with the back of Exton's head. The butler staggered forward, his hand raised to protect the wounded area. Spence hit him again, this time on the side of his head. Pink ooze flew and spattered the walls and portraits and Spence. Exton lurched away, both hands protecting his head. More of the pink stuff dripped from between his fingers.

He had managed to put ten feet between him and Spence. He placed his back to the wall and examined his hands. Even at a distance Spence could see they were covered with the pink fluid. Exton's eyes were wide, incredulous. His mouth worked but no sound escaped him.

Beyond him Scott pulled himself to his feet. He charged Exton and succeeded in wrapping his arms around the butler's midsection. Scott heaved and backpedaled toward the end of the hallway. He was off-balance and they made it nearly to the end before they went down in a tangle of arms and legs.

"Scott!" Spence could hear his friend swearing and struggling to free himself. Spence ran after them.

Scott succeeded in separating himself from Exton. He was first to regain his feet. He stumbled and his elbow cracked the glass of the window behind him. Exton lunged at him. He threw a haymaker that caught Scott across his jaw. Scott's feet left the floor. The window glass exploded and Scott disappeared through it.

"No!" Spence shot past Exton and reached the window. He could see little outside. The overhang of the front deck blocked his view of the yard below. Broken glass littered the overhang's roof; it sparkled in the light spilling from the hallway behind him.

"I'm going to take her to their Lordships," Exton was saying from somewhere behind Spence. "This one is all yours. Do with him as you will."

"Save some of her for me, will ya?" Jacoby replied.

Spence called to his friend but Scott made no reply. It was as if he had vanished into the darkness below. "Jesus, don't be dead, don't be dead, don't be dead." It was at that moment Spence became aware of the conversation taking place behind him. He turned in time to see Exton wrestle Amanda toward the staircase.

Jacoby squared his shoulders and smiled at Spence. "The little chickie got a, what do you call it, a temporary reprieve? I think that's it. If I had known you morons were gonna show up I wouldn't have wasted my load on Exton. Don't worry, though. I'm sure for her I'll be able to manage again in a few minutes."

"Manage *this*," Spence told him. He charged Jacoby and swung the shovel.

Jacoby ducked under the first swing. He backpedaled and avoided the second. The third swing struck the wall behind him. Plaster flew and the shovel snapped at the handle. Spence spun much as he did in the barn. He intended to bury the broken end in Jacoby's head. Jacoby ducked and shoved Spence with both hands.

Spence's feet went out from under him. He hit the floor and gasped for breath. He turned onto his stomach and spied Scott's shovel near the end of the hallway.

Jacoby's arm snaked around Spence's neck; his free hand pressed against the back of Spence's head. "Dude, seriously, that's all you got? I seen your picture in the paper a few times. I think we even shared the police blotter once or twice. I thought you were some kinda badass."

Spence found he had no leverage. Jacoby's grip felt like an iron vice. He sucked in a breath when Jacoby shifted his grip. The stars that had begun to sparkle at the corners of his vision dimmed but did not wink out entirely. Spence clawed at Jacoby's hands, his arm, but could not move them.

He let go with his left hand and threw it behind him. He was aiming for Jacoby's groin but his fist, when it did connect, glanced off the man's thigh.

"No, no, no. That was very naughty." He shifted his position again. His arm and hand applied even more pressure.

Spence's world started to darken. Both hands were clamped to Jacoby's arm but he could not move it. He became aware of Jacoby's voice in his ear. He could feel the man's breath.

"After you're dead I'm gonna rape the shit out of your corpse. Then it'll be the chickie's turn. Take that down with you."

Spence snapped his head in the direction of the voice. He felt and heard the satisfying *crunch* as Jacoby's nose gave way. The arm around his neck was gone. Spence collapsed forward and barely had the presence of mind to get his hands under him before he crashed to the floor. He gulped air and made a funny whooping sound as he did. Spence blinked several times; the stars winked happily back at him.

"By dose! You broke by fucking dose!"

Spence placed his hand on the wall and used it to leverage himself to his feet. He sagged against the wall, still sucking air. Jacoby leaned against the opposite wall. One hand covered his nose. Blood—*red* blood--gushed from between his fingers. It stained his shirt and jeans, the hardwood and the strip of carpet down the middle. It was the color of the blood that surprised Spence the most. After the others he had expected it to be the same milky-pink. Jacoby blinked tears from his eyes. The blood continued to seep between his fingers.

Spence pulled the hammer from his belt. Jacoby looked at it dumbly. Spence buried the claw in Jacoby's head. It produced a dull, wet sound when it broke through skin and skull. Blood flew from the wound; it painted the wall, the nearest portraits, and Spence himself. Jacoby froze. His expression was that of a man who had just witnessed a magic trick that left him utterly baffled. *How the hell did you manage that?* his eyes asked.

His free hand went to the hammer. His fingers wrapped themselves around the handle. They slipped on the blood and his arm fell to his side. The hammer remained in its place. Jacoby stared at Spence. "Dat was fucking weird, man." Then he slid down the wall until he seated himself on the floor. His expression never changed.

Spence dropped back to his knees. He was still gulping air, still trying to rid his vision of the stars that winked and blinked at him. It was several minutes more before he felt steady enough to push himself to his feet.

****

Exton apparently tired of her struggles. When they reached the second floor landing he suddenly hurled her the rest of the way down. Amanda hit every step, felt every impact. When she reached the bottom her momentum carried her across the hardwood of the foyer. She let out the last of several yelps when she came to a stop. Her back, her arms and legs, everything hurt. She managed to get her hands under her.

Before she could do more Exton reached her. His hand grasped the back of her collar and suddenly she was no longer on the floor. Her feet dangled in the air for several moments before she felt them touch the floor.

"*Walk*, Ms. Regan." His voice was stern, angry. It was the first time she heard anything approximating emotion from him. "Do not force me to drag you." His hand was still on the back of her neck. He shoved her toward the door.

Amanda opened the door and stepped out onto the deck. She whirled and brought up her arm. It connected with his and bounced off. In return Exton yanked her back, nearly off her feet.

"What happened upstairs was most unpleasant. I am afraid my patience is exhausted. Do not test me again."

She saw the pinkish fluid caked on the side and back of his head. It stained his uniform and several drops had landed on her shirt and hands. His eyes were glossy, his pupils dilated.

"Walk."

"Mr. Exton, please, let me go. I won't tell anyone what happened tonight. I swear! I'll leave right now and you'll never see me again! Just let me go!"

He guided her down the front steps.

She pleaded her case while he prodded her toward the driveway entrance. Amanda's voice died when she saw caught a glimpse of Scott. He lay flat on his back to the side of the front deck. One arm was raised toward the broken window on the third floor as if he were trying to touch it.

"Scott! Scott! Help me!"

His head tilted back at the sound of her shout. His eyes found hers. He mumbled something. It took several attempts but at last he managed to roll onto his stomach. "Hey. Hey, you." His words were slurred. He stretched his arm in her direction. "Leggo her." His eyes rolled up and he lay still.

Her first instinct was to run to him. She did try but Exton's hand was still on the back of her neck and he yanked her back roughly. Amanda squealed and just managed to get her feet under her before she fell. "Please, we have to see if he's okay," she pleaded.

Exton ignored her.

Amanda brought her foot down atop his with as much force as she could muster. At the same moment she threw her elbow into Exton's midsection. He *humphed* and doubled over and she was free. Amanda bolted for Scott. She knelt next to him and patted his cheeks. "Come on, Scott, wake up! I need you! *Spence* needs you! Snap out of it!"

Scott groaned.

Rough hands clamped down on Amanda's shoulders. She had time to scream before she was airborne. Exton had thrown her in the direction of the driveway. When she landed on the grass the breath exploded from her and her momentum carried her several more feet. She had enough time to get her hands and knees under her before Exton reached her.

He hauled her roughly to her feet. "You are a very slow learner, Ms. Regan. One more attempt such as that and I will be forced to discipline you most severely." He shoved her forward, one hand welded to her shoulder.

"Fuck you!" Amanda shouted at him. "Just wait, Exton. You'll get yours. I fucking promise you!"

His only response to her threat was a smile.

They made it to the end of the driveway. Amanda expected him to force her to the right, down Aldebaran Road. Instead he aimed her across the street to the empty field. It was a sea of darkness as far as Amanda could see.

He's going to kill me and bury me in that field, along with everyone else he's killed over the years. There's probably an army of corpses under that dirt. She acted without thinking. She slammed her fist into his groin. Exton grunted and doubled over. For a second she was free. Amanda took two strides back the way she had come.

Exton's hand clamped down on her wrist. She screamed when she felt the bones crack. He yanked her back, off her feet. Amanda sprawled onto the dirt road. Exton advanced on her. She pushed herself back as quickly as she was able but she was not fast enough.

"You were fairly warned. Stand, Ms. Regan." His voice quivered. His eyes bulged and a large vein pulsed inside his forehead. He leaned slightly forward, one hand protecting his groin. "I said *stand.*"

Amanda got her good hand under her and pushed herself to her knees. "Please, I'm sorry! Please don't hurt me!"

She did not even see the backhand coming. After it hit she saw nothing at all.

CHAPTER TWENTY-ONE

Spence found Jacoby's keys poking out the top pocket of his jeans. He pulled them loose, regarded them. Two were worn to the point of being almost perfectly smooth. Their shape indicated they belonged to the Olds in the driveway. Spence tossed them into the air and caught them. "Thanks, fuckhead." His voice sounded strange, as if it belonged to a life-long chain smoker. Spence coughed several times to clear it.

He pushed himself to his feet. His legs trembled a bit, and his throat hurt like hell. He eyed the shovel Scott dropped and made his way to it. His legs threatened collapse when he bent to retrieve the shovel but he willed them to keep him upright. He used it for support when he returned to Jacoby's side. Spence considered the hammer. It remained buried in the dead man's skull. He wanted to take it; God knew he might need it again. He suspected he would. But he found he could not bring himself to touch it. His hand got within three inches of the handle before he pulled back. He swallowed, then spat on the floor.

He made it three steps toward the stairs when he saw Amanda's pocketbook on the floor. Beside it were her car keys. Spence rummaged through her pocketbook. He came up with a cigarette lighter; it was the only thing he could find that might be remotely useful. *Burn this whole fucking place down*, he thought. He scooped up the keys and stuffed them into his pocket.

The stairs he navigated slowly. His legs still trembled, and he had to keep one hand on the railing. He paused at the second-floor landing to catch his breath. His legs still shook but the tremors were beginning to subside. When he reached the foyer he paused and willed his heart to slow its pace. The blood was pounding in his ears so loudly he thought it would give away his position. It was at that moment he realized the house was quiet. He heard nothing but the pounding in his ears and his heart thundering within his chest. *Not only are you inside Greystone Manor, it looks like you have the place all to yourself. This really is a night of firsts!* And all he wanted to do was get outside.

The front doors were open. A slight, cold breeze wafted through the foyer. It felt good on his skin and drove the last of the fog from his head. Spence breathed deeply, slowly. His heart began to slow and the sound of his blood receded in his ears. He closed his eyes and let the cold breeze finish its work. After several moments he felt better. He opened his eyes and made for the door.

At first he saw no one. When he made it down the steps to the lawn his eyes fell on Scott. He lay on the lawn surrounded by broken glass. It glittered in the light spilling from some of the windows. "Jesus!" Spence raced to his friend's side. He knelt next to him and placed his hand on Scott's back. "Scott! Scotty! Wake up, man. Tell me you're still alive."

Scott cooperated with a groan.

Spence released a breath he was unaware he was holding and patted his friend on the back. "Come on, man, do that again. Wake up, brother. Wake up!"

Scott groaned again. He rolled onto his back. His eyelids fluttered and opened. "Ow."

Spence giggled. "Jesus, fuck, you scared the shit out of me! You okay?"

Scott's eyes focused on his. "Do I look okay? I just got bounced out a fucking third floor window."

"Can you stand? Can you move?" Spence didn't know much about first aid but he knew enough not to try to move his friend. *Please be okay, please be okay, please be okay.*

"My back feels fucking weird. I can move my toes, though. That's a good sign, right?" He placed both hands upon the grass and pushed himself into a seated position. "Ow."

"You said that already."

Scott leaned to his side and looked at Greystone manor's front doors. "Where's the asshole who threw me through the window?"

Spence swallowed. Against his will his eyes moved to the broken window on the third floor. "Don't worry about him."

"Good." It was the only thing he said about the implication. He extended his hand. "A little help?"

"You sure?"

Scott nodded. Spence grasped his friend's hand and lifted him to his feet as gingerly as possible. "Ow a third time." He flexed his back and shoulders, lifted his feet one at a time like a military trainee marching in place. "Back still feels weird but I don't think anything's broken."

"It's your lucky night."

"Yeah, I oughta play all the lotteries."

Spence sobered. "Exton grabbed Amanda. I don't know where they went."

"He dragged her across the street," Scott told him. "I saw them. I mean, I think I did." He shrugged, winced at the pain.

"Toward the field?"

"Yeah."

Spence took a single step toward the driveway. He stopped, turned. He fished Amanda's keys from his pocket and tossed them to Scott. "Think you can drive?"

"Yeah. Why? Where am I going?"

"To get help. Those are Amanda's keys. I don't remember what kind of car she said she has. Hit the fob to see which one is hers and then take it to the cops."

"Fuck that noise. I'm going with you." He held up his hand. "And you're not stopping me."

Spence knew his friend well enough not to argue. Without another word he turned again and made for the driveway. The gravel crunched beneath his feet and this time he did not care if he made noise. They walked around the gate and across the dirt road and entered the field. Spence's feet slipped a few times on the wet grass. He heard a muffled grunt of pain from Scott as his friend tried to keep his balance.

They had penetrated perhaps twenty feet into the open field before Scott pointed a bit to their right. "Something's cooking. Look."

The slope of the hill hid the fire, but Spence could see the flickering light easily enough. "Bonfire probably." They changed direction.

After several more minutes they crested the hill. Spence immediately ducked and then hit the dirt. Scott mimicked him but not as quickly. He grunted again before he was able to lower himself onto his stomach.

Below them there was indeed a bonfire. The flames licked the sky and turned it orange. Several people stood in a wide circle around the fire.

"Fucking devil worshippers," Scott murmured. "Now they're wearing masks. This is some *Eyes Wide Shut* shit right here."

"Say that five times fast."

"Fuck off," Scott replied with a grin.

Spence's eyes found their target. At the bottom of the hill Exton dragged Amanda toward the fire. Spence's breath caught in his throat. *Holy fuck he's gonna burn her alive!* His first thought was to charge down the hill. He didn't even have time to get to his feet before he realized he was wrong. Exton did not toss Amanda into the bonfire. Some of the people stepped back and Exton threw Amanda to the ground beside someone who knelt perhaps ten feet from the blaze. The fire made a haze of the scene but it looked like Amanda sprang to her feet and tried to run. Exton slammed his fist into the side of her head and the woman dropped to the ground and didn't move again.

"Son of a bitch!" Scott's hands balled into fists. "He fucking levelled her! Jesus, Spence, I think they're gonna throw her into the fire!"

Spence did not offer comment mostly because he believed his friend was right. Instead, he said, "I think I see Phil. Down there, next to Amanda. See the guy on his knees? It might be him. I don't see Maria anywhere, though."

Scott's eyes narrowed. His hand covered his mouth. "Jesus H. Christ." His voice was barely a whisper. His hand slid slowly down his chin. "They're gonna kill them both."

Spence's lips compressed into a thin line. *He's right, you know*, his younger self agreed. *Those devil-worshipping assholes are about to burn Phil alive. And you're lying down up here in the bleachers with a nice view of the whole show.* "No. They're not." He turned toward his friend. "I have Jacoby's keys. I'll take the 442 down there, drive it right through their fucking circle, get them to scatter. You follow in Amanda's car. Get her and Phil and then take off. I'll try to keep the rest of them off you until you're clear."

Scott's expression gave away his opinion of Spence's plan.

"What? You have something better?"

"Spence, this grass is wet. That piece of shit is gonna fishtail all over the place. Those old muscle cars were worthless on wet surfaces. Rear wheel drive and all the weight's in the front. Going down this hill at full speed you'll be lucky if you don't flip the thing a dozen times."

Spence shrugged. "My question stands."

Scott grabbed a handful of grass and tore it from the ground. He held it in front of Spence's face as if it were evidence in a courtroom. "This shit is too wet. That's a steep slope. I'm telling you, you won't get anywhere near them. They'll see and hear you coming way before you get there. And getting yourself killed won't help Phil. We need to think this through."

Spence could no longer see Phil or Amanda. The circle of people had closed again. The bonfire burned merrily in the center of the circle. He eyed the slope to his left. It was gentler than the one he and Scott occupied. *It'll take longer to get to them. They'll have plenty of time to scatter. Or to throw Phil onto that bonfire.* "Yeah, but I have a better chance of making it there."

"Huh?"

Spence shook his head. "Doesn't matter. If you have a better plan I'm all ears. If not, let's get back to the cars.

Scott started to protest.

Spence started to stand.

That was when night became day.

****

"Hey, you okay? Lady, are you all right? Wake up!"

Amanda's head throbbed. She was both cold and warm. Light danced and flickered in the darkness. She wanted nothing more than to allow that darkness to envelop her. There was peace within its folds, the promise of the end of all her pain and, yes, suffering. But she was not alone. There was someone nearby. Their voice was intrusive, urgent. Against her will Amanda opened her eyes.

It came back to her all at once. She pushed herself onto her knees and screamed. A bolt of lightning lanced up her arm from her wrist. Amanda's free hand immediately wrapped itself around her shattered wrist. A second scream tried to rise in her throat but she gasped and willed it back down.

She became aware of the crackling of the fire. She had seen it on the way down the hill. She had even tried to put it between her and Exton when he threw her to the ground. She hadn't made it more than a step or two before her world went dark. Not that she had much of a plan even if she had made it. There were too many people standing around the fire, too many hands that could grab her, too many feet that could chase her. These were, of course, the same people with whom she had rubbed shoulders and served drinks earlier in the evening. Their faces were covered with the masks from the mask room but she recognized some of the outfits. She wasn't in much condition to run anyway, and certainly not after Exton dropped the hammer on her. Her head still rang and she could add a broken wrist to the night's tally.

"Lady, snap out of it," the nearby voice implored her.

Amanda looked to her right. "You're Phil."

Phil's brow wrinkled. "How'd you know that?"

"We were looking for you." She lowered her voice although no one seemed to be paying them any mind. "Spence and Scott."

"They're alive?"

"Last I saw them."

Phil swallowed. His eyes went to the fire. Tears welled up and sparkled in the flickering light. "My brother's in there." His voice was utterly without emotion.

Amanda's mouth opened, closed. Against her will her eyes moved to the bonfire. There were several bodies at the base of the pole. She could not tell how many; four, maybe five. The flames blurred them until they became a single, black mass. Small bits of ash and sparks drifted into the night sky. The smoke was thick but thankfully rose into the air and not into her nostrils. It seemed unaffected by the slight breeze that felt so cold against her skin. She raised her good hand to her mouth. Tears spilled down her cheeks.

"They burned him." Phil's voice remained flat. He did not look at her. "Maria, too. Marcus's wife. She's in there."

Amanda whimpered through her hand. Her tears flowed freely now. She found she could not turn away from the flames or the indistinguishable bodies therein. *You're next.* The thought hit her harder than Exton's fist. *Why else would they bring you down here? They're gonna throw you onto that fire and you're gonna burn until no one can tell you apart from Phil's brother or Maria.*

The image snapped the world back into focus. Amanda's eyes whipped about in every direction. The people were gathered close. One of them stood no more than a foot or two behind her. They were chanting something in a language she had never heard. It was low key, guttural. It raised the gooseflesh on her arms.

Her eyes settled on the two Morley brothers. They stood with their backs to the circle, facing another part of the open field. Amanda could see little detail beyond them. The field seemed empty, devoid of trees, people, anything at all. The two old monsters chanted along with their neighbors, their arms raised, their heads thrown back.

She would have to skirt the edges of the bonfire. If she moved quickly enough she thought she could reach them before anyone could grab her. Knock one of them down and grab the other. Use him to get her and Phil clear. If the neighbors tested her she did not know if she was capable of actually hurting the old bastards but she thought she might. If that left her with only one Morley so be it; the neighbors would have learned just how far she was willing to go.

She moved as slowly as she could. She got one foot under her. She chanced a glance at the person behind her. It was a man although she didn't think she knew his name. He must have been on Katie's side of the room. She could not see his eyes but it appeared he was looking into the fire. His mask sported an elongated chin and high, sharp cheekbones. *Thirty feet between you and the two old bastards. Just be fast.* She placed her good hand on the ground, felt the wet grass. Amanda tensed.

The field filled with light. Amanda yelped and threw her arm in front of her eyes. The breeze, cold against her skin, became warm, almost hot. The early-autumn air filled with a thick, unpleasant odor that seemed to stick to her skin. Her stomach clenched; had there been anything left inside it she would have emptied it onto the ground. As it was she dry heaved several times. Her head began to swim in the old, pleasant way it once had on any given Saturday night back in West Philly. She would have toppled over but she got her hand under her just in time.

The breeze continued. The unpleasant stench became thicker until she found it difficult to breathe. She gasped for air. Stars sparkled beneath her closed eyelids. It was not until that moment she realized the world had gone silent. She could no longer hear the crackle of the fire. The men and women of Aldebaran Road had ceased their strange chant. She thought perhaps she had been struck deaf. Or was she already dead? *You're not dead. Not unless dead people can still feel pain from broken bones.* Amanda opened her eyes a crack.

Daylight had come. Or, rather, something approximating daylight. The color was wrong. The light and everything it touched was tinged yellow. She could feel the heat from the fire but the flames had become all but indistinguishable from the light. Even the bodies within the flames no longer appeared as black.

Amanda turned her eyes in the direction of the light. She saw she had been wrong. The night sky was still there, still dark. It existed around the edges of what appeared to be a hole in the air. On the other side of that hole the gentle slopes of the open field stretched nearly to the horizon. The tall grass that covered those hills was yellow as was the sky. In the far distance she spotted trees that bordered the hills. They were no more than dark shapes to her eyes but something about them struck her as odd, even obscene. *They're* wrong, she thought. No better word came to mind. *Trees don't look like that.*

The Morleys stood where she had last seen them. Their arms were still raised although they had lowered their heads and looked into the hole in the air.

Amanda scanned the people around her. No one moved. No one spoke. Nor did they appear to show any reaction to what had just occurred. They simply stood in place, as if sculpted that way.

Her eyes went to Phil. He was as frozen as those around them. Unlike the others, he at least showed signs of life. His mouth hung open; his eyes squinted into the new landscape that presented itself. His every muscle shook.

"His Majesty approaches!" one of the Morleys shouted. His voice was filled with excitement, even elation. He raised his arms even higher, a boxer who had just seen his opponent get the ten count.

Amanda looked more closely at the hole in the air. She caught sight of movement on one of the yellow hills. Someone *was* approaching, the old monster was right about that. The figure wore a robe the color of mustard. The robe's hood was raised and obscured the figure's face. Amanda did not know why but this brought to her a sense of relief. She had no wish to see what kind of man called that yellow place his home. The figure glided through the yellow grass until it stood perhaps twenty feet from the opening.

"Your Majesty." Both Morleys lowered themselves to their knees. The people around them mimicked the gesture.

The robed figure seemed to regard the people in the green world. He made no move at first, appeared simply to take in the sight before him. Slowly he raised his yellow hands to his hood and removed it from his head.

Amanda did not know what she expected to see beneath the hood, but it was not this. The scream she had prepared on instinct died in her throat.

CHAPTER TWENTY-TWO

One For the Road

Spence got his hands up just in time to avoid being blinded by the sudden light. He squinted through his fingers, certain a bomb had just gone off. He heard no explosion, and from what little he could see the circle of Aldebaran Road residents was still in place. It took several moments for the spots to leave his vision. He opened his eyes tentatively, then all the way when his vision adjusted. "Holy Mother of God."

The hole—there was no other word for it—was wide enough for two semis to pass through abreast. It was tall enough to accommodate all of Greystone Manor. On the other side fields of tall yellow grass stirred in a breeze beneath a yellow sky. The scene reminded him of the painting he spotted in the third-floor bedroom.

"Jesus, Spence, is that hell?" Scott's voice was soft, little more than a whisper.

The breeze moving the yellow grass reached the bonfire and fanned the flames. Several of the masked people in the circle shifted their feet. Some turned their heads away. The two nearest the hole, the Morley brothers, simply stood, their arms raised high.

"It's hell, isn't it? Jesus, Spence. All the shit we thought about this place is true! We need to get out of here right fucking now!" He placed his hand on his friend's arm.

Spence jumped at the contact. At last he pulled his eyes away from the scene at the bottom of the hill. "Phil's still down there. We can't leave without him. Amanda, too. And Maria could be there."

Scott swallowed. "Spence, that's a gateway to fucking *hell*, man! What are we gonna do about it? Forget the cops, we need a fucking priest! Maybe a lot of priests!"

"I'm not leaving Phil and Amanda down there." He pushed himself to his feet. He looked down the hill at the circle of people. He avoided looking into the hole in the air again. He started back the way they had come.

Mister Johnson stood no more than ten feet from him.

Spence's breath caught in his throat.

The big man's eyes were glazed and half-lidded. Pink, viscous fluid dribbled from his mouth and collected on his chin; his shirt was caked with it. His hands were balled into fists large enough to envelop Spence's head.

The giant took a lurching step toward him. His legs shook and he swayed. His arms spread out as if he were walking a tightrope. He teetered for a moment before he took another step.

Scott gasped from somewhere behind him. Spence heard his friend scramble to his feet. "Fucking guy's unkillable! Run for it!"

Scott shot past him. He gave Johnson a wide berth but it was not wide enough. A large hand descended and landed heavily on Scott's shoulder. Scott cried out and tumbled to the ground.

Spence tightened his grip on the shovel and he lunged at the giant. He landed a blow to the side of the big man's head. Johnson staggered back. Spence pulled back the shovel for another swing. At that moment he caught sight of the garden shears still imbedded in the back of the man's neck. Spence tossed away the shovel and threw himself at the giant.

His hands grasped the shears and he drove down with all his weight. He felt the blades sink deeper into the man's flesh. The giant grunted. His knees buckled but he somehow kept his feet under him. He turned, hands trying to grasp the man on his back. More pink blood frothed from his mouth. The grunt became a gurgle. Spence put all his weight into another thrust. The blades penetrated right up to the handles. This time the giant could not remain vertical. He landed hard on his knees. More blood spurted from the wound; it erupted from his mouth in a geyser of pink spray. He tumbled backwards.

Spence released his hold and tried to roll away. He nearly made it. The giant came down on Spence's left leg. Spence felt and heard bones break under the impact. He howled.

Scott was there suddenly. He planted his hands on Spence's arms and pulled. "I gotcha, bro. Grab onto me."

It felt like his arms would tear from their sockets before he could be freed from Johnson's bulk. The bones in his leg ground together and Spence screamed. Had he been capable of coherent speech he would have told Scott to stop. As it was he could do nothing but grunt through his clenched teeth.

Scott pulled him free and tumbled onto his back. The pressure on Spence's leg was suddenly gone. Both hands went to his shin. There was no bone poking through the skin as far as he could tell. He gritted his teeth as his hands probed the injured area. "Fuck, this hurts!"

Scott crawled to him. He looked at the injured leg. "You're lucky that fucker didn't land right on top of you. You okay?"

"Leg's busted," he said through clenched teeth. Then, "Is he dead?"

Scott looked at the giant for several moments before he answered, "If he ain't he's one hell of an actor. We got lucky."

"Yeah, I feel really fucking lucky. Did he get you?"

"Yeah. On the shoulder. Not much strength behind it, though. Still hurt like a son of a bitch. I think he was already on his way out when he came at us. I don't mind telling ya, I thought I was dead when I felt the punch."

Spence grunted. "Yeah, me too."

"Come on, let's get you out of here." Scott knelt and lifted Spence to his feet.

Spence barely stifled a scream. It came out as a whimper. The broken bones ground together with every movement. Scott placed Spence's arm around his shoulder and was moving back toward Greystone. With every step Spence renewed his effort not to scream again.

Negotiating their way past the driveway gate was tricky. Scott sidestepped it and Spence's foot dragged along the gravel. Spence grunted and the sound became another scream. He nearly passed out. "Try not to do that again."

"Suck it up, you pussy."

When they were past the gate Scott hauled him toward the driveway.

"We gotta go, Spence. We can't help Phil, not right now. We'll come back with a fucking army if we have to but we're leaving."

"You go. I told you I'm not leaving them down there and I meant it."

"Are you fucking crazy? I said we're leaving!" He dragged Spence past the 442 and made for the silver Corolla. It beeped obediently when Scott aimed the key fob at it. He placed Spence against the Toyota's back door. Scott's hands went to his knees and he sucked in lungfuls of air. "Fuck me. I need to get my ass in shape after this."

"Well, a different shape." Spence laughed. It made him grimace and his hands returned to his broken leg.

"Yeah, you can fuck all the way off with that bullshit."

Spence eyed the Olds. It was no more than ten feet away. It may as well have been a mile. If Scott insisted on leaving he would have to crawl across the gravel to get to it. Daggers drove themselves into his leg with every breath. *Yeah, how do you plan to pull that off?*

Scott opened the Corolla's back door. "Go on, get in."

Spence shook his head. Beads of sweat flew from his hair. "Can't do it. I can't leave them down there, man." He pushed himself from Amanda's car. He hopped once and then crashed to the ground. This time he could not hold in the scream. His hands welded themselves to his leg. Stars danced and winked in front of his eyes.

"For fuck's sake!" Scott got his hands under Spence's arms and he hauled him to his feet.

Spence felt the car at his back again. The daggers continued to tear at his leg. His head swam. He thought he was falling and his hands scrambled for purchase on whatever he could find to keep himself upright. In the end he did not fall. He remained propped against Amanda's car. Sweat poured down his neck and back. He could swear the beads were freezing on his skin. "Why is it so cold?" His teeth chattered when he spoke.

"It ain't. I think you're going into shock, man. I ain't a doctor but I've seen it on TV and shit. People who go into shock get cold for some reason. I don't know why. Come on, let's get you to the hospital."

"I'm. Not. Leaving." He opened his eyes, wiped the sweat from them with the back of his arm.

Scott threw his arms in the air. "Hard-headed son of a bitch!"

"Scotty, this is my fault. All of it. Katie's dead because I didn't tell her about this place. Keith and Marcus are dead because I thought it would be fun to come back here with the old crew. And Phil will be next if we don't get down there." He swallowed. "This is all on me, man. I can't just leave Phil and Amanda down there. And maybe Maria, too. I can't."

Scott's expression softened. He licked his lips, started to speak, stopped. He took a deep breath. When he finally spoke his tone was subdued. "None of this is your fault, Spence. No one could have known what would happen tonight. I mean, a whole street of devil worshippers? I don't think any of us believed that, not deep down, not even back in high school. Well, maybe Marcus, but not anyone else." He nodded in the direction of the empty mansion behind them. "This whole place was just somewhere to go to kill time and feel like we were doing something dangerous on a Friday night. That's it. Nothing more."

He shrugged, winced at the pain in his shoulder. "So it turned out we were right. But no one could have predicted that shit. Right up until a few minutes ago I *still* wasn't a believer." He placed his hand on Spence's shoulder. "Don't blame yourself. This was those two old bastards down there and their merry group of fuckheads. Hear me?"

Spence frowned, did not reply.

Scott took several steps from the Corolla and breathed deeply the cold night air. Finally he turned. "Okay, you stubborn fuck, let's go get Phil and the maid. We'll swoop down that hill right at that gateway to hell and grab them."

Spence finally looked at his friend. "Thanks, bro." He smiled and it was genuine. "Help me to Jacoby's car."

"I still don't see how you're gonna accomplish this but okay." Scott placed Spence's arm around his shoulder again. His steps were quick, impatient. It took only a moment for him to deliver Spence to the 442. "Happy?"

"Ecstatic." Spence fished the keys out of his pocket. He used the time to blink away the stars in front of his eyes. He hopped back a step and tried to ignore the daggers. Fresh, cold sweat blossomed on his forehead and his neck. His heart slammed itself repeatedly against his ribcage. *Just do it, man. Fire this thing up and drive it right into the middle of those fuckers.* "That's the plan."

He opened the door. The interior of the Olds was in even worse shape than the exterior. The leather seats were torn, the dash sported several cracks, what little carpet remained was worn through, the headliner hung in tatters. The stench of old cigarettes and weed assaulted his nostrils. Spence recoiled, his hand moving to cover his face. "Christ on a crutch."

He was working out in his head how he would slide himself behind the wheel when his eyes fell on the clutch. Spence's shoulders sagged. "Oh, shit."

Scott peeked over his shoulder. "What a piece of shit," he remarked.

Spence nodded toward the floorboards.

"Oh, shit."

"Yeah." Spence had been unsure if he would be able to drive the car at all. The presence of the clutch removed all doubt from his mind. He thought of Phil and Amanda and wondered what the sick fucks would do to them.

"I guess I'm driving this one."

Spence raised an eyebrow. He regarded his friend. "You know how to drive stick?"

"My first car was my brother's old Cavalier. Remember that car?"

Spence did. He had forgotten about it until that very moment. Their high school student parking lot had been filled with Mustangs, Camaros, and Firebirds… and one Chevrolet Cavalier that was held together by rust and age. "That car sucked ass." He laughed, daggers be damned.

Scott joined him. "Yeah, it did! I as so fucking embarrassed to be seen driving it!"

"We were just as embarrassed to be seen *in* it!" Spence roared with laughter. For an instant he forgot about his broken leg, forgot about everything. He was back in high school and sliding down the front seat of the Cavalier so Kathy Canton from history class wouldn't see him. Being spotted in that rust bucket would do nothing for his chances with her. He laughed so hard and so long his gut began to cramp. Spence took several deep breaths to stop the laughter. He succeeded but started again when Scott couldn't hold it together. They leaned on each other and roared until tears streamed down their cheeks.

It took a while but they both managed to get themselves under control. The daggers returned to his leg, but the chill left him. If anything, he felt warm. He guffawed a few more times but now it caused the pain in his leg to ratchet up a few notches. Spence swallowed and returned himself fully to the present.

Scott was red-faced. He wiped tears from his eyes. "That fucking Cavalier." He started to laugh again but Spence placed his hand on his friend's shoulder. Scott's laughter subsided until he sniffled and wiped his eyes again.

"You're sure you can drive this thing?"

Scott slid past him and plopped himself down into the driver's seat. "Fucking reeks in here." He waved his hand in front of his face. He placed his hand on the shifter and moved it around a bit. He tested the brake pedal and the clutch. Finally he nodded. "Yeah, I think I can handle it." He reached beneath the seat until he found the lever he was looking for and slid the seat back as far as it would go. He tilted his head and continued to probe beneath the seat. He withdrew his hand and held a bottle in front of him. It was perhaps one-quarter full of dark amber fire. "JW black. He might have been a colossal douchebag but he knew what to drink." Scott twisted off the cap and took a slug. "God*damn* that's good!" He held the bottle out the car door. "One for the road?"

Spence accepted the bottle. "One for the road." It was strong but smooth. It burned its way down his throat and filled his belly with warmth. For a split second he forgot about the pain in his leg. He took another swig and handed it back.

Scott had found a pack of Marlboros on the dash. He sat behind the wheel and smoked and finished off the bottle. He tossed it over his shoulder into the backseat. "Okay, so what's the plan again?"

Spence told him.

****

The face beneath the hood was not that of a monster. The man was handsome. *Perfect*, in fact. His almond eyes were precisely the correct size and shape for his face. His nose was all sharp angles and ended in a rounded tip. His lips were full. His hair spilled past his shoulders and was ruler-straight and so blonde it was almost white. If Amanda ever tried to build the world's most handsome man in her imagination he would have fallen short of the being who stood within the tall yellow grass on the other side of the hole in the air. She did not feel the dampness between her legs for several more minutes.

"Herald," Arthur Morley said. "Where is His Majesty?"

The herald's white, perfect teeth revealed themselves when he answered. "He sent me in his place, Arthur Morley. I am to assess the quality of your offering. His Majesty was most disappointed last time. He does not wish to repeat the experience." The perfect man's voice was music.

Arthur lowered his arm and waved it behind him without looking.

Rough hands forced Amanda to her feet. She yelped and tried to dig her heels into the soft ground. The man who had been standing behind her had a solid grip on her arms. He forced her forward, directly at the hole in the air and the beautiful man who stood beyond it.

They came to a stop beside Arthur Morley. "This," the old monster announced.

The herald's beautiful eyes started at her feet and moved north quite methodically. Despite herself Amanda felt the dampness blossom. A soft moan escaped her lips.

His eyes at last found hers. Dark brown, almost black, they penetrated her own. The world began to fray at the edges. The field vanished, followed by the bonfire, the people of Aldebaran Road, even the Morley brothers. Somewhere deep within her mind she thought maybe the entire universe was gone now. Nothing existed in all creation but her and the perfect man before her.

She orgasmed so suddenly and forcefully she almost dropped to her knees. The moan became a scream and the sound filled her reality. Her body convulsed and she orgasmed again. This time her legs gave and the ground rushed up to meet her. She felt the cold wetness of the grass on her cheek. She moaned again. Her eyes were locked onto his. Nothing and no one existed but for the two of them.

All at once the world snapped back into being. The change was so sudden Amanda gasped. The pain in her wrist returned and she groaned and held the wounded appendage. The heat from the bonfire returned. The bodies within the conflagration continued to be consumed by it. The men and women of Aldebaran Road were back, as were the Morleys. Both men had half-turned and stared at her. They smiled their approval before they returned their attention to the herald.

"So, herald?" William Morley asked. He sounded quite pleased with himself.

The perfect man had not moved a muscle. He stood where she last saw him, hands folded together beneath the sleeves of his robe. His eyes were still fixed on her but there was something different about them. They held no warmth. In fact, Amanda could see nothing there at all. His eyes appeared blank, emotionless. A chill worked its way into her bones and stayed there.

"She is superior to your last offering," the herald announced. "Her response is most impressive. His Majesty may well not be disappointed."

The Morleys turned to each other and smiled. They bowed from the waist. Then they stepped aside as if inviting the herald to join them.

The herald's arms fell to his sides. The folds of his sleeves undulated as if a stiff breeze rippled the fabric. Something emerged from those sleeves, but they were not hands. Amanda's mind raced to find the correct word to codify what she saw. She decided there was no correct term for this. The closest she could get was *tentacles*.

They were impossibly long, far too long to have ever fit within the sleeves of his robe. They snaked along the tall yellow grass toward her. Round objects that might have been suction cups opened and closed along their length in anticipation. They reached the edge of the border between the green and yellow worlds. The air seemed to shimmer and sparkle when the tentacles crossed the threshold. They reached hungrily for her.

Amanda's voice failed her. She stared mutely at the tentacles right up until the moment they touched her. Then her voice returned. She screamed.

CHAPTER TWENTY-THREE

Bad Form

Spence stifled a scream as he maneuvered his body behind the steering wheel of Amanda's Corolla. Every movement of his left leg brought on more of the daggers. He had to use his hands to get his leg into the car. By the time he succeeded he was bathed in sweat. He leaned back in the seat, eyes closed, and breathed deeply. He could still taste the JW Black and he concentrated on that. The memory of it warming his insides seemed to help a bit with the pain. It was still several moments before he felt he could open his eyes safely. The world swam back into focus.

From somewhere close by he heard the 442 roar to life. Just as quickly it sputtered and died. He had time to think, *Phil is going to die because that piece of shit won't start*, before the engine came back to life. The old V8 roared again, the sound of a beast waiting to be let off the leash.

Scott pulled the car next to Amanda's and stopped. "Clutch is tight as fuck but goddamn! This thing has some power!"

"I'll give you ten seconds before I follow."

Scott nodded. "Hey, Spence. Get Phil and the chick. Just get them and get the fuck outta Dodge. As soon as you do I'll race you up the hill." He revved the engine a few times and smiled again.

"You're on." Spence turned the key and the Corolla fired right up. He revved the engine and smiled in spite of himself at how much quieter it was than the old beast idling beside him. "Ready?"

Scott revved the engine again. Then the car shot forward. Gravel kicked up behind the tires and pelted the house and some of the other cars in the driveway. The Olds fishtailed a bit but Scott got it under control quickly. He raced for the driveway exit. The gate shot into the air with a shriek when the Olds hit it. It reached a height of at least twenty feet before its mangled remains crashed onto the dirt road. Then it was lost from sight.

Spence began to count.

****

The tentacle—if that's what it was—was frigid. It caressed Amanda's hand and wormed its way up her arm. It left a trail of slime in its wake. She recoiled, or tried to. Her limbs refused to obey her. She managed to turn her head away but that was the extent of her control. She could feel the thing, could track its progress, but thankfully she no longer had to watch. The slime froze on her skin. Numbness began to creep into her arm. Amanda whimpered.

At the same moment Scott started the old muscle car the perfect man's tentacle swept across her shoulder and proceeded down her chest. The buttons of her blouse popped off as it passed. The cold worked its way through her breasts and into her heart. Amanda gasped. She was certain her heart was going to stop. If anything, the opposite occurred; her heart picked up the pace. It began hammering the inside of her ribcage. "Please." Her voice was weak, less than a whisper. She could barely hear it herself.

The perfect man seemed to hear her perfectly. "Begging is bad form, my dear."

The tentacle continued its trek south. It lingered between her legs, touching, probing. She could feel the ice forming on her panties. But it remained there for only a moment more before it proceeded down her leg. It ended its exploration at her feet. Her shoe slipped from her foot and the thing wrapped itself around the appendage. The slime found its way between her toes and froze there. Then the vile grasping thing was gone.

Amanda felt drained. She dropped to her knees. She had the presence of mind not to catch herself with her broken wrist. The pain, gone amidst the horror she had just endured, returned with its familiar dull throb.

"What else?" the perfect man asked.

"We do have one more for His Majesty," William Morley admitted. He indicated Phil with his arm. "But he is a male. We do not know if His Majesty would desire such a thing."

"Bring him," the perfect man beckoned.

Amanda heard Phil struggle. For the first time since the tentacle touched her she opened her eyes. It took two men to haul Phil to his feet. He pulled against them, tried to kick and bite them. They stayed well out of range of his feet and teeth.

"Get off me, you fuckers!" he shouted. "Let go!" He dug his heels into the ground. The wet grass offered no traction and the two masked men brought him closer to the hole in the air and the perfect man on the other side.

"Hmm. He doesn't look like much of a sacrifice," the perfect man announced. "But I suppose I should examine him all the same."

The ice had begun to melt from Amanda's skin. The numbness went with it. All she had left from the encounter was a trail of slime that stretched from her shoulders to her feet. She flicked her unbroken wrist and watched some of it fly off. Her hand curled into a fist.

Her eyes fell on the strap of leather that bound Phil's hands behind his back. She could not see how it was tied but that made no difference. She had to get it off him. Together they might be able to get away. *How? You lost your keys. Not to mention your whole plan is predicated on outrunning Exton and everyone else here.* It didn't matter. They could run if they had to, all the way back to Deacon's Landing if that's what it took.

The perfect man's tentacle crossed the threshold again and made for its new target. Phil struggled against the two men holding him in place. He even managed to jam his elbow into one of them. The man doubled over with a grunt. He kept one hand on Phil's arm while the other went to his gut.

Amanda launched herself at the other. She shouldered into him and knocked him off his feet. There were several gasps from some of the men and women. Amanda kicked the other man in the groin with as much force as she could muster. He howled and went down.

"Stop moving!" she shouted as she worked at the leather strap.

Phil did not stop moving. He backed away from the hole in the air as quickly as he was able. Amanda lost her grip on the strap. She ran after him.

"Stop them!" one of the Morleys shouted. "Exton! Stop them at once!"

Amanda caught up to Phil at the edge of the circle. The people of Aldebaran Road had backed up several feet. The women held their hands to their masked mouths; some of the men cursed her. None approached. Amanda grasped the leather strap with her good hand and tried to free her companion.

Phil twisted his wrists and grasped at the strap with his fingers. "Get it off! Get it off!"

"I'm trying!" she shouted.

Exton was walking toward them. No, not walking. He staggered in their direction. His body swayed with each step. He tried to maintain his balance with his arms. The pink fluid had stained his jacket and his shirt. It ran from the corners of his mouth and from his nose. Amanda estimated she had perhaps ten seconds before he reached them.

Her fingers worked at the knot. She almost had it when Exton grabbed for her. Amanda shoved Phil away and ducked under Exton's arm. He started to turn. Her bare foot found his groin. Exton grunted, nothing more. Amanda's jaw dropped. She looked him up and down and tried again.

This time he caught her foot. He flung her away from him with far more force than she would have expected. Amanda crashed to the ground several feet from where she had stood. Her broken wrist screamed at her. Amanda stifled a scream of her own and rolled into a crouched position. Exton advanced on her.

Jacoby's car crested the top of the hill and caught air before it landed amid a shriek of protest from the shock absorbers. The car swerved in every direction before its driver regained control.

He killed them. Spence and Scott. And now he's here for me. And he's not going to kill me straight away. He's going to have his fun, *first.*

Or perhaps Jacoby would not get his chance. Exton regarded the car for only a moment before he returned his attention to Amanda. He grabbed for her again. His fingers grasped her blouse. Amanda twisted out of it but lost her balance. She backpedaled and went down on her back. Exton tossed the blouse aside. He reached down and tangled his fingers in her hair. Amanda screamed. She felt herself being dragged across the wet grass toward the hole in the air.

Her eyes found Phil. He was still working at the strap. Several of the braver men of Aldebaran Road advanced on him. They seemed to have gotten over their surprise and looked determined to obey their Morley masters. Phil noticed them and ran as fast as he could in a random direction.

Jacoby had reached the level part of the field. The car fishtailed on the wet grass, its headlights sweeping the field like laser beams. He was clearly insane; at that speed he would have little or no control of the car. Someone was going to be killed.

The masked people did not seem to share her concern. Some watched the car impassively, others golf-clapped their approval of Jacoby's late arrival.

The car straightened and flew forward. The golf claps ceased. People gasped. Some lifted their masks as if they could not believe what they saw. The more nimble among them leaped clear; a few unfortunates stood rooted to the spot. The car plowed into them without slowing. Masks flew from faces and bodies flew through the air. Women screamed. Men shouted curses.

The car continued on its path. People scattered and dove out of the way. Jacoby spun the wheel and the car fishtailed again. More grass and mud shot out from under the tires. The big block V8 roared like the dinosaur it was. It looped around the bonfire and skirted dangerously close to the hole in the air before the driver regained control. "You devil-worshipping cocksuckers are all fucking *dead!*" the driver shouted.

Amanda felt Exton's grip falter and then disappear. She scrambled away from him and started after Phil. The car cut across her path. She pulled up short and felt the breeze on her bare skin. It was at that moment she caught her first look at the driver. "Scott!"

He waved as he drove past. The car swerved again. The rear fender struck Exton with a loud *thud* and he sailed through the air. Still Scott had yet to stop or even slow down.

A beam of light caught her eye. Another car was already halfway down the hill and headed in her direction. It took her a moment to recognize her Corolla. She could not see the driver but it could be only one person. She leaped and waved her arms. "Spence! Over here! Phil, it's Spence!" The driver saw her and turned in her direction.

Phil had made it perhaps one hundred yards from the bonfire but he seemed to hear her. He stopped, turned. At the same moment he at last freed his hands. He rubbed his wrists and shouted something before he reversed course. He sprinted back toward the bonfire.

"Stop this madness!" William Morley shouted. He was waving his arms, too, frantically, pathetically. The people of Aldebaran Road ignored him and continued to run for cover. Scott was circling the bonfire at a high rate of speed, kicking up grass and mud. Amanda was forced to smile when she saw a fist-sized glob of mud splatter onto William Morley's tuxedo.

Amanda's eyes fell on the perfect man. He had moved to the edge of the hole for a better look at this unscheduled addition to the proceedings. He stood, arms folded in front of him, his tentacles hidden within the fabric of his sleeves. He watched the car in its widening circles around the bonfire, saw the people trying to avoid it. His expression was neutral.

Arthur Morley ran to the edge and stopped inches from the perfect man. He was shouting and pointing behind him but Amanda could hear nothing but the roar of the old muscle car. The perfect man did not move, did not reply. He did not even look at the old man before him.

Two masked women in elegant evening dresses, their fingers adorned with rings of gold and silver, froze in the old car's headlights. They clutched each other. The car plowed into them and they fell beneath the tires. Blood that looked black in the flickering light of the bonfire sprayed across the hood and the windshield. The masks flew from their faces; several rings bounced off the hood and vanished into the grass.

Amanda caught sight of her Corolla. It was handling the wet grass better than Jacoby's car but she could see Spence behind the wheel fighting to stay in control. More people scattered at its approach. Amanda found her blouse on the ground. Without much thought she scooped it up and slipped her arms through it. She didn't bother with the buttons. She ran for her Corolla.

****

Spence had seen Amanda even from a distance. She jumped up and down and waved her arms in the air. He course-corrected and headed for her. Not far from her Scott was wreaking havoc with the people of Denham. Spence noted there were far fewer of them on their feet than he had seen standing around the bonfire. The 442 had made a mess of the field; there was virtually no grass left in the car's wake. The deep grooves in the mud reminded Spence of the tilled soil in the cornfield. Now that he was closer he could see several bodies seated around the pole in the center of the fire. They were black shapes, nothing more. He was thankful for the lack of detail.

He caught his first real glimpse of the hole in the air. The sky on the other side was bright, a shade of yellow that hurt his eyes. The topography of the open field continued uninterrupted on the other side of the hole. Someone stood on the edge of the gateway to hell, a robed figure who seemed content to watch what was happening in this world. One of the old men stood before this robed figure and gesticulated wildly at the scene playing out behind him.

Spence watched two more Aldebaran residents, a man in an expensive suit and a woman in an equally expensive gown, leap out of his way. He paid them no mind. Amanda was running toward him, waving one arm in the air. Perhaps fifty feet behind her he spotted Phil. "Thank God," Spence said to no one.

He slowed and then stopped. Amanda reached the car and opened the passenger door. "Spence! Thank God! Let's get out of here!" She threw herself into the front seat.

Spence eyed the scene around them. No one had rushed the car. If anything the few people still on their feet were doing their best to put distance between them and what was happening around the bonfire. A few were running as fast as they could up the hill toward the road. Spence shouted out the window, "Phil! Move your ass!"

Phil ran past the gateway to hell. He saw the old man standing in front of the portal, still gesticulating wildly. Without breaking stride he slugged the bastard. The old man's head snapped back and he staggered a few steps. Phil did not press his attack. He made straight for the Corolla.

Amanda scooted forward and pulled the seat with her. Phil dove headfirst into the backseat and shouted, "Spence!"

Amanda slammed her door closed.

Spence took his foot off the brake pedal.

A hand shot through the open window and wrapped itself around his throat. Spence gasped.

Exton stood outside the car. His face was covered with thick, pink ooze. His hair was plastered with it. His uniform was torn and covered with grass, mud, and more of the pink stuff. His lips pulled back from his teeth. He snarled something incomprehensible.

Amanda screamed.

Phil shouted, "Jesus!"

Spence couldn't breathe. Despite the man's apparent injuries his grip was like iron. Spence's hands clawed at the man's arm, his hand, but Exton's grip was unbreakable. Amanda and Phil both tried to pull him loose. They had no more luck than he.

Spence shifted into reverse. He slammed his foot on the gas pedal. The Corolla's transmission whined a bit as the car lurched backward. Exton somehow kept pace with the car. His hand remained welded in place. The edges of Spence's vision began to darken.

He heard the roar before he saw the car. The 442 shot past in the opposite direction at a high rate of speed. The Corolla rocked to one side with the impact. Exton's hand was suddenly no longer around Spence's throat. Spence sucked in a deep breath. The Corolla's windshield was cracked. Exton, or at least the top half of him, sprawled on the hood. Pink ooze leaked from the large, new injury on his forehead, the same size as the crack in the windshield.

The Olds, headed directly for the portal, tried to turn. The front fender clipped the bonfire. Sparks shot high into the night sky. The impact flipped the car onto its side. It cartwheeled, sending clumps of dirt and grass shooting into the air. One of the front tires flew off and bounced across the field.

The car flipped end over end. The Morley brothers saw it coming too late. It struck both of them. The impact did nothing to slow the 442's momentum. It somersaulted straight through the hole in the air. The robed man on the other side took a single, nonchalant step to his right as the car tumbled past him. It flipped several more times before it came to a stop on its roof. Steam or smoke rose into the yellow air.

"*Scott!*" Spence jammed the Corolla into park and threw open the door.

"Spence, what are you doing? Don't go out there!"

He barely heard her. He was aware enough not to put weight on his broken leg. His hand found the Corolla's roof and he used it to keep his balance. He did not look at the half-body of the dead butler on the hood. His eyes were fixed on the ruined Oldsmobile in the yellow field. When he moved past the Corolla he hopped as best he could on his good leg until he found a piece of tree branch that had been expelled from the bonfire during the collision. It was thick enough and intact enough to support his weight. The heat scorched his fingers but Spence did not care. His leg screamed at him with every movement but he could barely feel it.

Spence limped closer to the portal. The robed man had resumed his place in the center. He did not move, did not speak. He simply stood and watched Spence's progress. Spence didn't look at him. His eyes were glued to the Olds. "Come on, Scott. Come on, bro. Climb out of there. Come on, man, do it." From this distance and angle he could see nothing of the car's interior.

Maybe he was thrown clear. With great reluctance Spence scanned the ground between the bonfire and the wreck. He found only empty space.

When he neared the portal he came across the Morley brothers lying where they fell. One was clearly dead. Most of his face was gone. White blood covered the remains of his head and most of his tuxedo. The second clung to life. He lifted his arm, his fingers brushed Spence's right leg. "Get me to the manor." He coughed blood when he spoke. Spence ignored him.

This close to the portal Spence felt a warm, foul breeze coming from the other side. It was not brimstone, as he might have expected. It smelled of fruit left on the vine a few days too long. His free hand moved to cover his nose.

There was no movement from within the Olds. The smoke/steam continued to rise until the breeze dissipated it. The tall yellow grass swayed slightly, caressing the vehicle's ruined body.

Spence turned his attention to the man on the other side. "My friend."

The man's lips turned up at the corners. He shook his head slowly. His eyes moved to the two old men on the ground a few feet behind Spence. His robe undulated far more than could be accounted for by the breeze. He returned his eyes to Spence. His smile widened. Then he turned away.

"My friend!" Spence said again with more force. The robed man did not react. When he reached the overturned Olds something emerged from the sleeve of his robe. It was not an arm but Spence's mind refused to identify it. The limb, whatever it was, glided along the rocker panel as the man walked past.

Getting to the wrecked Olds and hauling Scott out of there was all that occupied his mind. It took Spence a few seconds to understand what happened next. He had time to take a single step closer to the portal. All the light in the world winked out suddenly. The temperature dropped many degrees in an instant.

Spence took a startled step back. He lost his grip on his makeshift cane. When he fell it was blind luck that he landed on his good side. The impact was still enough to send a lightning bolt up his broken leg. He screamed something incoherent and clutched his leg.

Two pairs of hands grasped his arms and pulled him back several feet. Spence struggled to free himself even after one of the voices said, "Spence! It's me, man. Chill. We got you."

It took him a few moments to recognize Phil's voice. He looked up at his friend, then at Amanda who had a grip on his other arm. "No, we have to get Scott." He turned his attention to the portal.

It was gone. The field was dark save for the light of the bonfire. The yellow field beneath the yellow sky had vanished as if it had never been. The wrecked 442 was gone as well.

"No, no, *no!*" Spence struggled against the hands that dragged him away from where the portal had existed a few seconds before. "Scott! Scotty!"

"He's gone, bro." Phil's voice cracked and he sniffled. "They're all gone."

"I'm so sorry, Spence," Amanda added.

"*No!*" But his struggles subsided. He could not free himself from them, nor could he stop them from dragging him back toward the idling Corolla. When they reached it Amanda pulled the passenger seat forward. Between them they maneuvered Spence into the backseat. He grunted against the pain and lay still. His chest heaved and the blood pounded in his ears.

Amanda walked around to the other side and slid into the driver's seat.

"Hang on," Phil told her.

"What are you doing? Get back here! We have to go!"

"Be right back," Phil answered.

Spence lifted himself into a half-seated position and looked through the windshield. Phil stopped at the bonfire. He knelt in front of it and remained there for several moments.

Spence eyed the field. He saw several bodies lying where they fell. Two men in ruined, expensive suits crawled along the grass in the direction of the hill. Their movements were slow, tortured. No one else moved.

Phil regained his feet. He walked to where the portal had been. Spence saw the living Morley brother raise his arm much as he had with Spence. Phil said something but they were too far away for Spence to hear anything. Phil grasped the arm and started walking toward the bonfire. Morley struggled but he was no more capable of freeing himself than Spence had been.

They reached the bonfire. Phil knelt, placed both hands under the old man's body, and lifted with everything he had. The body tumbled into the fire. Sparks rose into the sky and the flames leaped higher. They were near enough now for Spence to hear the old man's scream. Phil stood there for a moment and watched the fire. Then he headed back to the Corolla.

"Feel better?" Spence asked when Phil sat himself in the passenger seat.

"No."

"Can we go now?" Amanda asked. She did not wait for an answer. She put the car in drive and drove slowly up the hill. The tires slipped a bit on the wet grass but she maintained control.

They reached the top of the hill and emerged onto the dirt road directly across from the driveway to Greystone Manor. Amanda turned the wheel to the left.

The mansion looked as it did when last he saw it just a few minutes before. It looked the same as it did on any number of nights when he and his friends kept to the shadows until they worked up the courage to actually look through the windows.

Greystone's outward appearance had not changed at all since the night Marcus dared Vic to sneak a peek inside the barn.

It looked identical to the night Scott and Spence brought their dates here because the girls had the nerve not to believe the stories. His date's name was Cindy but he would be damned if he could remember the name of the girl Scott brought. It didn't matter anyway since it was the last time Spence and Scott ever saw them. The windows facing the downward slope of the field had witnessed Glen ripping donuts with his Camaro, one hand out the window flipping the bird to the house and anyone who chose that moment to look outside. It would probably look the same ten years from now. Or one hundred. The goddamned house was eternal.

Those within were not. Neither were those who snuck around the edges for a peek inside. Scott and Marcus had seen Greystone for the last time. So had Keith and Maria, whose first visit was also their last. And Katie.

Amanda stopped at the section of road next to the bottom of the cornfield. She and Phil stepped out and Spence was alone inside the Corolla. Habit made him cast his eyes in both directions of Aldebaran. He saw no one. The people who lived here were either already headed for home or were lying in the field by the bonfire. He allowed himself a moment to close his eyes.

Phil and Amanda returned to the car with Katie's body. Phil opened the back door and Spence took hold of his sister and helped Phil get her into the backseat. Her head rested on his lap. Spence brushed the hair out of her eyes and cradled her.

"I'm sorry, bro," Phil said as he sat in the front seat. "I'm so, so sorry."

"So am I," Spence replied. He looked into Katie's still, expressionless face. He would bring her away from Denham and bury her and beg her forgiveness.

And while he was at it he would beg everyone else as well. Only Phil would be able to forgive him, assuming he could. The others were beyond granting him anything. Spence thought of his friends and he thought of Katie and he did not try to tamp down the *Remember Whens…* when they came. For the first time in his life, he welcomed them.

Spence watched out the rear window until the trees and the course of the road removed Aldebaran from his sight. Then he returned his attention to his sister. When the tears came, he did not fight them.

JOSEPH J. CHRISTIANO

Photographed by Taria A Reed

JJC grew up in Connecticut's Naugatuck Valley where he still resides.

He doesn't go to Oshkosh anymore.

OTHER WORKS BY
JOSEPH J. CHRISTIANO

The Last Battleship
Moon Dust
Dark Annie
Old Ghosts
The Shadow Man
The Cemetery Game

Works as JC Logan
The Raven Queen (YA)